The Shape of Things to Come

THE SHAPE
OF THINGS
TO COME

Maud Casey

Perennial

An Imprint of HarperCollinsPublishers

A hardcover edition of this book was published in 2001 by
William Morrow, an imprint of HarperCollins Publishers.

HarperCollins books may be purchased for educational, business, or sales
promotional use. For information please write: Special Markets Department,
HarperCollins Publishers Inc., 10 East 53rd Street, New York, NY 10022.

First Perennial edition published 2002.

Designed by Bernard Klein

Library of Congress Cataloging-in-Publication Data is available.

ISBN 0-06-008441-3

02   03   04   05   06   JT/RRD   10   9   8   7   6   5   4   3   2

for my parents

Acknowledgments

I am especially thankful for the wisdom and counsel of the following friends and readers: my beloved sister Nell Casey, Jeremy Chatzky, Caitlin Dixon, Jesse Drucker, Elizabeth Evans, Dwight Garner, Daniel Greenberg, Julia Greenberg, Janet McNew, Jan Miner, Dr. Mitchell Newmark, Timothy Schaffert, Robbie Dale Smith, Lorraine Tobias, and everyone at the Lee Strasberg Theatre Institute. Many, many thanks to Colin Dickerman; Rob Weisbach; my editor, Meaghan Dowling; her assistant, Kelli Martin; and my agent, Alice Tasman, whose amazing talents and friendship are without equal. Thanks to Clare, Julia, and Rosamond Casey for their love and support. Thanks to my grandmother Janet Barnes Lawrence for her literary passion and intelligence. Big thanks to my literary role models — my superstar mother, Jane Barnes, and my honorable father, John Casey. Finally, thanks to Bob Perry, who inspires and sustains me every day. For his love and company, I am eternally grateful.

Portions of this novel appeared in story form in the following publications: "Days at Home," *The Georgia Review*, Summer 1997, volume 51, number 2; "First Date," *Wholesome*, Summer 1992, volume 1, issue 4.

THE SHAPE OF THINGS TO COME

1

I N the office bathroom, my image trembles back at me. Today marks my first-year anniversary at the installation division of a San Francisco phone company where I spend my days, when I'm not answering the phones, copying oversize cable installation maps. Every morning, I brace myself for the white-hot flash, flash, flash of the giant copy machine. Under the fluorescent yellow of the bathroom lights, my face has the glow of a freshly made-up corpse. The bathroom smells like a re-creation of a pine forest. "You'll look back on this someday and laugh and laugh and laugh," I say to myself in the mirror. I fake laughter. But, today, my hair pulled away from my face with a motley collection of barrettes and bobby pins, I have a grim realization. I am officially "in my thirties," and I have never had a grown-up hairdo.

I began at the phone company as a temp, then floated as a floater into a permanent position, under the catchall title of "administrative assistant." My hair never made the leap. Always in some transitional stage, aspiring to be longer or shorter, it is perpetually on the verge of an actual hairstyle.

What if I become the female version of those men who are constantly experimenting with facial hair—one day a mustache, another day a five o'clock shadow, sometimes sideburns, occasionally a goatee? People, in describing me, will refer to me as that woman with the—well, she had hair practically shaved to the scalp but now it seems to be growing out. You know, that girl, the one who is always experimenting with her hair. Isn't she getting a little *old* for that? I reclip a chunk of loose hair with a pink barrette I found last night, abandoned in a bar bathroom where I'd gone to seek refuge from my date, a man who went on at length about "spiritual athleticism." This morning, my hair stuck in permanent adolescence, I've lost the ability to deny life's weight.

Until today, my life had been a source of amusement. Bad dates and worse jobs were fodder for future stories told to my future husband and a close-knit circle of future friends in the comfort of my future home. I'd always harbored hope for better things, operating on the guarantee theory: Eventually you find yourself in that home, with that husband, with some small children who need you—at the very least to reach things for them—with a job that makes you occasionally happy, with some money to buy your kids the things they need you to reach. But today my quivering reflection says to me: It is conceivable that you will work at the phone company and go home to Jell-O for the rest of your life.

"Jell-O?" My reflection nods.

I walk out into the empty office, all brown wall-to-wall nubbly carpet and the sharp edges of file cabinets stuffed with papers saved for an unspecified emergency. Flying toasters and bubbling fish screen savers are the only evidence of life. It is still early and I am the first one here. It's my day to prepare the coffee on the office chore wheel—my boss's idea of office community.

I have no other option. I unbutton my white work blouse and let it slide to the floor. I unhook my bra, tossing it onto Louise's desk where it lands in her inbox. I kick one flat off at a time, sending them clanging into the warped metal of Simon's desk. I step out of my sexless work skirt, roll off my nylons, climb on top of the copy machine, and go to work. I make a copy of my breasts and my torso. I've just finished my pelvis and the front of my thighs and flipped myself over when my supervisor, a fidgety man who sports a pencil-thin mustache, finds me on my back, pulling the top of the copy machine over me like a coffin lid.

"In this sort of situation," he says after clearing his throat, as if he were reading from the chapter in an office rules and regulations manual entitled "this sort of situation," "I won't be asking any questions. I'm afraid I have no choice but to let you go." He rocks back and forth on his heels. He nibbles on his pen.

But I want him to ask me questions. I want to explain that I am creating a life-size version of myself to stand in for me while I figure out how I ended up at this dead-end job, in this dead-end life, alone and without a plan. Instead, I laugh. Last-ditch, end-of-your-rope, completely inappropriate, hysterical laughter.

"I mean, come on," I say, when I can talk again. "This is just a little bit funny, right? Me, naked, on top of the copy machine?" For a second, it seems as though this is the kind of ridiculous scene that could bridge the chasm between two people with no hope of connecting otherwise. I feel deep, and on a roll—deeply rolling, rolling deeply. I am a nine-to-five philosopher. "I mean, the *copy machine*."

He can't even look me in the eye, though he's made looking me in the eye the main point whenever he asks me to answer the phones more politely or to call the copy machine repairman.

"Put your clothes back on and climb down from there," he says, blinking hard at the bubbling fish on a nearby computer screen. He turns and walks into the break room. I am wrestling with my nylons when I hear a loud "Christ on a crutch!" He stomps back in, his tiny mustache twitching. "You didn't even make the freaking coffee?" He breathes deeply in an effort to contain his rage. "Get out. Just get out."

WHEN the electricity and the phone were turned off in my apartment, my work friends—Louise and her husband, Simon—offered me the foldout couch in their living room. They were very understanding. They would have killed me with their kindness.

"That flash, flash, flash couldn't be good for anyone," Louise said. Simon stood behind her, flashing his hands, a visual aid. They are one of those couples who complement each other; one is crucial for the other to make sense in conversation with the outside world. Living by candlelight was more romantic, I convinced myself, and who needed a phone—that pesky mode of communication? My days of waiting for the phone to ring were over.

It wasn't clear how long Louise and Simon would be in San Francisco anyway. They called themselves "freelance telemarketers," working long enough at one company to save money to travel. Once their funds ran out, they moved on to another set of phones, another "I'm sorry to interrupt your breakfast, lunch, dinner, life" speech. Instead, when my landlord finally evicted me because his new tenant was willing to pay double what I hadn't paid in three months, I came home to live with my mother.

"HONEY, darling, sweetie, pooch," my mother calls from downstairs, a month later. "Sweetie, darling, honey, pooch." Her voice does not waver as she bends to pick somebody's discarded sweater up off the floor, spot-cleaning the house though she's meeting her date at a restaurant. The only time she cleans is in the last few minutes before she goes out. Just before she leaves, she gets fidgety and suddenly she's polishing or sweeping. We live in a house of half-polished tables and half-swept rooms.

"Honey, sweetie, darling." She's forgotten why she's saying these words, forgotten that she wants my attention. She is thinking of the evening ahead of her, whether to wear her hair up or down.

"Yes, dear?" I call down from my old bedroom strewn with objects I used to love. My mother has always said there is a specific satisfaction to bottoming out but you have to wait years. "You're happily married, have a fulfilling job. You have the haircut that you will have the rest of your life. You're finally happy with your body. Then, suddenly, one day, you remember the shit fondly."

Nostalgie de la boue. It's my mother's favorite phrase. It was her mantra years ago as she walked the edges of my room like a detective solving a mystery, when I was a dreamy little girl lolling on my frilly bed and dreaming of what it must be like to be her—to know how to put my hair up in a bun with only two pencils, to feel the bone of my cheek make someone want to look closer.

"Nostalgia for the shit that your life once was," my mother would say, her voice slow to savor the line we both knew by heart while her reflection floated in the night framed by the window. I'd watch car headlights go by the end of our cul-de-sac like possibilities in the suburban night, past the shops down the street with their EVERYTHING MUST GO signs dated weeks before. The street was constantly shedding its skin in order to be born again—what was once an ice cream parlor became a yogurt hut, the old stationery store became a papeterie, and the vacant warehouse became somebody else's vacant warehouse. My stomach dropped deliciously at the dramatic beat of silence just before my mother began to tell her stories.

"I'm going out," she calls up now, as if to say this is how you do it. I imagine her looking at herself in the mirror in the front hall, smoothing an eyebrow. These days, she goes out almost every night after she gets home from her job as the senior administrative assistant of the obstetrics division of the local hospital. She meets men through the classifieds. The report after a recent date: "We'll call him George. He's a horticulturalist who is developing a line of plants that need no care. A garden that does itself. We danced to the car radio in the A&P parking lot where we went to get beers." She never went out with

George again and the A&P parking lot is heavily patroled by policemen looking for teenagers like her. Facts don't play much of a role in my mother's postdate assessments. I've learned these things since I came back home, here at the age of thirty-three.

"You know," she calls up now. "Thirty-three's as old as Jesus ever got." This is something that classified-ad, former Sunday school teacher turned soccer coach ("Kick that ball up to God!"), Tuesday-night Ted, allegedly said to my mother when he asked my age.

"Yes," I call down. "How funny it was the first time you told me that." I stay in my room. Our conversations are often better when we are in different rooms, on different floors.

"I think Jesus probably got out of the house more than you do."

"And look where it got him."

"Whatever," my mother stage-mumbles. She turns on the vacuum.

"You can recoup," my mother said when she invited me home to Illinois for the summer upon hearing the news of my life, as if living without love or money were an illness.

"Honey, sweetie, pooch," she said, her words like outstretched arms.

"This is your fault. You should have told me to live my own life. San Francisco was your town. How could it be mine?" But my heart just wasn't in this analysis. Neither of us was buying it.

"At least you tried, little soldier," my mother replied, countering hostility with cute talk. She was pleased that I'd referred to San Francisco as her town.

I protested, though I knew what I had to do.

The first week home, I spent nights accidentally on the couch, falling asleep during the late movie—a sane woman locked away in a mental institution, all spinning scenery and tough talk, or gangsters speaking in a staccato dialogue that matched the background noise of constant machine-gun fire. When I woke up, a blanket would be draped over me and a box of tissues placed strategically near my head. I'd remember my mother's hand on my shoulder in the middle of the night, the way it worked its way into my dreams and became the soft touch of one of my failed love experiments in San Francisco. At the start, my mother was willing to treat my malaise as a physical problem, one that required waking up only long enough to eat whole pints of ice cream. She bought me a pack of cigarettes though I'd quit years ago. "Smoke, honey," she said. "Smoke if you feel anxious."

A month later, her patience has run out. She turns off the vacuum and stomps her feet to hurry me downstairs. I come down in the sweat suit that I put on and stay in after I get home from this week's temp job at a graphic design firm. They are sponsoring a benefit ball for cancer so I've tried to use this to help me feel more involved. My job has been to hand-write the names of the guests on one thousand invitations. The firm learned from Temporama, my temp agency, that I know a little calligraphy and they thought it would be charming for a graphic design firm to have handwritten invitations. That sometimes the pen gets away from me was all right with them. It was that much more of a personal touch; it lent character. For the past three days, I've sat at a desk in the middle of the office—each invitation balanced on a clutter of papers—and carefully carved out a name.

My mother's flowery, chemical drugstore perfume washes over me as I step into the front hall. It makes me dizzy. I need another nap though my life is a cycle of naps and recovering from naps.

"Where are you meeting him?" I ask.

"Well-lighted, busy, don't worry," my mother says, putting on very red lipstick. Her powder clings to the soft hair on her cheeks. She has gotten her second wind of beauty, here, twenty-five years after my father left her. She has a deep relationship with a hairdresser named Ralph—Ralph is his entire name—and together they have arrived at a short gray-free hairdo that suits her dark almond-shaped eyes, a feature she highlights in her personal ad.

I step out onto the front porch with her, into a neighborhood filled with houses exactly like this one, only sometimes they are backward on the inside. Across the street, Raymond stands in his kitchen window, pausing as he does the dishes to watch us.

"Poor, sweet guy," my mother says as she smiles at Raymond, wiggling fingers in his direction. She says it in her dog-and-cat voice: silly, silly curious little creature. Raymond looks down quickly, scrubbing a dish with sudden intensity.

"I'll call if it's late," my mother says, heading for her car. Her slip shows a little but these days it's charming. "Ta ta," she says. "I'll shake my hips and hope for the best." She slaps herself on the ass. Once she's in the car, she pokes her head out the window. "Just kidding?" she offers.

"I'm as old as Jesus ever got," I say. "I can handle the fact that my mother has a libido."

I turn toward the front door with my hands on my hips, doing my best impression for my mother of a grown woman who can handle the fact that her mother has a libido. After my mother's long gone, I linger in the doorway, offering Raymond my profile.

2

In the living room, I settle in for the night in front of the TV with a glass of wine and near-stale potato chips I find forgotten in the back of the kitchen pantry by the briquettes. A sitcom married couple decide whether it's the right time in their lives to have a child. What they are learning, between commercials, is that there is no right time. You just have to take the plunge, the woman's childless best friend assures her. The plunge? the woman says suggestively to studio audience laughter.

"Then I was married with a child," was how my mother's stories ended, in the days of wandering my childhood room. The way that she said "child" instead of my name made me feel more included, as if I were someone she met on a train, a stranger to whom she could more easily tell her whole life. She had a whole repertoire—tales of regret ("I could have been a singer. People used to pay to hear me sing."), missed opportunity ("I know there's a painter inside me somewhere."), the one that got away ("My college boyfriend was an artist of sorts. He moved to Paris, where he lives on the Ile St-Louis and sees Grace Jones buying croissants at the bakery where he gets his baguettes in the morning.")—but only one that she returned to again and again.

She first told me about Henry when I was eight. My father had left us the week before and her voice filled the empty rooms like music.

"Pay attention," she said. "I am telling you this now because this is an important story. Henry was that thing that happens early on in life, that thing that becomes the root of everything else you do." Her eyes were wet with tears I had seen only on rare occasions, shining in the dark when she took me to see sad movies.

I sat up, hungry for a secret that would alleviate the dull grind in my gut that accompanied my father's sudden departure, something my mother treated as a routine occurrence. What happened to you today? I woke up, had some breakfast, read the paper, my husband left me, went to work, came home, watched TV, went to bed. She never talked about my father after he was gone.

She met Henry when she was twenty, in a café where she waitressed in San Francisco.

"You lived in San Francisco?" I asked. A citizen of Standardsville all my young life, I was in awe.

"Briefly," she said. "I ran away from home and secretarial school." She waved her hand dismissively as though I were a fan hounding her for an autograph. "Your father doesn't even know." Was my father ever worthy of this wonderfully haughty, beautiful woman?

Henry slid cigarettes out of my mother's pack without asking as she sat at a table taking a break. "You can't imagine how they worked us there," she said. But I imagined it all—her feet throbbing though she'd bought comfortable sneakers especially for waitressing, the ache in her lower back from too much standing, the smell of coffee deep in her pores.

Henry didn't say anything at first. He just smoked with his steady, yellow-tipped fingers. He was handsome but had a crooked face close up. He told her he had other girlfriends, that she shouldn't be so old-fashioned as to expect to be the only one. "I didn't realize I wanted to be your girlfriend," my mother said she told him, hiding her trembling hands underneath the table. He was full of himself, a guy with an attitude, but one so obvious she was charmed. My mother paused then to give me the weathered look of a smoker, though the only cigarettes I'd ever seen her smoke weren't lit.

"He sounds like a jerk," I said the first time she told the story, tired of the mean boys at school.

"He *pretended* to be a jerk," my mother said, correcting me.

Henry drew a picture on a napkin for my mother—a stick-figure version of her lying in a stick-figure bed.

"What is the last thing you thought of before you went to sleep last night?" he asked, handing the napkin to her.

"I thought about meeting you," she told him, because she had thought of meeting someone like him.

My mother left my room abruptly. A master of leaving her audience wanting more, she was through for the night. She left me trembling with the hope that when I grew up I would be a completely different person than I was as a child. My hair would be thicker; my skin wouldn't be so pale. I'd be beautiful and tall, and I'd think thoughts that had never occurred to me before. As I fell asleep, I imagined my future, telling stories of the way I was years before—drinking and kissing and smoking for hours. Propelled by these adventures through grown-up cocktail parties, I would pause only to brush some invisible thing off my impossibly long leg as men and women watched with fascination, their minds eagerly filling in the details of the life of cloudy despair that I'd recovered from.

The first time through, my mother told the story of Henry every night for fourteen nights, an installment for every day of their relationship. The second day, he returned to the café to offer her a bit of plaster from the place on his ceiling where he stared while thinking of her before falling asleep. The third day, they promised that they would always think of each other right before they fell asleep, and on the fourth, they spent the night together. They stayed up all night because they would miss each other too much if they fell asleep. On the fifth day, he told her he loved her. Eight days in a row, he told her he loved her, and my mother said she loved him back.

"I loved him more than my parents," she said. "More than myself. I loved him so much I thought I would die from this love. But whether I loved him or not was not the point. I was wide open. That's what was important. With Henry, I was skinless. Tingling with sensation. Exposed to the elements."

I couldn't wait to feel something that painful. Every night, I pleaded for her to tell me more but she refused, pulling the door shut behind her. "Remember," she would whisper, "this is our secret."

She didn't need to say more. My father was gone. He had stopped listening long before he left anyway. He would ask me how school was on his way to some other part of the house. He and my mother slid past each other without speaking when they met accidentally on the stairs. My father's arm was leaden when he rubbed my mother's shoulder for my benefit as she stood at the sink doing dishes while I leaned over homework and dinner crumbs at the table. When he was at home, he squandered most of his nights in remote and empty rooms. The rest of the time he spent in bed. Some nights, he and my mother whispered all night, their words indiscernible. Their muted, thudding tones were like heavy rocks dropped over and over onto a dirt path. The week before he left, he stopped joining my mother and me for dinner, and I brought him dinner on a tray. He would stroke my hair and say my name as though I were someone long dead.

On the fourteenth night, my mother came in to my room holding something behind her back. "Henry died" was all she said, laying the napkin on the foot of my bed. There it was: Henry's faded napkin drawing. My stick-figure mother in her stick-figure bed, dreaming the dream of him. I traced the napkin drawing until all I could see was a blur of black against white.

She returned night after night—until teenage hormones made it impossible for me to sit still for that long—to tell stories about Henry. He was a lesson in the fleeting nature of innocence, lurking behind everything my mother said or did.

Henry died one of those horrifyingly random, ridiculous deaths. His coat caught in the back door of a bus just as he and my mother stepped off. Henry had paused on the stairs to fish for something in his pocket. To this day, my mother swears it was an engagement ring.

My mother watched the bus drag the life out of Henry. The bus driver was unaware until Henry slid, slow motion, underneath and, by the time the driver felt the bump and slam of Henry's body against the bottom of the bus, it was too late.

"Henry died," my mother said again and again, "for no reason. Death popped out of nowhere, a mocking jack-in-the-box, demanding my attention. It laughed in my face. Death forced me to be its audience. And after that, nothing would ever be the same." After Henry died, my mother returned to Standardsville to live with her mother and re-enroll in secretarial school, but she was an entirely different person.

"I understood that people could be taken away," she said. "And I understood nothing." She would snap her fingers. "Like that. The illusion that all was right with the world was just that—an illusion. The ground could give way beneath you at any moment. I could never unlearn that."

I don't need *TV Guide* anymore to tell me what's on each night. Anyway, it's filled with ads for the cable my mother refuses to order ("I don't want to be out on a horrible date knowing there was something good on television. I like to experience a bad date as better than any of my other options and if I had cable, forget it."). Most nights I lose myself in the endless loop of half-hour shows. During commercials, I turn down the sound to hear the cars whoosh by, stealthily guarding the secrets to life. I want to eventually limit myself to the shows I really like, the ones I think I can learn something from: a mother who comes to realize her daughter is envious and protective rather than just plain mean, friends who realize that they are better friends than lovers. My goal is to watch only the shows I can apply to my life.

On the coffee table, there's an old photo album that my mother brought down from where it was folded in towels in the linen closet by the bathroom. She brought it down so that I could look at pictures of myself as a baby, pictures of me learning to walk, climbing up on the toilet, mouthing mashed carrots from a spoon. She wants to show me these pictures because they are evidence that I have accomplished something and that, quite possibly, I will accomplish something again. What interests me more are the pictures of my mother. She is slimmer and wears sleeveless dresses that end above her knees. In one picture, she looks coyly out from under her wedding veil while her mother stands in the background, feigning irritation.

The picture that I always return to is the picture of my mother in a jaunty hat. She sits on a park bench with pigeons at her feet. Her head is turned and the profile of the long slope of her nose, a gentle root erupting, is the center of the picture. She looks sure of herself. Henry took this picture, which my mother keeps in her underwear drawer.

"He snapped it when I wasn't looking," my mother used to say shyly. "I didn't even know he had a camera." But in the picture, she is a young woman waiting for someone to capture her beauty. A year ago, when I had first moved to San Francisco, I asked her to send me the picture Henry took because I wanted to see if it was taken in a park near my apartment. She refused.

"It's your city now," she said. "I'm through with it. I'm moving on. Henry was a lesson I've learned. Past tense. End of discussion." She'd gone to Ralph for the first time and gotten rid of her gray. After almost twenty-five years of living on her own, she was starting to talk about the possibility of dating. In the picture, I am an idea she will have one year later.

There is a rustling on the front porch, the sound of denim pant leg swiping denim pant leg, and Raymond from across the street appears in the doorway, timid as if he hasn't been a regular guest since I've been home, whenever my mother is not here.

"What's on TV tonight?" Raymond asks. He told me that he doesn't have a television but when I was locked out the other day and went over to use his phone, I saw the inside of his house—the mirror image of ours—with the stairway to the left instead of to the right. Raymond's house doesn't have very much furniture, but it does have a television. It remained on and unwatched—blasting images of lifeguards running on a beach aimlessly and in slow motion at an empty wall—while I called my mother at work.

"Come in and see for yourself," I say.

I've grown accustomed to Raymond's companionship—the smell of his Bay Rum, his broad hand placed solidly on the arm of the couch. One night after my mother had left on a date, Raymond didn't appear as quickly as he usually does and I panicked. It was like an essential piece of furniture had been removed from the living room. I couldn't sit down. I wandered around the house, peering through windows to see if I could catch a glimpse of him across the street. I was on the verge of calling the police, having convinced myself that Raymond was dead in his house, all alone, when I heard the familiar shuffle on the front porch and suddenly, the evening was right again.

Raymond's claim to fame is that, in his twenties, he won a contest to be a guest on *The Honeymooners*. It was an episode in which the Grand Exalted Leader of the Raccoon Lodge is coming to town and one member is to be chosen as his escort. Ralph desperately wants this coveted role, but it is Raymond's character, a fellow lodge member, who is given the opportunity instead.

"It was a big moment for me," Raymond told me the other night as we watched a late-night *Honeymooners* marathon. "The biggest."

"I escorted the hell out of the Grand Exalted Leader," he said.

"Did you meet Jackie Gleason?" I asked.

"I spoke with Mr. Gleason briefly. And he told me: Opportunity comes where you can find it. And sometimes you find it on TV."

My mother told me that a year ago, when Raymond first moved into the house across the street, she invited him to dinner. She laughed about how timid Raymond was with an "unattended woman." He left a small bite of each thing—carrots, mashed potatoes, chicken—on his plate at the end of the meal, an offering, and he didn't say a word. "I must have scared him," my mother explained with pride. Now, when Raymond and my mother pass on the sidewalk or see each other from across the street, Raymond looks down, nodding his head quickly in restrained acknowledgment of what she will never offer him.

There were nights in San Francisco when I would come home from work with fingers stained red with ink from trying to reset the date on the phone company's date stamp. The third blind date of the week would pretend he was a vampire and the ink was blood, sucking my fingers until I wished it was real blood that he was taking. Raymond was kind from the moment I met him, asking nothing of me. From the beginning, Raymond and I have been comfortable with each other's lethargy.

The first time we met, I was watching TV on a night that my mother was out on a date. He knocked on the door and when I opened it, he shrugged, though he was the one asking the question. "Would you mind if I watched with you?" It's been a ritual ever since.

My mother and I don't know much about Raymond except what we see as the people who live across the street from him: He doesn't work and rarely leaves his house; he washes the same set of dishes every night (this detail we guess), holding them up to the light in his window to make sure they are clean; and he checks his mail three times a day, although the postman only comes once—at three in the afternoon. My mother often wonders aloud if he is waiting for a winning sweepstakes or a letter from someone who has never written him before because he never seems to get any mail or send any letters himself. Some days when we see him heading down his grassy slope to his mailbox with an American flag indicator, my mother will say in a dramatic drumroll sort of voice, "Could it be the winning sweepstakes?" She has that kind of energy.

That first night, we fell into the trance of the sleepy TV rhythm. We sat in the comfortable silence of longtime friends until, at the end of the first show, Raymond turned to me and asked, "Why are you here?"

I told him the whole story—how I'd left Standardsville to go to college a few hours away, how after I graduated I sunk there—for ten years—in the spongy turf of a steady boyfriend and a steady job doing research on Benedictine monks for one of my old professors until I couldn't take it anymore. It was an all-or-nothing moment. There had to be something else, something more. So I left my very nice boyfriend, quit my interesting job, and headed west to the city I had heard about all of my life: San Francisco.

"Did you find something more?" Raymond asked patiently.

"Yes and no," I said. I slid my shoes off, moved the photo album out of the way, and put my feet up on the coffee table.

"No more than yes?" Raymond shrugged for the second time that night, a shrug I'd later recognize as his signature gesture.

"Yes," I said and started to cry in front of this man I'd just met. In San Francisco, I'd sit by my open window alone late at night, listening to the sounds of people laughing and drinking in the bar down the street. I'd pretend they were talking about me, and my name would drift down the street to me: *Isabelle, Isabelle, Isabelle.*

Raymond nodded, not in the least embarrassed by my tears. He crossed his legs, put his arm across the back of the couch, and continued to nod until I finished crying. He wasn't going anywhere.

Tonight Raymond takes a seat at his end of the couch and I return to my old place near the other end. Raymond has become bolder over the course of the last month. Now as we watch TV, he interjects comments like "What jackassery!" or "That person's a boatload of trouble." Flickering images of men and women solving their problems swiftly and efficiently fill our eyes until, after the first family plot in which a wayward daughter does right, Raymond speaks about my mother.

"I was thinking about telling your mother about the boy who comes to do my yard," he says. "I was thinking that she might want him to do your yard too. The boy has a nice touch." From the table, he picks up the photo album, flipping to the picture of my mother looking out from behind her bridal veil. He holds the album up to catch the light as though this glimpse into somebody else's past will carry him through next week. "That's a pretty picture," he says, crunching ice, and then we watch family plot after family plot ("That young man should learn to think with his heart, not with his pants," Raymond says. "He should never have turned his back on his family.") until the ten o'clock news.

"How's your grandmother?" Raymond asks, a little of his drink spilling over the side of the glass as he raises it to his lips. Raymond doesn't know my grandmother, but he asks the question as if he is a friend of the family. It seems out of the blue, but he is looking at a picture of me, my mother, and my grandmother, standing in that order, in front of a ride at the local fair. The ride is called the Twister and it's made out of two baskets that twirl around like eggbeaters. A girl in my junior high once threw up while the ride was going full speed. In the picture, the three of us are pretending to be dragged toward the stairs to the Twister by some invisible force. My grandmother has placed her Panama hat on the ground several feet away, as if the invisible force has blown it off and it landed there. My mother and I have our hands above our heads to demonstrate our horror, eyes bugged, and behind us all, the Twister is a mere yellow blur, people strapped to the sides of the baskets, trying to resist its pull and twist.

"She's been dead for years," I say, remembering the way my

mother wore a clouded face that uttered only apologies when her mother died. I was in my teens and my mother was constantly sorry—sorry dinner was late, sorry her husband was gone, sorry for always being sorry, especially sorry that her mother died thinking my mother was a failure. My grandmother was unhappy with my mother in the end for losing her husband. She was upset that there was so long a pause in my mother's life after my father left, fearing that if she took too deep a breath, my mother might have passed out.

"Hmm," Raymond grunts thoughtfully and shrugs. He doesn't particularly regret the question. When the news is over, he rises abruptly without saying good-bye as he always does. He puts his glass down on the table, next to the coaster, then stands in the living room for a minute, looking down at the picture of me, my mother, and my grandmother.

"The Twister?" he asks. He points at the yellow blur, though he is looking at my mother. "You all look alike," he says, running his finger along the row of us.

I slide down the couch to look and see what I've seen before, but never through Raymond's laser gaze. It's true, we do. We are variations on a theme: the same thin hair and almond-shaped eyes, the same exaggerated pose, the same look of mock astonishment. I've studied these pictures since I've been home, but the way Raymond searches my mother's image for the source of her magic makes me look again.

"The boy who does my lawn is really good," Raymond says.

I want to offer Raymond something for his companionship. "My mother had such a lovely time the night you had dinner together," I say.

The lie is a gift to both of us. It's as if I've thrown a sandbag from my grounded balloon—I hover ever so slightly above the floor. I've never used the word "lovely" before. It even seems a little bit true, something my mother should have said, even though she makes a point of avoiding Raymond as much as he makes a point of avoiding her. "She was charmed. She talks about it still."

"Charmed?" Raymond says, flustered. He is out the door and into the night filled with the hum of telephone wires. I watch him skitter across the street, pausing only to peer into the dark cave of his mailbox. He reaches deep inside, up to his elbow. Nothing yet again, and he trots into his backward house empty-handed. I imagine the sound of his shoes landing on the linoleum as he kicks them off, sits down on his couch, and flicks on *his* TV. He stares into the TV but thinks about the angle of my mother's elbow as she raised her fork to her lips that night.

I take a glass of wine upstairs and drink it in bed with the lights off, scanning my closet for tomorrow's temp outfit, one that suggests a richer, sleeker, more effective me. Then I remember I've forgotten to put away the picture Henry took of my mother in San Francisco, so I stumble downstairs again. The photo album is still open to the Twister picture and I realize that I have always thought of my mother, my grandmother, and myself being dragged toward the Twister as somehow real; the fact that the picture has brought a reality to the pose when the pose was just something that my father shouted from behind the camera makes me suspect that, deep down, all desire is fake.

I return the San Francisco picture to my mother's underwear drawer and take the Twister picture to my room where I tear it into tiny pieces. I throw the scraps out my bedroom window to flutter, pieces of our faces pushing through the air while the sky falls away. They land randomly on the lawn, ready to stick to my mother's heels when she makes her way back to the front door tonight. It's something to counter this endless process of recovery—my grandmother waiting for my mother to recover from my father's desertion and now me waiting to recover from a badly scripted life. As my mother moves toward the vacancy left by my grandmother, and I move reluctantly toward my mother's cast-off ages, I wonder how one recovers from trying to make a life.

Sometime later, I hear a car, a key in the door, and then my mother's whispering voice and that of a man's. Out my window I watch the movement of light from the TV in Raymond's living room. Raymond has no curtains in his living room and I can see him doing stretches on the floor. He leans forward over his legs, pulsing in an effort to reach his toes, maybe thinking about what a lovely time my mother had the night he thought it had gone so badly, afraid that he didn't have enough to say, that he'd run out of all the words he knew to describe his life.

I hear my mother downstairs in the kitchen, putting the kettle on to boil while she sizes up this man, measuring her desire for him. It's strange to be in such close quarters with my mother's sexual desire, and each time I hear her giggle or the wet sound of kissing, a foreign source administers small shocks to let me know this is forbidden territory. The hushed tones of my mother and this man drift up to me as I finish the wine and set the glass by my bed next to other glasses from other nights.

The quick bursts of light from Raymond's TV tell me he's watching a Western, or a cop show. One if by land, two if by sea, I pretend that he is sending me signals through the flashes of TV light. *I know you're watching. Thank you. Good night.*

It is the moment when the low tones turn to carefully suppressed laughter, at a minute gesture of my mother's or at a joke told by this man that I hear only fragments of—bar, cow, dart board—something silly and quickly forgotten but shared between them, that I am most an outsider in this house. I lie in such a way as to be the smallest I can be, deciphering the flash of Raymond's TV light, heading for sleep, while downstairs my mother's life continues.

3

"THIS isn't about getting a life, Isabelle," Marla, my temp counselor, says to me when I sit down across from her at Temporama. "It's about getting someone else's life." She leans in so close I can smell her breath mint. She called this morning at 6:00 and asked me to come into the office. "I can't give you this assignment over the phone," she whispered urgently. From the beginning, she's maintained the tone of a slightly hysterical secret-service agent.

"This is about being . . ." Marla pauses, raising a meticulously sculpted eyebrow. "A spy for movie theaters worldwide." With her gleaming, star-and-moon-adorned nail tips, she pulls several strands of hair off my dress jacket, borrowed from my mother.

I'm dressed in my temp wear—the skirt to match the jacket with heels that have me walking like I sat on something sharp, all borrowed from my mother who has always dressed as if she meant it. She's the kind of woman who is constantly updating her wardrobe in her mind and could tell you at any given moment what, if anything, is missing—the perfect black pants, a scarf to top off an outfit. I inherited my father's haphazard sense of fashion. My closet is filled with the same sweater bought again and again, the occasional wildly patterned and never appropriate pants. Given the choice, I would wear the same pair of cutoffs and tank top every day. Yet my mother's clothes fit me perfectly, as if after years of resistance my body has become hers.

"It's a *mystery shop*, Isabelle," Marla is saying. "The idea is to go into a movie theater pretending to be a regular customer in order to evaluate its services. The movie theater's parent company needs you to get certain answers, but you have to do it secretly—that's why it's a *mystery*. Are you following me?"

Temporama is bustling with activity today. Behind the front desk, a radio plays a "lite" AM radio station on low. The DJ has a voice so smooth it's inaudible at this level, a meditative hum between the instrumental versions of Top 40 hits. A woman in a nearby cubicle, also dressed in a mix-and-match jacket and skirt, laughs nervously as her temp counselor explains something to her. We are a whole legion of impersonators.

"You're sending me to the movies?" I'm indignant. "I'm dressed for the office."

"Isabelle," Marla says sharply. Her fiercely cheerful voice pushes friendliness to its outer limits. "I wouldn't give this job to just anyone. I had to make sure that I could trust you first." She looks me up and down—from my shoulder pads to my pointy toes—and then looks me in the eyes as if she were looking into my soul and, finally, sees something useful. "I had to make sure you had the right personality for this job."

"What kind of personality is that?"

"You know," she says. "Blank slate-ish—someone who could be anyone."

"And this is supposed to make me feel special?"

"Isabelle," Marla says. "What I'm trying to tell you is, you're an actress and you don't even know it. I want to tap your dramatic potential."

Like talk-show psychologists, Marla has a hypnotizing effect. Deep down, I know I'm being hustled, but I don't care. I'm unable to change the channel. No one has ever told me I have dramatic potential.

When I walked into my initial temp interview a month ago, my hair was still wet from the shower. Marla began reading over my answers to the requisite temp-questionnaire questions but almost immediately put it down again. "Before we begin, I need you to know something," she said. "I've never left the house with wet hair *in my life.*" She touched her complex, multilayered, multiblonded hair—a real hairdo. "It takes me twenty-seven minutes to achieve this." She took my hand in hers, baby soft from the lotion she keeps in her desk. "If you don't take care of yourself, Isabelle, no one else will." The oldest self-help line in the book, but I could hear how many times she'd said it to herself, how it had gotten her out of bed every morning of her forty-something years, helped her through her hair routine, pushed her out the door to work.

"Trust me," she said, and I do.

Marla snaps two fingers in front of my face. "Earth to Isabelle, come in, Isabelle."

"Isabelle reporting to Earth," I say. I salute.

"Here are some 'for examples.'" Marla pulls a list of sample mystery-shop questions from a file labeled MYSTERY SHOP. "For example, sometimes the parent company creates a form for you, the mystery shopper, to fill out. The local managers come up with their own. This is a local: *Is there an adequate supply of popcorn? Are the ushers wearing their bow ties? Do they tear the ticket properly or do they palm it to give to their friends for later use? Do they ask to see your ticket when you leave the theater to use the restroom facilities?*"

As Marla continues reading the questions, I imagine myself wearing a veil, a mysterious veil, a "mystery shop" veil, with long, glossy nails in place of my chewed stubs. I dance down my mother's street, past the Thortons' carefully arranged faux Stonehenge garden, past Mrs. Morton's fountain whose bare-ass cherub caused such a stir when she first had it installed, past Raymond's house where he stands on his lawn wondering who I am and whether I will dance his way. My mother stands on her porch, riveted and curious as I twirl like opportunity down the driveway.

"I've got a job for you right away," Marla says. "But, let's get down to brass tacks here. Do you even look in the mirror before you leave the house? Your face is absolutely naked."

"I'm going to the *movies*," I say.

"Isabelle, you are not going to the movies, you are mystery shopping," Marla snaps. "You have got to trust me. Don't you trust me?"

"I do, I do." I want to please her. Like a therapist, she is paid to be nurturing, but still, when she tells me I am the one for this job, that she needs me to be a part of her team, I am willing to be convinced.

"Follow me." She rises boldly from her desk, purse in hand.

P-S-Y-C-H-E-D. Psyched is what we want to be! Get psyched! My mind fills with pep rally cheers from high school that I never knew I knew. I hardly ever attended pep rallies. Yeah, yeah, get psyched!

In the bathroom, Marla applies rouge and eyeliner like war paint to my naked face. She whips out a curling iron, plugs it in, and gives my straight, shoulder-length hair a crinkly flip at the bottom.

"You have such potential, Isabelle," she says. She sprays a cloud of perfume into the air. "Walk through it," she instructs. I do. Rowdy, let's get rowdy!

"You really think I have potential?" I ask.

"You have to ask?" Marla hands me a questionnaire on my way out of the bathroom. "Your first assignment: the matinee mystery shop at the Super Cineplex. Just be yourself."

I head for the door, trying my best to walk confidently in my heels for Marla.

"Isabelle," Marla calls after me. "Be yourself, but remember: Don't tell anybody who you are."

"Gotcha." I give her the thumbs-up.

I climb into the Chevy that I drove during high school, a hand-me-down from my mother who, after I left home, could never bring herself to get rid of it. "Sentimental value," she'd say. It's been parked in the driveway, untouched, ever since. The entire car is green—a mint-green exterior with a dark green vinyl roof, and what might generously be described as a kelly-green interior. The kelly-green vinyl of the bench seat is ripped so the foam bursts out in spots. The springs of the seat creak and occasionally poke out, jabbing me in the ass as I buck down the road with my legs stretched to capacity in order to reach the gas pedal and the brakes. Because the windshield leaks, the seat mechanism has rusted and the seat is stuck in a position appropriate for someone a foot taller than I am.

I cruise past the collage of strip malls, car dealerships, palm readers, and restaurants pasted to the landscape to meet the needs of the residents of the housing developments that have popped up farther and farther along the highway, lurking behind scraggly remnants of roadside forest. A city billboard hangs from a tree outside a gunshop built long before the malls, an ancient relic with roots deep in the Illinois mud. A mural on the side of the gunshop depicts a hunter shooting a rifle. At his feet are several dead rabbits, a few dead birds, and a deer. The billboard, which shudders against the tree when cars speed by, reads CITY LIMITS? THERE ARE NO LIMITS TO THIS CITY. Huge tractors claw at bare earth around the tangled highway system, a mass of intersections and perilous yield lanes designed by a man rumored to have had a nervous breakdown as soon as he lay the last stretch of tar.

Aside from my weeklong stint at the graphic design firm, my Temporama career has consisted of random days spent here and there covering for a sick secretary, days spent stealing hard, old candy from a musty jar hidden underneath scribbled-on first drafts of letters. A "Stars of the NFL" cup filled with pens that don't work sits on the desk next to computer manuals still in their plastic wrap, and the ever present Jaws of Life staple remover. As the day wears on, my panty hose pile up in loose rolls around my ankles.

In a top drawer, there is accidental art made out of pats of butter that have melted and then frozen again into the slips of wax paper and tiny squares of cardboard once they hit the

32

high-impact office air-conditioning. In a bottom drawer, there are sneakers in a plastic bag, or worse: hopeful high heels. One day, I stood in for a "lifer out sick for the second time in twenty years," at a car insurance company. A secretary wearing a wrist brace at a neighboring desk bitterly refused to tell me where to find the wrist bar meant to prevent carpal tunnel syndrome. She was the same woman who escorted me around the break room. After showing me the industrial-size coffeemaker and the basket overflowing with sugar substitutes, we made our way back to the cubicle, Styrofoam cups in hand. She took a sip from hers, leaving fuscia lipstick on its rim.

"It's not a hard job," she explained. "It just makes you want to shoot yourself."

If I read slowly, the instructions and environmental warnings on air fresheners rolling around in otherwise empty side drawers occupy exactly three minutes. Naming the sick secretary's children in pictures tacked to her corkboard strip can last all day. On these day-to-day stints, I'm hired to answer the phone, but I branch out as it occurs to people that a temp is a minefield of possibilities, someone who is there to do whatever. "You look so together—I bet you would do a great job straightening up the break room. Feel free to give it your own personal touch." or "You look like a real alphabet whiz—I bet you'd do a fabulous job filing that stack of papers that's been cluttering the conference room for the past year." My name on those days is "you're not Tiffany" or "you're definitely not Sarah," so today, driving to a temp's idea of a paradise vacation at the Super Cineplex, I am grateful to decide for myself who I'm not.

In my mother's clothes, I feel the confidence that comes from having lived longer—through the death of her first love and her husband's abandonment—and come out the other side. I smell the arm of her jacket, a combination of her drugstore perfume and the cedar chips she keeps in her drawers and sprinkles on the floor of her closet.

This morning, as I pushed her clothes around on their hangers looking for an outfit, she sat up in bed. "Take all of my clothes," she announced. "Take them all!" She wet her finger in the glass of water on her bedside table to dab at the lipstick stain on the pillowcase.

"That bad?" If the dates are good, they are very, very good. When they are bad, she stays in bed.

"He was perfectly nice," she mumbles, falling back and putting a pillow over her face. "He's still living with his ex-wife."

In the month since I've been home, she's been on fifteen dates. One proposed on the first date, on his knees in a Mexican restaurant with a mariachi band backup; one's toupee got caught on an overhanging tree branch and a bird flew away with it, causing him to burst into tears; another picked her up and then swung by the house of an old girlfriend to ask her to join them. He thought she could tell my mother what she needed to know so they could skip to the deeper stuff. "This is deep enough—I've got the bends already," my mother said before calling a cab.

But she is always hopeful at the beginning of the night, spritzed with that awful perfume and decked out in a carefully chosen outfit. "How are my pillows?" she'll ask cheerfully, referring to the lines under her eyes.

"It'll happen," I said this morning, as useless and cryptic as the fortunes she sometimes buys for me out of bubble-gum machines. The last one: *Love is like a flower in someone else's yard.* I left the house quickly, pretending not to hear her as she called after me in a tone gone desperate at the thought of being left alone with herself.

Are the movie theater employees upstanding citizens? As I maneuver around the construction that surrounds the entrance to the Super Cineplex, I peek at the questions the theater owner gave Marla. I can hear his voice in these questions, the voice of a tired, lonely man who wants to befriend his employees but who ends up telling jokes they don't get. This man's questionnaire is an act of revenge. *Do the workers charge the proper bargain matinee rate or do they pocket the extra cash?* I say the questions out loud in the car, trying on an older woman's voice, throaty like Lauren Bacall.

With time to kill, I swing through the neighboring Walgreens for my drugstore fix. Drugstores have always soothed me with their aisles full of cheap solutions to anything. I roam the Hair and Nail Products aisle, where a teenage girl is taking the top off a bottle of nail polish remover to inhale the fumes. Her friend catches her in the act.

"No, stupid. Glue gets you high," she says. They both turn to look at me and run out of the store laughing in their outfits that are the same as what I wear most of the time—cutoffs, a tank top with a bra strap sneaking down one shoulder, sneakers with no socks. The girls look familiar, but everyone looks familiar when you come back to live in your hometown. Everyone is interchangeable—a relative, a best friend, someone you slept with, an enemy.

I comparison shop in the toothpaste aisle, studying the pictures of men and women with toothy grins meant to tell me more than just about their good teeth. Their lives, so their teeth say, are just as big and shiny. I read the Hallmark cards for your new baby, your grieving aunt, just because.

For some inexplicable reason there are polyfiber workout suits in the Sanitary Needs aisle. The couple on the package face each other, jogging furiously in place. The suit covers your whole body as you exercise, collecting the heat so that you actually shrink as you run. The couple jogs eternally toward each other, so, eventually, all that will be left are two puddles of sweat.

The overwhelmingly sweet smell of the candy aisle reminds me, as it always does, of San Francisco's salty-sweet wharf and pastel front. The neon martini glasses, the symbol for bars, nauseated me when I first arrived. They were part of a secret code, proof that a city is something you need to be born into. There were secrets that no one would ever tell you, like the names of fancy drinks or how to be comfortable in a bar; where that tiny shop is where you could buy the thing you've been looking for all of your life; how to find the perfect man, the sort of man who is the only man for you; how to find the perfect career, the sort of job that is the only job for you. These were city secrets I never learned, designed to protect you from your rawest self.

Across the street from the Walgreens, there's an old bank that was recently turned into a restaurant. The restroom doors have been fashioned out of the old vault doors. People eat their pan-Asian-American-Mexican food in tellers' booths. My mother has always said there is something magical about the way a city constantly reinvents itself. But it is the untouched land outside the boundaries of Standardsville that contains mystery for me. Growing up, the town seemed built out of the fear of that untouched land, the earth layers of unread history in sloughed-off dead skin, someone's old bones gone to dust. Whenever I thought of my own death, I imagined myself lying in a pile of leaves, slowly turning to dirt a few miles from a Freedom Mart.

A tiny woman with dark eyebrows that meet when she looks puzzled—as she does now—guides her lanky boyfriend up the Sanitary Needs aisle, past douches and tampons, past the polyfiber workout suits, toward me. Her long brown hair flips up at the ends dramatically, her hair poised to ask me a question too.

"Is that a church?" she says, pointing out the window toward the restaurant that used to be a bank.

"What?" I ask, looking to her boyfriend for help but he's looking down the aisle, wishing he were pricing mouthwash. He slouches sadly like someone who has spent all day with her. He looks at my feet as he pushes Coke bottle–lens glasses up the bridge of his nose. They are both of indistinguishable age—they could be anywhere from twenty to forty.

"Is that a *church*?" the tiny woman says again. She is gnome-like—powerful in her compactness.

"A church?" Maybe she is a gnome.

"Don't you know anything?" she says. She takes her exasperation out on her boyfriend, squeezing his arm to bring him back from his mouthwash fantasy. She punishes me with her stern, bunched-up eyebrows, then uses them to guide her boyfriend toward the door. She takes surprisingly long, swift strides with her short legs, creating her own breeze as she cuts through the thick summer air.

On my way across the enormous parking lot to the Super Cineplex, I take long, swift strides too. In the adjoining field, there is a muddy man-made duck pond without ducks. Beyond are endlessly flat fields. There is nothing for miles, a landscape waiting for its costume. Somewhere out there, I think I hear my name being called in a voice gravelly and deep like an engine breaking down. I spin around, expecting gnome lady and instead collide with my high school boyfriend.

"Isabelle," Dennis says again.

"Oh, shit," I say.

"Nice to see you too," he says.

"You know what I mean." I kiss his cheek and inhale his familiar scent—the warm, sweet smell of a baby with a hint of tobacco, a baby who smokes.

When I first met him, he was lying on the floor, in the middle of a parents-out-of-town party, singing along to an Otis Redding album as people stepped over him to get to the line for the bathroom. I waited in line too, forced to straddle one of his outstretched arms. He looked up and held out his hand for me to help him to his feet. When he stood up, I told him he smelled like a baby who smokes because I thought he was cute and, as a result, couldn't think of anything intelligent to say. He looked at me with resignation—pausing in the middle of "Pain in My Heart"—and said, "I know, man." Nothing fazed him and, at the time, that seemed like an admirable quality.

"What are you doing here?" Dennis asks, then spots the Chevy. "That thing still runs?"

"What are *you* doing here?" I ask back.

"Working." He takes a step back, arms wide apart so that I can get a good look at him in his black pants and vest, his white shirt, the "Manager" tag with his name printed on it. From the questionnaire: *Does the manager spend inordinate amounts of his precious time playing video games?* He sweeps his arm toward the Super Cineplex. "My kingdom," he says. "The latest addition to Standardsville's newest shopping island, Shop Op. Super Cineplex: movies for the mindless masses."

"I guess that means me."

"Movies for the mindless masses. And Isabelle"

"I'm going to be late for my movie, your highness." I take his arm and move him toward the doors.

He shakes his head as I pull out my wallet to pay for a ticket, and sneaks me in. "Ex-girlfriend discount," he says, putting his hand on the small of my back. He's trying to impress the pimply teenage-boy ushers flocking to the ticket counter to gossip. He guides me toward the manager's office.

"Aren't you in San Francisco?" he asks.

Does it look like I'm in San Francisco? I want to scream. And, no, we are nothing alike, even though here we are, back in the town where we started.

"On some weird time continuum, I am in San Francisco right now," I say instead. I'm going for coy and evasive, but instead I just sound weird.

"Isabelle," he says. His sympathetic tone makes me want to punch him. He uses my name to lay claim to whatever he still can. "Why are you dressed like a business lady?"

"Because." I take a deep breath and exhale the words that offer themselves, helpless sound sacrifices launched from my tongue. "I am here on business, Dennis. As difficult as it may be for you to believe, I *am* a business lady now. I do business."

"You're at the Super Cineplex on business? Driving that thing?" Dennis's Adam's apple looks trapped in the top button of his too-tight white shirt. His features seem huge, like he's under a microscope. Out the window behind him, a father uses a butterfly net to fish for a ball floating away on the murky surface of the duck pond while his young son jumps up and down on the shore.

"I've just come from a business meeting," I say quickly. "I'm taking a breather. I'm a business lady, business*woman*, taking a breather. The Chevy's on loan from my mother." A businesswoman taking a breather? The Chevy's on loan? But Dennis looks just confused enough to buy it.

"Businesswoman," Dennis says, trying it out. "What kind of business?" The unfinished construction around the duck pond, where the father is still fishing for the ball with his net and the boy is still jumping, reminds me of Dennis's favorite places to go in high school. "Still some mystery to them," he would say cryptically whenever he took me to one of the construction sites just outside town. What Dennis really liked about these places was that, like Dennis at that age, they still had the chance to make something of themselves, even if they looked like hell at the moment. Dennis's obviousness drew me, someone who could never get to the bottom line, to him. But even then, I knew he wouldn't be my Henry, the root of everything that came after. Dennis would allow me to remain rootless.

"I got a promotion at the phone company," I say. Last week, a phone solicitor tried to sell me a new long-distance phone service and I told him I had no friends or family just to get him off the phone. "Surely you must have one friend," he said, exasperated and desperate for the commission. "Not a one," I said, completely sincere in my dishonesty. He believed me because, in a voice different from his salesman's pitch, he said, "You have a friend in me."

"I'm a sales rep," I tell Dennis. I pause, pleased at the use of the word "rep." "I'm a traveling sales rep." No one questions a job with a nickname. "There's a conference at the Hotel Fugor," I continue.

"You're staying at that weird medieval place with the jousters?" Dennis asks.

"Actually, the jousters have their own rooms."

Dennis just gives me his look that means he'll stand there solidly until he gets some real answers. With Dennis, patience has always verged on obtuseness.

I can't face telling Dennis I'm single right now. "I have a fiancé," I blurt out. "Sebastian. He's British." I'm not sure where the British part came from, but it sounds intimidating.

"Your movie is about to start," Dennis says, choosing to ignore me. "You know, you should really lay off the perfume." He takes my hand and holds it between his cold palms. The air conditioner in the theater is turned on so high that the leaves of the potted palm in the corner of his office rustle.

The last man to touch me was a painter working as a paralegal in San Francisco. I touched him as though I were touching an electric fence: fast for the jolting thrill of it, then anxious to get away. The last night in his bed, I dreamt that his apartment was a ship, floating away on choppy seas until it reached an island where my mother stood on the shore in a phone booth trying to call me. The phone wouldn't take her quarters. My search for love seemed both gratingly minute—a day when pay phones don't work, you've lost your fifth umbrella, and you drop your wallet in a puddle because you're carrying too many things—and impossibly vague, like trying to describe something you've never seen. Here in the Super Cineplex, Dennis's hands are like a cold compress, comforting and steady.

"Let's hang out," he says, nodding dismissively to an usher who hovers with a question. "Can I take my break now?" the usher asks, but Dennis continues to look at me. *Does the person who tears your ticket look you respectfully in the eye?*

"Don't be a dumb-ass," Dennis says to the boy, looking me in the eye.

"Sure, let's hang out," I say, and the usher wanders away.

"Damn," he mumbles under his breath loud enough for us to hear. "Serious harshness."

Dennis pouts like I'm blowing him off, so I add, "I mean it. Let's really hang out. Really." Already we've abandoned the formality of two people who haven't seen each other in years. We're back to pleading teenage tones.

In the dark anonymity of the movie theater, I still feel Dennis's touch. The movie is a romantic comedy about a man and a woman who have been in love for years. Their love is tested by other love interests, other men and women who offer new sexual positions, a hairless chest or a hairier chest, smaller breasts or bigger breasts, new definitions of themselves, innovative methods for maneuvering through life. Ultimately, the movie helps the original couple return to each other and stick with a good thing. Don't look a gift horse in the mouth. Home is where the heart is. Why go looking for trouble? What you've been looking for all your life has been right in front of you all along. "I just didn't know how to look," the woman says, jumping into the man's arms. It's a terrible movie, but part of me never wants the lights to come up again, wants the credits to roll and roll so that I can remain slouched down in the movie theater darkness, perfectly erased.

About a year ago when I first moved to San Francisco, my

mother called me and, after twenty-plus years of acting as though he had disappeared off the face of the earth, said, "We have to find your father."

"I have to see him," she said. "He has all of my Curtis Mayfield albums."

"Mom," I said. "You don't even have a turntable anymore."

"I don't care. I want them back." She cried inconsolably for an hour. I came home immediately. I thought she was losing her mind. I came home and ran meaningless errands—taking clothes my mother had never worn to the tailors to be altered as she worried pounds away, shopping for the weed whacker my mother suddenly had to have right at that very moment though she'd never whacked a weed in her life.

I thought I saw my father once in a check-in line at the San Francisco airport. I'd taken to spending afternoons in the arrival/departure area, watching people get on and off planes. This man I thought was my father—based on my own rough estimation of what he might look like twenty-five years since the last time I'd seen him—didn't see me. He riffled through his bag, checked his ticket, brushed lint from his pants, unwrapped a piece of gum, and put it in his mouth. He picked up his luggage and boarded the plane. The most remarkable thing about this possible sighting was how unremarkable it was. In my mind, I had turned him into a stranger standing in line at an airport long ago.

My mother made a list of things she claimed my father had taken from her: a hand-knit Irish sweater, a rare book on the Galápagos, and the Curtis Mayfield albums.

"A rare book on the Galápagos?" I asked. "What are you talking about?"

"And a fancy pen with my name engraved on it," she said.

I decided to run some more errands. I went to the copy shop to copy anything—I'd just gotten my job at the phone company and I thought making copies might lull me into the zombielike state of calm I achieved at work. I recognized Dennis behind the counter, despite the new braided tail down his back. His facial features seemed to have grown with the rest of his body since high school; the changes in his physical appearance seemed grotesque. I put on my sunglasses and quietly copied loose receipts I'd found in the back of the Chevy, hoping to leave the store unnoticed, but he came from behind.

"I know you," Dennis said. "I know you," he said again like he was blowing my cover. He leaned against the copy machine and told me how his band broke up, how his girlfriend had a baby with his old drummer, how they all ran into each other around town, and that it was a bad scene.

"Man," he said. I copied my hand by accident.

"Better watch that," he said. A copy of my hand slid out of the machine. "Stuff's radioactive." I could have gone home with him and maybe we would have pushed against each other for a few hours, found meaning in skin. His warm, thick self pressed against mine would hide my life until it was safe to look again. But I could see the future, or at least the next morning, when I would want Dennis gone, so I offered him a blank face.

When I returned home, my mother made an announcement. "I never really liked Curtis Mayfield that much anyway."

"Mom," I protested. "I thought you wanted me to help you find Dad."

"I know, honey. I don't know what got into me." She got out the furniture polish and went to work on the wooden legs of the dining room table.

"I think I need to get out more," she said, looking up from her crouch. I went back to San Francisco the next day.

The credits are finished rolling and the lights come up in the theater. On my way through the lobby, I wave to Dennis, who is reprimanding an usher, shaking a bossy finger. He yells, "See you around" in his rock-and-roll voice, a voice he probably heard Robert Plant or Jimi Hendrix use in one of the midnight movie concerts he dragged me to in high school. I swagger a little on the way to the car, to give Dennis something to watch.

AT home, my mother is standing in front of the mirror in the foyer, dabbing at her curled eyelashes with a tentative fingertip.

"How do I look?" She turns so that I get the full effect of her floor-length blue chiffon dress. "We're going ballroom dancing at the Y. He called himself Twinkle Toes in his ad, which, let's face it, spells disaster, but you know I like to dance."

"You look stunning," I say. I feel a prick of jealousy at her good looks and the way she knows what she wants, even if it's just for tonight. I decide not to tell her that I saw Dennis at the movies. He will stay my secret, like mystery shopping. She never liked him anyhow—not as my lazy high school boyfriend, not in any of his incarnations. I told her when Dennis worked at the copy shop, she said "It just proves what I've known all along, he's probably never had an original idea in his whole life."

She pauses in her primping to give my reflection a meaningful look.

"I'm fine," I say, squirming under her gaze and irritated by her perceptiveness. Our relationship seems too easy sometimes, as if when I moved back home I was fulfilling the final step in our relationship as a mother and daughter married to each other.

"Tell me later," she says.

I'm choking on that drugstore perfume, so I walk outside onto the front steps to get some air. From where I'm standing, our street is a movie set with the sun setting on identical houses; it shines through the water dribbling from Mrs. Morton's cherub fountain, making the water sparkle like champagne. Somewhere far away in the distance is the sound of a car alarm, making everyone feel secure.

Across the street, Raymond washes his one dish, cup, fork, spoon, and knife as he pretends not to watch our house, waiting for my mother to leave so that he can come over and stand in her lingering perfume. Through Raymond's eyes and the gauzy yellow of the setting sun, our house must look like heaven.

My mother twirls on the lawn—a fairy-tale princess all grown up. She blows me a kiss. "Don't drink too much, sweetie," she says, pretending to toss back an imaginary glass of wine.

"How very parental of you."

She rolls her eyes at me, arranging her chiffon as she climbs into her car. As soon as her car leaves the cul-de-sac, Raymond is out the door and headed for our house. I fluff the pillows on the couch, turn on the television, then wait for him to knock. Though he spends a lot of time crouched in our bushes spying on us, he likes to maintain this formality.

I discovered Raymond's secret the first week I was home. I'd spent an afternoon cruising Standardsville, looking for anything recognizable. Feeling like an alien, I pulled into the driveway and saw Raymond's hightops poking out of the bushes that line my mother's house, and recognized a fellow spaceman. I pretended not to notice him as I walked up the front stairs, and I've kept his secret ever since. In most cases, having someone spy on your life is creepy, but with Raymond, it's like having a witness. He keeps track of our lives. He's the person who could say: It's true, Adeline and Isabelle really do exist.

When Raymond arrives, we watch a cop show. In this episode, a detective falls in love with a beautiful murder suspect.

"I'm not an actor, but I play one in real life," Raymond says out of the blue during the commercial break, after the detective discovers a bloody knife under the bed of the beautiful murder suspect. "You know, that old commercial, 'I'm not a doctor, but I play one on TV.' "

"I get it," I say. "I know exactly what you're talking about."

I take Raymond's hand as he continues to stare at the TV. Our hand-holding isn't sweaty or hot or tense. There's nothing uncomfortable about it. It's like we've been holding hands all our lives.

4

THE phone ringing startles my mother in her blue chiffon off the couch. When she got home from dancing at the Y, this is where she collapsed. I hear a thud. "Twinkle Toes, my ass," she says. Dating has become her second job. Some nights she gets home and doesn't have the energy to make it up the stairs.

Twinkle Toes had a blue-tinted rinse in his thinning hair that made her want to cry. "Is the aging process mandatory?" she said when I went down to check on her last night. "I mean, is it absolutely necessary? Are there no options?"

"Twinkle Toes?" Marla asks when I pick up the upstairs phone.

"Go back to bed," my mother says. She has trouble hanging up the downstairs phone so it clatters and bangs until it finally comes to rest in its cradle.

"Marla, do you always make calls at this hour?" Outside, the sun is a burning orange line on the horizon.

"You've got to be ready for anything in the business of temporary services," she says. "You never know who might need you and when. You've got to be ready to go, go, go. Any time of the day or night."

"And you are calling because . . . ?"

"Don't get smart with me, Isabelle," Marla barks. "Just because you're the chosen one doesn't mean you can mouth off. You're special, but not that special."

"I'm sorry," I say meekly.

"I need you here immediately." She hangs up.

Sweat-soaked construction workers tear down the old pizza place that has stood a couple of blocks from our cul-de-sac since I was in high school. They are replacing it with a new pizza place. On my way to Temporama, I maneuver the bulky frame of the Chevy to avoid hitting the chunks of brick from the original building as they roll stupidly onto the road.

High school legend had it that a girl was buried in the foundation of the first pizza place. I didn't know her, but I passed her every day in the hall. Her name was Susan, but she called herself Star. Her hair was shaved on one side and the other side was dyed bright orange, the color of a highway cone. There was a boy, later forced by his parents to wear corrective headgear, who once passed Star in the hall and said through naked, crooked teeth not yet gripped in the vice of braces, "Ready for hunting season?" "Yeah," Star said. "And I've got a matching vest, so you better watch out or I'll shoot your sorry ass." After that, word got out that she was a girl who fought back.

Her clutziness was appealing. The first time I noticed her, she stumbled over nothing on the flat of the corridor linoleum.

Her drifty, fluttery eye contact—looking and then cutting away in nervous invitation—comforted me in high school when nothing else did. I counted on her presence to help me through the daily smell of acne medication, cakey makeup, and rotting locker food. Around the smelly lockers, unremarkable Sea Breeze–drenched girls with their less-than-streamlined wardrobes were suddenly elevated to a status almost as good as that of the prettiest girls, tragically having the best years of their lives. This status boost was a direct result of their claim that they were at the slumber party where Star sleepwalked into the woods. The police found her underwear hanging from a tree branch and for years, whenever I felt sad, I saw her young-girl underwear hanging in the woods like a symbol of protest. The same locker crowd who said that she had sleepwalked out of the party were also convinced that whoever murdered her (the police found strands of orange hair caught in trees and in bloody clumps in the dirt, but no one ever found her body) had buried her in the newly laid concrete of the pizza place under construction at the time.

A man in his early twenties named Jay Delaney turned up months later claiming that he did it. Even at his young age, he seemed to know that this was the only thing he would ever lay claim to. Before the trial, Jay Delaney disappeared as if to prove he could be no one just as easily as he could be infamous. The police never found him, and now, according to teenage-girl legend, Star's body lies like a fossil in the hardened bottom layers of the pizza place being razed.

Star had been one of those interclique wild cards, maneuvering between nerds and popular kids with apparent ease, seeming to let the whole tiny world of high school pass easily through her. One day, I saw her talking to the school math whiz who had just returned from an all-state competition where he'd won second prize. Star touched his arm, and his tight, pointy shoulders went round. In a voice that was unusual for its leveled consistency—not raised at the end of every sentence like a question—she said, "You're just warming up. They won't even recognize you next year." That she, a teenage girl, put him, a teenage boy, so at ease seemed like a miracle. Even more remarkable was that I'd heard the very same lines spoken the night before by a little-known actress in the movie of the week. Star lifted them directly from a scene in which the little-known actress comforted her character's brother who had lost a leg in a horrible car accident and was struggling with physical therapy.

"I try to live in the moment," she said on a different day to a football player. He nodded awkwardly in his newly muscular body. The day before he'd missed a crucial pass and lost the game for the team. Star perfectly imitated the end-of-an-episode speech of a sitcom mother who, when her daughter didn't get a callback for a school play, said, "That's all we have as human beings on this earth. That and each other." The football player smiled dimly and chucked her on the shoulder in agreement.

Now, as I drive by the construction, I hope that they are careful with her crumbling bones. After she disappeared, I pretended that she spoke to me from beyond the grave. She would let me know that it was okay to fall up stairs or to feel bottomless despair while listening to Led Zeppelin alone in my room. In return, I kept her presence strong in the world by thinking about her on a daily basis. She was my Henry and I promised her that I would be the audience to her death, that I would tell the story of her short life to myself as a lesson. But then I left town and forgot all about her.

"And look at you now," I imagine she says as I drive by. "You need me again." Her voice is lost in the rumble of demolition.

Star is the first reason I believe in ghosts when I'm home. A city can hide the fact of nature with seamless concrete and buildings that cover every inch of bare earth, but here in the suburbs, hulking trees and fields not yet touched surround the scattered, squat buildings like reminders that life is raw unless you dress it up. In the empty fields adjacent to the mall farthest out of town, and in the patch of forest behind the Dairy Queen, there are moving, shadowy shapes—light filtered through trees, wind blowing grass in lush rhythms, and the occasional dark figure that's neither light nor wind.

I drive by the Hotel Fugor, where Sebastian supposedly waits for me in our room decorated with sabers and stuffed boars' heads. He waits for me to come home for dinner, to sit with him in the hard-back chairs of the dark oak dining room where we'll be serenaded by a man in tights playing a flügel-horn. He still feels passionately about me, though we've been together for years. As we make our way down to dinner, he pushes me against the wall with manly yet gentle aggression and kisses me. He uses expletives, in his sexy British accent, when he says he loves me: I love you so fucking much. God damn it, I love you. Shit, could I love you any more? Marriage will be our safety net, the mesh swinging gently below us as we fly through the air, performing the acrobatics of love. The lady in the car behind me honks and gives me the finger. I'm crawling along the highway and she's right on my ass. I give her two fingers as she screeches by, screaming mutely at me from the cool confines of her station wagon.

Next to the Hotel Fugor is an idyllic park, which marks the center of town. Until Dennis had other ideas, like rolling in playground dirt behind the junior high school, I always imagined my first kiss would be in the park's gazebo. But Dennis lived under a tyrannical reign of immediate satisfaction. Everything—eating, drinking, sexual pleasure—was a small, miraculous event. That he could seem so completely fulfilled was a miracle in itself, as amazing as Star's hall counsel, and I was astonished into what I thought of as love.

Temporama is a low brick building, indistinguishable among a row of low brick buildings. At the entrance is a sign that Temporama shares with a business called The Healing Arts and a personal-injury lawyer. When I was growing up, this building was my kindergarten, the windows filled with colorful cutout letters and their animal companions—aardvark, baboon, camel. My kindergarten classmates and I wished for an animal rebellion that would lead us out of the building and down the street to Carvel.

Sometime in the middle of that year, I told my mother and father I was tired of having a name. It was like the aardvark in the window being reduced to a construction-paper A, an inadequate symbol of its rambunctious, ant-eating self.

"But how will we call you in for dinner?" my father would ask while my mother smiled and looked out the window into the night, beyond the outskirts of town, past our lives. "Little girl, little girl," my father would call, cupping his hands to his mouth like the shepherd calling his lost sheep in a book I loved then. "Little girl," he called, laughing like someone who was used to entertaining himself. He'd turn to my mother and pretend to call her back from wherever she had drifted. I longed for my father to throw me into the air until my flat cardboard colors went round and galloped away.

When I walk into the Temporama office, Marla is on the phone with her husband. She distinguishes between his man world and our world of women by winking at me while telling him in a sugar-sweet voice, "You're absolutely right, honey." Today's rose fingernails glide lazily over the computer keys, seemingly too slow to be accurate but always reaching their mark as Marla moves numbers around in a chart.

While I wait for her, I read the ever changing scraps of paper she has taped all over her desk. *Treat me no differently than you would a Queen. Life can be understood backward but it must be lived forward. Winning is not a sometimes thing (Vince Lombardi).* Next to her computer is a poem that she wrote. *You must learn to relish my tears. And when love beckons, you should join him though his ways are hard and steep.* There is an asterisk by the word "relish" and, at the bottom of the page, relish is defined: "enjoyment, zest."

The other day, she read to me from a writing manual she swears by: "For many people, having to write something causes more heartache and anxiety than the Cubs in a play-off game. Unfortunately, such anxiety makes it hard to approach a task calmly and confidently." Marla turned to me and mouthed, "*And how.*" She continued: "Sometimes, we fatten up our prose out of linguistic insecurity." She stopped reading and looked at me, " 'Linguistic insecurity.' *That* is poetry, Isabelle. The freaking directions. Poetry."

"You're right, honey," Marla says now to her husband,

rolling her eyes to indicate he's not. "Absolutely right. Okay, gotta go."

When she hangs up, she turns to me with an energy that always startles me. Her amused blue eyes widen like she's got a secret only the two of us can know. "Here's my fact for the week, Isabelle. An ongoing survey has recently shown that sixty percent of people who have rekindled an old romance are still together with most saying that the sex is better than ever. Something to think about in this day and age of elusive love. My husband and myself, for instance, have rekindled our flame on numerous occasions." She giggles and nods vigorously, which she does whenever I don't respond adequately.

"I've fallen off the romance wagon," I say in an effort to define myself. The air conditioner rustles the huge leaves of the potted plant in the corner of Temporama and Dennis holding my hands in the Super Cineplex office returns to me as a tingle of remembered pleasure. I'm not sure what the romance wagon is, but I'm almost certain I've never been on it. In the face of Marla's easy summation of mysterious lands—romance, true love—I find myself using terms like "romance wagon."

"Oldies are the goodies," Marla says. I imagine her at home in front of the mirror after she's removed layers of makeup with wads of cotton balls and rows of elaborate cleanser, her pink skin scrubbed raw.

"No hitches with the Super Cineplex, right? Cake. Baby stuff. I knew you were the right woman for this job. Okay, you need to find a date for this next one. We're going to have some fun." She's bouncing in her chair a little.

Scrub, scrub. Raw, pink skin. I nod so that she doesn't have to.

"I'm sending you to the Other Movie Theater. The artsy movie theater. You like those artsy movies, right? You need to dress all in black, like someone who sees a lot of movies with subtitles."

"Why do I need a date?"

"Because it'll make you look less like a spy, and frankly, you look like you need one. You look like you have a headache. Maybe your bra straps are too thin. Thin bra straps can dig into your shoulders and cause headaches." All of Marla's advice comes from the women's magazines she has piled under her desk. She doesn't discriminate—*Vogue, McCall's, Young and Modern*—on the basis of target age or taste, constantly recycling and referring back to information she gleaned five years ago. She has an amazing memory for this sort of information. "Get some bras with wide straps," she says. She leans in close, pulls her blouse over her shoulder, and shows me hers—pink and wide.

"I don't need a date. Just because I *look* like I have a headache doesn't mean I need a date. There are other things women need besides dates, you know. Ibuprofen, for instance."

Marla ignores me as she continues to shuffle papers, looking for the correct form. "It's another local questionnaire," she says. "The theater owner thinks the manager is too snooty to the customers. He laughs at moviegoers who say 'movie' instead of 'film.' "

Marla pushes paper around and furrows her brow, touching the tip of her pen to her forehead and tapping. Maybe Marla saw her mother looking for something in a similar way. Maybe it was a gesture that struck Marla as grown-up. I have a horrifying vision of the romance wagon overflowing with mothers and daughters.

"What are you looking at?" Marla asks. She's found the questionnaire. "Tomorrow night. Remember: all black, take a date."

"I don't need a date," I repeat.

"Check your bra straps," Marla says, dismissing me with the brisk click of her rose talons on her desk. "You know, eighty percent of employees are chronically angry, Isabelle. Think about it. You don't need thin bra straps making matters worse."

On the way home, I turn on the Chevy's crackly radio. A DJ is gleefully reporting the weather. He giggles as he announces that the temperature has officially reached 110. He is just one of the many Standardsville weather shock jocks who act as if they are gaining in some secret weather race, thrilled every time the temperature climbs one more degree. The banks are in on this mysterious race too, their time-and-temperature clocks displaying a different temperature on every corner, as if here in the land of strip malls, the wilds of suburbia, there is nothing left to do but play god with the weather. On one block, United Bank & Trust reads 108, and around the corner Federal Savings has them beat by two degrees.

Before their stint at the phone company in San Francisco, Louise and Simon were telemarketers for a chain of Old West amusement parks in Tucson, Arizona. The parks offered a tour with an extensive menu. Visitors could participate in re-enacted gunfights, shooting blanks at pistol-toting cowboys with droopy mustaches and shit-kicking boots with spurs, or they could learn to cheat at poker and swig apple juice meant to look like liquor out of dusty shot glasses in a saloon full of Old West prostitutes wearing little more than Miracle Bras and garter belts. Another option in the tour package was death. Death involved squeezing sacks of stage blood at any point during one of the reenacted gunfights or learning how to fall off the roof of the saloon. Louise and Simon would describe Tucson as we sat around the breakroom at the phone company drinking just enough coffee to make us sweat and distract us from the numbing boredom of our jobs. Tucson, they said, was built around the saguaro cacti that were everywhere—in people's front yards, in the parking lots of Circle Ks, lining the median strips of minor and major highways. Some people, Louise and Simon claimed, built their houses around them, incorporating them into the design of their homes. One particularly boring day, Louise said the cactus was like a "triumphant totem pole."

"Triumphant totem poles?" Simon said, laughing. "You're so melodramatic."

But Louise was carried away, and I didn't mind her melodrama lifting me out of my day.

"These cactus are reminders of our mortality," she said. "Some live over one hundred years." I admired the way she read the landscape for clues. She conjured up black widows, scorpions, javelinas, flash floods, heat that melted pens on your dashboard, all proof that humans were mere specks in the face of nature.

"It's a land that should never have been settled," Simon said while Louise shook her head and waved her hands in front of her like she was passing in a game of blackjack.

"The settlers must have shown up in the winter," Louise said. "They built, then couldn't afford to leave by the time a hundred and twenty degrees was a good day in June."

The DJ laughs out loud now as he provides tomorrow's forecast—more of the same—but, like everybody else, he has to climb into his car at the end of the day, burning his hands on the steering wheel as he heads to the nearest Walgreens, where he can finally feel the breeze.

5

THE cashier at the downtown Walgreens, where Dennis and I go to buy candy cheaper than the dusty assortment at the movie concession stands, has a red, white, and blue flag painted on her forehead. Temporama doesn't give me a popcorn and candy allowance. After you do ten mystery shops, Marla claims, you get perks like that.

"It's the Fourth of freaking July," the cashier says when she catches me staring. She points to the back of the store where restless children stand in swervy lines waiting for a lone clown with a rainbow afro to paint stars and shooting rockets on their cheeks.

"Sorry," I say, sliding my jumbo pack of M&Ms off the counter before she can put it in a bag. "I've stopped looking at calendars as a rule."

"What do you expect?" Dennis says to the cashier, looking up from rows and rows of gum. "People are going to stare if you have a flag painted on your forehead."

"Dennis, I can speak for myself," I say.

"Yeah," Dennis says to the cashier. "She can speak for herself."

"Dennis." I protest, and he laughs.

"*Kidding*," he says.

"She doesn't have to speak for herself, the nose ring says it all," the cashier says, scanning my outfit with unabashed disapproval. I've got my own black jeans on, a black fitted T-shirt of my mother's, a clip-on nose ring from a different Walgreens, and a new, hardback copy of *Ulysses*, its spine barely broken, that Marla borrowed from her husband's Classic Literature Library. "Not that you don't look smart already," she said. "But this is like your passport to smartness. Sting carried a copy around for a while, you know." At Marla's request, my face is dusted with pale powder and my lips are wine red. I am Marla's idea of an artsy chick, today is my grown-up Halloween.

"How do you blow your nose with that thing in?" the cashier asks.

"I've been wanting to ask the same thing all night . . ." Dennis says. He looked slightly alarmed when I picked him up, then decided to play it cool. But as long as the nose ring is up for discussion, he's decided to get some answers.

I pull the clip-on out of my nose, and the cashier and Dennis wince and duck like I've pulled a gun on them.

"Gross," the cashier says.

"Why are you carrying a book?" Now that we've broached the subject of the nose ring, Dennis feels free to get to the bottom of my whole look.

"In case you started to bore me? Can we just go to the movies now?" I steer Dennis toward the door.

The cashier looks away, down the aisle of cold remedies and other pain relievers.

In the Other Movie Theater, a sky-blue wood building that used to be somebody's house, Dennis and I sit cross-legged in tattered armchairs as we watch a shadowy futuristic French movie, made entirely out of still photographs. The movie's gaunt, nameless, unshaved hero lives underground because a nuclear war has made surface-living impossible. Everything is musty and brown in the postapocalyptic world. The hollow-cheeked hero dreams that he is a child in an airport, watching as a beautiful woman runs toward an anonymous man crumpling to the ground. Over the course of the movie, the hero grows a full beard, even as he travels backward through time where he falls in love and decides to abandon the postapocalyptic underground world for the past. That is where we are now—the hero has just resolved to abandon his foothold in the present to be with the woman he loves.

Dennis nudges me. "Which is the present?"

"Hang on." I offer him M&Ms from my jumbo pack. I saw this movie as a child with my mother, and then I was the one asking the questions. My mother told me that everything would become clear once the movie was over and, if not then, in a week or two. The key was to stop asking questions long enough to let the information settle, she said. At the time, this seemed like an adult piece of knowledge, a rare jewel to admire and consider. Dennis will have a better chance of understanding if he lets the movie pass through him like a spirit. Also, Dennis has always been a big talker during movies. My hope is that the M&Ms will keep him quiet for a minute or two.

When I called to invite Dennis to the movies, he asked whether I'd be bringing my fiancé.

"Sebastian?" I said nonchalantly. "He had to go back to San Francisco this afternoon to take care of the house and the cats." The house and the cats and Sebastian all sounded so nice that for a minute, I was jealous of myself.

"*Sebastian* won't be jealous if you go to the movies with your high school ex?"

"Why should he be?" I asked coyly, and then felt guilty for cheating on my imaginary boyfriend. According to Marla's instructions—"Don't tell anyone! No pillow talk, no nothing!"—I haven't told Dennis about the mystery shop aspect of going to the movies.

The theater isn't crowded in the middle of the day—a clinging couple, a group of three whispering girls who complain loudly about the subtitles, a distinguished row of very serious fifty-plus academics. Dennis and I slouch familiarly near the back of the theater, our knees touching lightly to prove how comfortable we are with each other.

Dennis has always objected to the Other Movie Theater. He says the marquee looks like somebody's refrigerator because of the way the theater uses different-size, different-color letters to spell out the names of the movies in jagged sentences. "I'm a Super Cineplex man," Dennis said on our way into the theater. "For you, Isabelle, I'll take the risk. But I still can't believe I took the day off from the movie theater to go to the movies." The way Dennis chooses our seats without hesitation, seats that provide a perfect view of the slightly off-center, small screen, makes me suspect he's been here before. Artsy movies and higher education were always my territory and Dennis likes to play this up. Dennis never went to college. He took a few anthropology classes at the community college after high school but stopped when one of his teachers took an interest in his work. As soon as it became clear that he had a knack for school when he applied himself, he got a job selling engraved pencils out of the back of his car. Then there was his stint with the exterminating company, his career as a bar back, the year he spent as a children's birthday party clown (donating sperm when he needed to supplement his income). He became a so-called travel agent for a while, until the class-action lawsuit. After that, he devoted himself to finding steadier jobs — waiting tables, working in a Laundromat, the copy shop, and now the Super Cineplex. When I first went away to college, Dennis called every day for the first week until I had fully described a world that didn't include him. Then he didn't call again for a year.

Does the movie remain within the four corners of the screen? Does it sometimes decapitate the hero/heroine? Do the movies sometimes go blurry, as if you have been drinking? Another bitter, local questionnaire. I excuse myself to investigate the restrooms. Marla warned me that, until I'd gotten the hang of reconnaissance work, I might surprise a stray man in the men's room. Tonight I'm lucky, the coast is clear. After I check the men's room, which appears clean except for a loose roll of toilet paper that has unfurled itself along the length of the bathroom, I sit on the lid of a toilet seat in a stall of the women's room with the door closed. Under Other Comments, I make a note of the unruly toilet paper and the gum that Dennis stepped in on his way down the aisle in the theater. I put the questionnaire back in my purse and flush the toilet to cover my tracks.

When I get back to my seat, the hero's menacing underground bosses are following him through time in an effort to bring him back to the present. Dennis turns to me and I hand him a fistful of M&Ms. The menacing bosses follow the hero into the very moment of his dream. There, his child self looks on as the woman he loves watches his adult self fall to the ground, shot by the underground bosses of the future. As the man's body curls like burning paper, the audience recognizes the curl toward death. The distinguished over-fifty crowd nods solemnly to each other and the teenage girls go quiet as it becomes clear that this moment of dying is the moment the hero has been obsessed with all his life.

"Oh shit," Dennis says softly. "Man."

When I saw this movie with my mother, I watched the side of her face in the movie light as the hero died. While there was no way out of life's forward thrust for either of us, she was much closer to death than I was, to that moment when obsession meets reality. And she'd borne witness to Henry's death. She had been to mysterious places in her mind that I hadn't even conceived of yet. She knew so much that I wondered how I would ever know as much as her, how I would ever endure what she had endured in order to know that much. At the time, the thought made me want to run home and listen to my mother's favorite home-cooking radio program, hosted by a woman with a relentlessly bright and chirpy voice.

When the lights come up, I gasp.

"What's wrong?" Dennis says. He slaps me on the back. "Wrong pipe?"

"Stop pounding on my back," I say, coughing. "I'm fine." But there is gnome lady from Walgreens, with her caterpillar eyebrows, in the corner with her skulking boyfriend. Like the time I saw the local news anchor in the grocery store smelling melons for ripeness, this has the feel of a star spotting. It seems like seeing a stranger more than once should have significance. There's a certain comfort in it. The world—or at least the particular world of Standardsville—is not so big after all. We're all wandering the same drugstore aisles and seeing the same movies. Gnome lady strokes her boyfriend's shoulder as if he were her pet as she gathers her purse from the aisle.

The lights come on and I look her way and smile, but she bunches up her caterpillar eyebrows and turns away.

"Do you know that girl?" Dennis asks as we make our way out of the theater.

"Not really," I say. I don't want to explain how I'm looking for a sign from twice-seen strangers so I tell a joke instead. It's a joke that I told a blind date in San Francisco during a lapse in conversation as we walked from the car to a cafeteria-style burrito place in the Mission.

"What's the difference between a new mistress, an old mistress, and a wife?"

Dennis hops on one leg beside me, trying to pull the gum off his shoe.

"I give up," he says. He puts his hand on my shoulder for balance. "Tell me."

"A new mistress says faster, faster, an old mistress says slower, slower, and a wife . . ." I put on a face of utter boredom and look at the ceiling, the way I did for my date who was still in his suit from work (he worked in publishing but really wanted to be a writer). "Says beige, I'll paint it beige."

Dennis throws his head back the way he does when he thinks something is really funny. He doesn't make a sound at first, like a baby when it starts to cry, and then he lets loose with a noise that sounds like wild birds. When I first heard his laugh, I loved the way it was like a bodily function—a sneeze or a fart—something he couldn't help or control. I appreciate his enthusiasm. The publishing/writer guy didn't laugh out loud. He smiled a world-weary smile to prove he was beyond laughter.

Dennis hums on the way out of the theater, loudly so that I will ask him what he's humming.

"Dennis?" I play along. "What are you humming?"

Next to the movie theater is a beauty parlor that strives for the esoteric aesthetics of a big city. A naked mannequin with a birdcage full of towels for a head extends her arms toward a chair, hands reaching for something that isn't there anymore. The mannequin that used to sit in front of her has toppled out of her chair. Facedown, bent awkwardly at the waist, towels spill out of her own birdcage head.

"My head would spill popcorn," Dennis says, then continues humming.

"Humming?" I remind him. "What are you humming, Dennis?"

"ABBA—they're everywhere. Where have you been, Isabelle?" Dennis says. "San Francisco?" He laughs at himself so I don't have to.

"Did you even like them during the seventies, when they really were everywhere?"

"Of course," he says, but he's lying because he looks away,

the way he did in high school when I asked him if he thought another girl was beautiful and he said no, definitely not. Even when I said, "Really, you can tell me the truth." I thought I wanted to know the truth, thinking I was more interested in a socioanthropological sort of way than jealous. I remember his tricks the way I remember songs I used to love—every word, every nuance, returns to me involuntarily from dusty corners of my brain.

As we climb into the Chevy, the smell of cigarettes and air freshener envelops me the way it did every morning on the days I drove Dennis to school and, for a minute, no time has passed at all. Like the movie's gaunt, nameless hero I've returned not to the crucial moment of my death but to the steady mindlessness of adolescence. Even Dennis's fake nostalgia for ABBA makes sense. Anchored in the faraway of the here and now, he can enjoy the ugliness of bell-bottoms, the awkward feel of his then-changing body, even ABBA. Dennis pulls out a tape he's got stashed like drugs in the inside pocket of his jean jacket and pops it into the tape deck as we follow the elaborate maze of the parking lot toward the highway. He knows every word and he sings them to me, wanting to prove that he knows these songs by heart, that he's known them for years.

"If you change your mind, I'm the first in line," he croons in a Swedish accent. "Honey, I'm still free, take a chance on me."

Barreling down the highway, we pass a man jogging on the side of the road. He wears a mask over his mouth to protect himself from car fumes. Dennis smiles and waves out the window, letting him in on the secret of our reckless abandon. We're two crazy kids returning to a love that never existed.

"If you're all alone, when the pretty birds have flown . . ." Dennis sings.

The Chevy windows are open until the air conditioner kicks in, so we have to turn the shitty tape deck up really loud to hear it. I light a cigarette—Marla gave me a pack as a prop— and halfway through I have a coughing fit that has Dennis pounding me on the back for the second time this afternoon.

"Enough. Enough," I say. "Do you want to go to my mother's house? She's having a barbecue and I'm tired of the pig roasts at the Hotel Fugor. A girl can only eat so much pork."

"What the hell?" Dennis says, as nonchalantly as possible.

WE find my mother and this evening's date, a paunchy man wearing a faded red T-shirt and jean cutoffs, in the backyard. The sloppy outfit looks studied—he must have tried on several combinations to attain this fresh-from-the-dirty-hamper look. He and my mother poke tentatively at hamburgers with long metal forks, as if performing some ancient ritual. My mother looks up gratefully when she sees us.

"Dennis," she says enthusiastically, and now I know the date's been going badly. She's never been glad to see Dennis.

"Isabelle, Dennis, this is Clifford." She points the tines of her long fork in his direction as if he were a specimen.

"Mmmm," Clifford says. The experience of meeting us requires deep thought. He extends his soft, tiny hand for us to shake. "Hello, hello," he says diplomatically, one for each of us.

"He's the Highway Psychic," my mother says in a tone that tells me she's as surprised as I am. My mother and I have driven past the Highway Psychic's shack, just beyond the far-thest housing development, on the way to the airport. We always assumed that the Highway Psychic was a lonely woman with many lovers lured from the highway through a tchotchke-ridden living room—a collection of tiny china animals perched on top of shelves and doilied tabletops—into a candlelit bedroom filled with bead-fringed objects. The sign outside the shack reads: IF THIS IS YOUR LIFE PATH, I'M ON IT.

"Your mother was a little surprised," Clifford says, sounding more and more like someone who is about to tell my fortune. "In the personals, I describe myself as a web designer. Which I am, but only part-time to support the divining." He smiles in an ironic way that stops me from taking my mother inside to call the police. The smile works on my mother as well because she moves a little closer to Clifford and smiles too.

Dennis, still excited that my mother was glad to see him, jumps in, wanting to offer something. "Divining. Cool job." He looks at me as he speaks, as though we are a couple again.

"Definitely," Clifford says. With the tentativeness of some-one unused to meat, he uses a fork to gently prod a burger and then flips it efficiently. My mother, pulling the buns out of their plastic wrapping, looks at me and shrugs.

"How does someone qualify to be a psychic?" Dennis asks. He is genuinely interested, the same way he was genuinely in-terested when an Amway salesman came to his door in high school. Even though he's worked his way up to the secure po-sition of Super Cineplex manager, he is always looking for a foolproof scheme and, right now, reading other people's futures is looking like the next big thing.

"Your voice is your ticket," Clifford says. He is using what he believes to be the perfect voice—part public radio talk-show host, part used-car salesman. "Your voice should convey to the seeker that while you can't undo your past, you can make a better future for yourself."

Dennis is transfixed. He sees his better future written on Clifford's face.

"So how exactly do you do that?" he asks.

"I'll be back with the salad," my mother says.

"Me too," I say. I'm worried the Highway Psychic might expose me if my mother leaves me here alone with him, so I follow her into the kitchen. Outside, Clifford tells Dennis that he used to own a restaurant. He began offering psychic advice as an option on the menu, right next to dessert.

"It's all about comfort," Clifford says. "People want to feel stuffed with comfort."

"I'm not sure I want him to stuff me with his comfort," my mother says, her head in the refrigerator.

"I didn't want Dennis to know that, at the age of thirty-three, as old as Jesus ever got, I'm living at home with my mother so I told him that I'm here on business at the Hotel Fugor eating a lot of roast pig." It just comes out. The words jump out of my mouth, abandoning ship. "And I told him I have a fiancé."

"Hotel Fugor?" is all my mother says after closing the refrigerator door. My mother holds the salad in her arms like a baby—a niçoise with olives and hard-boiled eggs so perfectly sliced that it breaks my heart a little. "Isn't that the hotel with the jousters?"

"Yes, I believe they have jousters."

"It's your life, honey," she says.

"Don't give me that it's-your-life-honey shit." She hasn't even asked what I'm doing with Dennis. She thinks he's the best I can do? That I won't leave at the end of the summer? That I'll settle down in one of the gated communities going up at the edge of the Super Cineplex and watch the other residents wander aimlessly through shrub mazes? "Will you cover for me or not?"

She looks at me solemnly, the way she does when she wants me to understand that there are things she knows because she's lived longer.

"You can count on me," she says. "Now let's get back to our dates."

"Dennis is not my date." Her resignation is so much worse than her disapproval.

"Whatever he is," she says, and heads for the door like a waitress who has more important customers.

"Since when did you become such a grown-up?" The way my mother embraces everything wholeheartedly these days makes me want to puke. What happened to the woman I used to know? The one who pined alone in her house for so long? What's happened to my fellow languisher? She's suddenly filled with such get-up-and-go, she gives languishing a bad name.

"Isabelle," she says, pausing in the doorway. "*I'm* trying to take my date seriously."

"The Highway Psychic is on your life's path? Give me a break."

She lets the screen door slam behind her and I lean my burning cheek against the refrigerator. When the pounding in my head stops, I venture out. Clifford is still talking to Dennis while my mother, pretending not to notice my existence, arranges the salad on plates with the precision of a curator.

"We're nannies of the nineties," Clifford says. "We all float around lost with no one to protect us. Psychics give people the thrill of being known." Dennis nods, taking careful note of Clifford's voice, every subtle inflection.

I edge toward my mother to whisper an apology, but she makes it impossible. She moves around the table, slightly ahead of me, just out of earshot. I follow her in circles around the salad plates. She stops suddenly and I bump into her.

"What do you want?" she demands. Clifford and Dennis don't notice. They are still talking, otherwise engaged.

"I'm sorry," I say.

"Why are you dressed like that?" She's going to make me pay. "That lipstick makes you look like a corpse made up for a wake." I'm grateful that the nose ring is safely in my pocket. But she won't let on that I'm living here. She's careful when it comes to a good story, and a good secret. She's never told anyone else how people used to pay to hear her sing, or about her boyfriend who now lives on the Ile St-Louis. And she's never breathed a word about Henry. He has always been our secret because she understands the power of secrets, the way a thing can bloom mythically behind secrecy's veil.

"I can't tell you your future, Dennis," Clifford is saying in a commanding voice. "You'll have to come to the shack sometime." He speaks briskly, trying to shake Dennis off. He's lost his patience. His perfect voice is starting to fray around the edges.

"What about Isabelle?" Dennis asks. "Just a hint. Come on, one little hint."

Clifford looks over to where I hover around my mother.

"She's a tricky one," he says in a voice that is like a slap, one that makes me glad I never stopped at his shack. He stares at me with his psychic stare—the stare of politicians, TV evangelists, and high school boys desperate to lose their virginity—an unwavering gaze meant to stand in for depth and truth.

"Isabelle's star will soon be on the rise," he says. "Slowly, she will recoup all that she thinks she has lost."

My mother smiles coyly. She's starting to like this guy. "Not bad," she says. "How about me?"

"Intense planetary activity." Clifford moves toward her, his psychic stare gone woozy with the effort of seduction. His voice is deep with prediction and hope. "It is said that when the rug is pulled out from under you, you must learn to dance on a shifting carpet."

"Ooooo, aren't you clever?" My mother rolls her eyes, but he has won her over.

"Come on, what about me? I've got a future too you know," Dennis pipes in. Clifford glares at him as my mother offers Clifford a plate of food with a flourish, a dating symbol meant to encourage.

"Say what you truly feel and the resulting passion will smolder for months to come." Clifford spits this out quickly, like a child who has been forced to apologize. He's pat as a fortune cookie. He can't even look at Dennis, who was never very good at sensing other people's annoyance. Fortunately, Clifford is too busy receiving a plate filled with lettuce, olives, perfectly sliced eggs, and my mother's gratitude to care about Dennis for long.

Dennis looks to me to confirm Clifford's prediction, and I look at the stars, pretending to search for meaning there.

After we finish eating, Dennis finds Magic Wands sparklers in a kitchen drawer. My mother calls them "gentle firecrackers" because they never explode, only fizzle. Dennis lights one and waves it, casting a spell on us all in the blue movie-light of evening sneaking toward night. Clifford cries, "Bravo" and digs in his pocket for something with a bang. He pulls out Black Cats and hands them to Dennis, who tries to light them using the clicker for the pilot light on the gas stove. He stands half in, half out of the house, clicking futilely and waiting for something to happen, his shadow dancing behind him. Thick and jerky, this shadow is familiar to me from nights spent creeping behind it through dimly lit parking lots looking for a place to linger, drink beers, and make out. There were many nights this shadow lurked outside my bedroom window, waiting for me to drop from the sill and sneak away with it.

We all watch Dennis intently, poised for the noise loud enough to startle us out of ourselves, and I wonder whether this life in Standardsville is what I was destined to return to all along. Maybe what I'm most afraid of is the smallness of my desires.

Dennis can't light Clifford's firecrackers. "Must have gotten wet," Clifford says.

"Let's take a ride," my mother says, meaning Clifford and herself. "We'll drive over to the gazebo and watch the town fireworks from the car." They disappear around the corner of the house.

This is the cue Dennis has been waiting for all evening. He walks toward me slowly. He knows I've been studying him so he doesn't touch me right away. He sits on the picnic bench, leaving distance between us. Fireflies surround us, flashing on and off in protest to the series of loud bangs that is the town's fireworks display. By now, the mayor stands in the gazebo near the Hotel Fugor, where the jousters are in red, white, and blue armor tonight, and the fireworks commissioner loads up the cannon. When Dennis and I watched the fireworks in high school, we'd sip warm beer and kiss with an intensity inspired by the melodrama of a blown firecracker as it fell to earth. There's something Pavlovian about the two of us together again, watching minor explosions.

At a high school party in the yard of somebody's parents' half-built empty house on the outskirts of town, Dennis found me in a crowd and led me to his car where he had cued up "When a Man Loves a Woman." When I turned, touched at this rare, premeditated gesture of affection, he had fallen asleep, slouched over the wheel, too exhausted from his efforts and keg beer to savor the moment. So I let him sleep, enjoy-ing the song the way it's best enjoyed—alone, the possibility of love just out of reach.

"I'm glad you're home, Isabelle," Dennis says now, touching my cheek with the back of his hand like he's taking my tem-perature. We've returned to that comfortable, unthinking place of skin and smell.

"Sebastian's a lucky guy." Sebastian who? I suspect that if Dennis kissed me and pulled me into some dark corner it would help. On dates in San Francisco, the urgent press of lips at the end of the night was more satisfying than the endless dance of words. Dennis tries to brood, but he ends up pucker-ing his face like he's eaten something disgusting.

"Good night," he says, realizing that if he leaves now it will add to his charm. As he turns to go, he trips over my mother's garden hose, and I am charmed. I look up in time to see the finale, fireworks overlapping in their ecstatic climax. For a moment, as a giant gold flag reveals itself in the sky, I am that long-ago version of myself, the girl on the blanket with Dennis, the girl who truly believed that one of those fireworks stars might someday tumble to earth.

MY mother is still out with Clifford, so Raymond slinks over to join me in front of the TV. He takes his place on his end of the couch, sipping his scotch. He is always nervous when he first arrives, my mother's presence still lingering—she's always just left, but tonight he seems especially jittery.

"Are you okay, Raymond?"

Startled, he spills some of his drink down the front of his shirt. "Oh, fine," he says. "I'm just fine."

We both look back at the screen, embarrassed. Five hipsters linger in a café over giant mugs of cappuccino on a show about a group of young, beautiful, single friends who work crappy jobs but somehow afford spacious, exquisitely appointed apartments in a bustling metropolis.

"I always thought marriage would just happen to me at a certain age," Raymond says suddenly. "Like *The Honeymooners* contest when I was twenty-three—I'd fill out a form and it would just come in the mail."

I laugh because I don't know what else to do.

"Yes," he says solemnly. "Candor is amusing, isn't it?"

"Do you want to watch something different tonight?" I ask. The world of sitcoms is more disturbing than usual. The canned laughter verges on hysteria. "*This* is not so amusing."

I change the channel to a show on public television about

the construction of the first surf-making man-made reef in Los Angeles. It's part one of a three-part series about the packaging of nature in the United States—rain forest cafés, animal kingdoms, and a re-created Kilimanjaro exactly like the one in Africa, minus the bad weather and bugs.

"I wasn't laughing at you, Raymond," I say.

"With me," Raymond says, considering this. "You were laughing with me."

I give him a playful shove. What I mean is: me too.

"I always thought that it would happen when I was thirty-six. That seemed like the next magical age," Raymond says, not playful at all. I think about the picture that Henry took of my mother in San Francisco when she was twenty. Twenty had seemed like a magical age too, until it came and went.

Raymond stares at the ice cubes in his drink. "All that stuff—adventure, a lady." He pushes an ice cube around the glass with his thumb.

"I'm sorry to bother you," he says, touching his face. The contours of his younger features—the hopeful boy who beat Ralph Cramden out to be escort to the Grand Exalted Leader of the Raccoon Lodge—hover handsomely in the background of his fleshier, older face. "It's pure jackassery. I'm going to have to call that boy about my lawn."

"It's ten-thirty, Raymond. Isn't it a little late to be calling him? Raymond? Stay and talk to me."

He's slipped out the door. Through the window, I watch him cross the street, moving through time with all his clumsy yearning. Those moves are not so foreign. He pauses only to check his empty mailbox before starting up the slope of his lawn.

When my mother comes home, I'm still on the couch, keeping watch over Raymond's house. On TV, the manager of Surf City in L.A. is explaining to the documentarian how the surf reef will be made out of polyethylene pipes.

"Polyethylene is as much a part of nature as sand or rocks." He sits at a big desk on top of which sits a small-scale model of Surf City, complete with tiny people standing in line and carrying tiny surfboards. The Surf City manager adjusts his tie and looks directly into the camera. "You have to understand. Surf City is as much a part of the real world as, say, Atlantic City or even L.A."

"Clifford predicted that I will be married within the year," my mother says, unpacking her purse to restore order. "To someone else." She puts her wallet and her keys in the ceramic bowl by the door, which is where she always puts them, so I know she will recover from this night. "He said we'll be very happy together. And he predicted that he'll be alone and miserable, wishing he hadn't missed his chance with me. Then I kissed him just enough so that he really will be sorry." She has the stand-up comic's gift of knowing how to leave a room, leaving me wanting more. She takes the stairs two at a time, leaving a cloud of eau de drugstore behind like the ghost of her own fireworks.

I go upstairs with a glass of wine. Before settling in for my nightly Raymond watch, I decide to follow my mother's example and make an effort, so I take the collection of sour-smelling empty wineglasses off my bedside table and slide them under the bed. That accomplished, I keep the steady beat of Raymond's TV light out my window. My attention, like a kind hand on his shoulder, is the deal we've cut.

6

WIGGED Out looms above the row of low, square office buildings in downtown Standardsville. Mannequin heads, some wearing wigs, some bald, line the old warehouse's store window. Long cracks run down their cheeks, and spots of discoloration mark their plastic faces like bruises. Dennis's ABBA tape got stuck in the Chevy's tape deck so I've been forced to listen to it on a constant loop. "Knowing Me, Knowing You" is playing full volume as I cruise the main downtown drag. Marla has sent me on a mission.

"Enough of this child's play," she said on the phone this morning. "It's time for a more sophisticated disguise. Go get yourself a wig."

A fiery orange wig in the display window catches my eye. The wig is cut at an ear-length bob on a mannequin head with only one ear. The other ear lies at the base of the mannequin's neck.

When the door opens, a bell rings and a slight woman

standing behind the counter reaches a protective hand toward a little boy playing with a pile of toothpicks. She wears thin silver bracelets on one arm that clink against each other like the chimes my mother hangs in her backyard and calls "the sound of summer." Wigged Out must not get many customers because the woman raises an eyebrow in annoyance, like I'm one more person stopping in to ask for directions.

Her eyes are big and sad. A cow disguised as a pretty girl, a "bovine beauty," is how Dennis described her when he told me about his new girlfriend, Peoria, on the phone the other day. Dennis and I talk on the phone frequently. There's comfort in having once existed together for so long on the same small piece of earth. I made a deal with the receptionist, Hugo, at the Hotel Fugor. I slipped him a twenty to tell Dennis I've stepped out of my hotel room whenever Dennis calls for me there. Then Hugo calls my mother's to alert me. When Dennis told me Peoria works at Wigged Out, I considered stopping in to check her out. Then Marla called and gave me an excuse.

"Does Peoria know you refer to her as cattle?" I asked Dennis.

"You should hear what I call you behind *your* back," he said.

Peoria was named for the town that would later become famous for its riverboat gambling. "Appropriate," Dennis said. "Spending time with her is like feeling seasick and losing money at the same time."

"She gets better and better," I said.

"It's a good quality. You should try it sometime."

"Can I help you?" Peoria asks curtly. She's unaccustomed to asking this question in this store filled with mannequin heads. There are rows and rows of heads but only four different types of faces: a perky face with a demonic smile; a brooding face with high cheekbones; a laughing face with big, white teeth; and a post-collagen-implant-face with swollen lips, long lashes, and a beauty mark. All the heads perch on skinny necks that end in a puddle of flesh, suggesting a little bit of shoulder and chest.

"Yes, as a matter of fact, I think you can," I say. She has lovely high cheekbones, not unlike the brooding mannequin. A flicker of jealousy makes me blush and I suddenly want to see more of the cow than the pretty girl. Seizing a golden opportunity to try out my newfound mystery-shop skills, I decide not to introduce myself. Marla would be proud.

"Well, help yourself." She has zero sales skills. She gestures grandly, waving her thin, elegant fingers at the heads, as if she were reversing a spell, changing all these beauties back into frogs.

"I was hoping you might be able to suggest something."

The little boy with the toothpicks looks at me as if I've started something I'm going to regret. "Don't poke yourself, honey," Peoria says.

"He's adorable," I say.

"Thanks." She starts to braid a section of her hair.

"I'm in town with a bus-and-truck theater company performing a show at the community theater about a woman who has become a man and then becomes a woman again." Marla would be prouder and prouder. "It's called *She Said He Said She Said*. The director borrowed the idea from a one-man show that's running in San Francisco. Gave it a twist."

Peoria looks at me with vague interest, as though I've just told her tomorrow's weather forecast. She strokes the boy's hair.

"I'm playing the lead."

"Interesting," Peoria says. This speck of enthusiasm eggs me on. My energy zings around the room, bouncing off the mannequin heads. The boy shoots me a jaded look like he's witnessed these transformations every day of his young life and he has his doubts.

"I was thinking maybe that one," I say, pointing at the orange wig on the one-eared mannequin in the window. I have a vision of Star from one day in the hallway. She was inhabiting the persona of an unhappy, dark teenage character in a movie out at the time about a group of unhappy, dark teenage characters.

"Do you have the time?" a bright, preppy girl wearing pearl earrings and layers of shirts asked Star. She said it as though she were the one doing Star a favor. Star scratched her head violently. "No one *has* the time," she said. "Time is a societal construct designed to control the chaos of the universe." If Star were alive today, she'd be able to convince Raymond that thirty-six is no magical age, that there is no magical age. She'd know how to help us make our own magic.

"I'm not sure that wig's for you," Peoria says. She walks around the counter and looks back and forth between other wigs and my face. She's not impressed.

"I'm writing a book on highway psychics too," I blurt out. I'm desperate. I want to be worthy of that orange wig, the one like Star's hair. "It's a side project. When I'm not performing."

"Really," she says. "What about highway psychics in particular?" She pulls a plain, curly, mousy brown wig off a collagen-lipped mannequin head. It could be my own hair, just curlier.

"You know, their personal lives, stuff like that," I say, deflated by the wig she's deemed appropriate for me. "I just started the project, really. And I've been so busy with the show."

"Right," Peoria says flatly. "You must not have much spare time with rehearsal and everything." She leads me to the three-way mirror. The boy on the counter doesn't even look up. He makes grunting noises and says, "Take that!" as he forces two toothpicks into battle.

"Have you ever worn a wig?" I want to steer the conversation away from the particulars of my highway psychic book. It is the most normal question I can think of, given the circumstances.

"Yeah. It's very liberating." She rises to the occasion, cozying up to the sound of her own voice. "I sometimes wear them home from work to freak my boyfriend out." I'm sorry I asked and not sorry at all. I don't want to hear more but I want to hear everything.

"So he *doesn't* like it when you wear wigs?"

"No," she says, then pauses just enough so that I know she's remembering a specific sexual experience with Dennis. "He likes it."

"Ohhhhh," I say, aware of just how bad I'm being but unable to stop myself. "So you wear it *during*?"

"Sometimes," she says with bobby pins sticking out of her mouth. "Don't make me laugh. I'll drop these things." She pins my real hair tightly to my head. "You know, the unfamiliar is exciting. That whole thing."

"Do you act like you but with a wig on, or do you pretend to be somebody else?"

"A little of both," she says. She pauses again as she pins my hair in order to collect the bits and pieces of the story she is about to tell me. She's beginning to relax—her face is wide open and beautiful in its vulnerability. She believes this is one of those intimate moments with a stranger she'll never see again, to whom she can try out secrets she's never told anyone else. "You're not going to believe this. *I* can't believe I'm telling you this." She laughs and her cheeks go rosy pink.

I don't say anything. I just smile an invitation to continue.

"Sometimes," she begins. "Sometimes my boyfriend likes me to wear a long red wig. He likes to pretend he's Captain Jean-Luc Picard from *Star Trek* and I'm Dr. Beverly Crusher." She giggles.

I nod encouragingly. "I'm an *actress*," I say, as if to say, Nothing surprises me.

"He's Captain Picard and I'm Dr. Crusher. When we're actually doing it, he gets really into it. He likes to say 'Make it so.' " She looks at my face in the mirror for a reaction.

"While he's thrusting," she whispers. " 'Make it so.' "

"Do you like it?" I ask, wondering why Dennis never told me he was such a *Star Trek* fan.

"Yeah, I guess. Sometimes," she says. Her face closes down. She is no longer relaxed. She's through talking. "There." She slides the last bobby pin into place. "You're all set. How does it feel?"

"Like a phantom limb returned to my body," I say. Emptiness might be my specific talent. There are rooms and rooms in me for other people, a sprawling mansion of space.

"You really are an actress," Peoria says, then backpedals. "In a good way." She holds up two hands, surrendering. "I mean it in a good way."

"I'll take the wig," I say. I turn to look at my profile in the mirror. My nose erupts in the same rootlike way as my mother's in Henry's picture.

Peoria searches for a bag behind the counter.

"Don't bother," I say. "I'll wear it out. Just give me the receipt." I pocket the receipt for Marla's expense report later.

TODAY'S mystery shop is in a theater that used to be an ice-skating rink. The rink's mural is still on the side of the building—children wearing brightly colored scarves and oversize mittens skating loopy figure eights. The theater is colder than any other here in town. Marla warned me to bring gloves, which makes filling out the questionnaire difficult. I make a sloppy, swooping check mark in the NO box after *Does the theater maintain a suitable temperature to enhance your movie-going pleasure?*

I am one of three people in the theater watching a movie about three women who take a road trip to escape the men in their lives. One of the other moviegoers is a middle-aged woman who cries throughout the movie before anything sad happens. She cries soundlessly for minutes at a time, then breathes deeply and makes a small swallowing sound. She's wearing heels, a pleated skirt, and has salon-styled hair. She appears to have fled here from somewhere else—a job interview? home? the apartment of the man she's having an affair with? The other audience member is a man in his thirties who, I notice when I go to check bathrooms, has his fly unzipped and his hand down his pants. When I return, the three women cry together in a motel room and then walk out into the sweeping desert landscape that reflects their true beauty back to them at twice its normal size—which is better than having any man is the implication. By the end of the movie, they abandon this charade and find hunky, sensitive cowboys with sexy Southern accents.

On a napkin I pick up off the theater floor—after recording the slovenly nature of the theater on my questionnaire—I write a note to the crying woman. *Please don't be sad. You deserve to be happier than this.* When the movie ends after the triple wedding of the three women and their cowboys, I return the napkin to the aisle and leave quickly, hoping that the crying woman picks it up. She strikes me as the fastidious type. She will think that it was a note meant for somebody else, but she'll read it as people tend to read things, as if every word were meant for her.

AT home, my mother and Samantha, a friend of my mother's who works as an administrator at the community health-care clinic, are standing in the kitchen eating a pound cake out of the box. Samantha is a new friend, someone my mother met on a double date. Neither of them ever saw their dates again, but the two of them hit it off. They spend hours on the phone together at work under the guise of making referrals, then meet at each other's homes after work to eat and talk men.

"I was never this girlish when I was a girl," my mother said, defending herself this morning when I pointed out the way she and Samantha behave when they get together. "I'm making up for lost time."

"No one was ever this girlish," I said. "Ever. Even as a girl."

"Well . . ." she said, letting the word trail behind her as she walked out the door to go to work. Translation: Loosen up and try it sometime.

When I walk into the kitchen tonight, Samantha, divorced and miserably childless, is in the middle of describing her date last night.

"His pants split right there on the dance floor," she says, breaking off a chunk of cake. "The worst part was, he wasn't even a good dancer."

"Here she is," my mother announces, pointing to me like I'm Miss America coming down the runway. "Fresh from the front lines of the temp battlefield . . ." She thinks I'm still at the graphic design firm. I told her I got a long-term job there because they liked my handwritten invitations to the cancer ball so much.

"You look fabulous," Samantha says. It's clear they've been plotting this attack of compliments.

"Doesn't she?" my mother says. "Honey, did you get a perm?"

"Curlers." I touch the wig, thrilled that my mother could be so attentively inattentive.

"It looks great," my mother says. "You should do that more often." She turns to Samantha. "Doesn't it look great?"

"Fantastic," Samantha says, nodding vigorously. My mother has told her that she's worried about me.

"It's no big deal," I say, keeping my distance.

"That's a great skirt too," Samantha says. She's relentless. "I *love* that skirt. It really flatters your figure." It is the same straight, knee-length denim skirt that every other woman in America owns and has shoved into the back of her closet. Its day came and went long ago. I hadn't realized my mother thought I was this pathetic. Even she sees that things are spinning out of control. She puts her hand on Samantha's arm in an effort to stop her.

"Tall," my mother says. "I love tall men. Last night my date was very tall—willowy thin and slightly hunched."

"I'm going upstairs," I say.

"I came inside last night, looked in the mirror, and found a fennel seed stuck in my teeth," my mother says, hopefully.

"That's hilarious," I say. I'm not smiling as I leave the room to head upstairs.

"We're going to make sundaes," Samantha calls after me.

In my room, I change into my sweat suit. I'm careful not to muss the wig, though Peoria pinned it so securely, it barely moves. Once I'm settled on the bed, I open the curtains to let Raymond know I'm home while I drink the sour remains of last night's glass of wine.

I've tried to love tall men too. In San Francisco, there was a tall carpenter/aspiring actor who I tried to love. He tried to love me back. He had beautiful, nimble hands, miracles of human architecture.

"I know it's what I want," the carpenter/actor said to me, describing his failing career on our second date in a café. "It's what I've always wanted." I nodded. It was an idea that anyone could get behind—wanting. I enjoyed the sound of his voice as much as he did—each word slow and crisp and edible. So I listened as he told me about wanting a good role, wanting health insurance, wanting money, wanting to move to the East Coast to get away from it all, wanting and wanting.

"Isabelle?" the carpenter/actor said, touching my arm. We'd kissed after our first date, which consisted of a play in which he had a walk-on. It was a Greek tragedy and he wore only a loincloth. His nudity in the theater seemed like foreplay and, after seeing so much of him, the kiss seemed strangely insufficient.

"Where are you?" he asked.

It was true—I was not with him.

"I'm sorry," I said, leaning over to kiss the carpenter/actor the way I thought it should be done. The kiss seemed like an acceptable form of apology. In the same way that all his life the only thing the carpenter wanted was to be an actor, I realized that all my life I'd wanted only to want something that purely.

Later, we walked on the piers. I wondered, as I held his beautiful hand in mine, what this link should mean. It seemed so random. As the carpenter/actor and I walked, it was hard to fill my body, to send myself to those points where our hands met.

Raymond walks into his living room, then walks in circles like a dog about to lie down. As night falls, his TV flashes urgent light on the wall. Downstairs, the wood floors creak as my mother and Samantha jump to their feet to add gestures to their stories. Their voices rise up to me, shrill with hope. I can't be in this house any longer.

The grass is wet on my bare feet as I let myself out the front door, leaving my mother and Samantha in the kitchen. "You did *not* do that! I don't *believe* it!" Samantha shrieks with approval.

"Come in," Raymond says when he answers the door. He's not surprised to see me. It's as if he were expecting me. He's wearing sweatpants too. I've never seen him out of his one pair of jeans.

"Look," he says. "We match."

"I can't be in my house right now," I say.

"Right." He doesn't require an explanation. We both head

for the wall opposite the TV and slide to the floor. "Interesting headpiece," he says, touching my wig with the tips of his fingers, carefully, as if it might bite him.

"Do you like it?" I ask.

"Not particularly," he says.

There's an entertainment news journal on TV—a man and a leggy blonde at a news desk with the front cut out to highlight the leggy blonde's legs.

Raymond has a bottle of scotch next to him.

"I've got a glass in the kitchen," he says, holding up the bottle.

Scotch has always tasted like soap to me, but when in Rome. . . . "I'll drink from the bottle too."

We pass the bottle back and forth and watch the entertainment news journal's segment on an angry star who spent a night in jail for punching out a journalist.

"He definitely had it coming," Raymond says. I'm not sure who he's referring to—the star or the journalist. To ask seems far too complex.

"Raymond, why don't you have any furniture?" I figure as long as we're drinking out of the same bottle, I'll get to the bottom of a few things.

"I always thought I'd eventually go somewhere else. I wanted to be ready to pick up and go at any moment."

"Where did you think you'd go?"

"Hollywood, maybe." He's not kidding, and it's not funny. "Or somewhere like that."

There is a segment on a new theme park that allows its guests to be any celebrity they choose. For one night, they are given the red carpet treatment—klieg lights aimed at the sky, throngs of hungry fans, and theme park employees desperate for autographs. In this clip, a woman is receiving a phony Oscar. "You like me!" she squeals. "You really like me!"

"Duh," I say. I look to Raymond to agree with me, but he is staring at the TV with more than his usual rapt attention.

"I can't *believe* this," he finally says. "I just can't believe it."

"Which part?" I ask. "The dress she's wearing or the interpretive dance segment before her?"

Raymond puts his hands over his eyes, shaking his head.

"The interpretive dance segment really got to you?" I pat his leg. His sweatpants are worn and soft, and I leave my hand there.

"This was my idea," Raymond says, looking through his fingers. "Tinseltown."

"Tell me," I say. I want to comfort him. I want him to tell me everything, his secrets, the pulsing, hidden heart of his life. It might be the soapy scotch, but Raymond is beginning to seem like someone who could tell me something important. If this is my life path, Raymond's on it. His nose in profile has none of the gentleness of my mother's—it is a bold arc, the terrifying end of a roller coaster. I imagine it on the faces of his family—the same nose living entirely different lives, stuck over mouths that speak other sentences.

"It was my big idea. It was all I had left after *The Honeymooners*. It's too pathetic to talk about."

Quick images of people dancing, running, embracing, walking on the beach, playing football, rolling in the grass, flash on the TV. It's a commercial, but it's unclear what is being sold.

"No, it's not. Raymond, tell me," I say. "Please."

"I didn't know what to do. I knew my spot on *The Honey-*

mooners was a one-shot deal. But I remembered what Jackie told me—opportunity's where you find it and sometimes you find it on TV—so I came up with Tinseltown. I brought Hollywood to southern Illinois. The idea was to let regular people in on the action, let them dress up like their favorite TV stars. It was just me and my parents, so really it was just us dressing up like Ralph and Alice Cramden, Ed Lily White Norton and his wife, Trixie. I'd play two parts—sometimes Ralph and Alice, sometimes Ed and Trixie. Always a couple—easier that way."

"That sounds like fun," I say. I mean it.

"I wanted to patent it, sell it, make a little money, go somewhere," Raymond says.

"What happened?" I ask. I put my arm around him.

"Nothing," he continues. "Nothing happened. I lived with my parents on their farm in southern Illinois until they died and then I stayed on until the farm fell apart. A cousin willed me this house so I moved in because what else was I going to do?"

I slide closer to him so that our legs touch. I squeeze his shoulder.

"I need to be alone, Isabelle," he says suddenly.

"Right," I say, wishing he would ask me to stay. I'd sleep curled up in a ball at the foot of his bed and not make a sound.

Through the living room window, I see my mother and Samantha, their arms flailing as they dance wildly to the radio, so I stumble around to the back of the house to lie in the thick grass. My head buzzes from the scotch and I only mean to rest here to gather my strength, but the click and whir of the sprinkler lulls me to sleep.

I dream Star back to life. The yellow smell of her long

buried body is the smell of sleep. She shakes dust off brittle bones, too tired to speak at first from having been dead for so long. When she recovers her voice, she tells me she can help Raymond build Tinseltown.

"You will learn your lines," she says. "Then we will build it out of bones."

7

◡

I N the middle of the night, I wake with a start, facedown in the damp backyard. Something is clawing at my head, catching its nails in the wig and tugging. At first I think it's Star, who in my dream has been scolding me for wearing such a pathetic hairpiece. "I promise! I'll never wear it again!" I say. But the pulling continues, and a hiss rises above the click and whir of the sprinkler. I look up to find myself face-to-face with Creampuff, the obese cat owned by the Rogers, the couple in the house on the corner. He twists and turns his giant body, struggling to free the paw caught in my wig.

Mrs. Morton has had it in for Creampuff ever since he began to leave half-dead baby rabbits to drown in her cherub fountain. In the middle of the night, the high-pitched shrieks of the drowning, limbless rabbits could be heard up and down the street. When the Rogers refused to keep the cat inside or to have him declawed, Mrs. Morton began a poster campaign around the neighborhood: CREAMPUFF IS A MURDERER! CREAMPUFF MUST GO!

Creampuff wiggles his enormous fluffy white body back and forth, staring into my eyes with the rage of a cat who is all good looks and bad intentions. I manage to get on all fours, reach for his stuck paw, and pull him toward me in order to unhook him. But he thrashes wildly and I end up flinging him as hard as I can away from me. He flies across the yard like a furious, screeching meteor.

"Murderer!" I yell after him. He rolls to his fat little feet. I pull the wig off my head and attempt to comb it with my fingers.

Stumbling into the kitchen, wet from the sprinkler spray, I catch my reflection in the microwave. I have wig head—my hair matted and full of bobby pins. Just as I am about to go upstairs to lie in my bed and wonder how my life has been reduced to fighting with an overweight cat in my mother's backyard, the phone rings. It's the heart-stopping, something-terrible-has-happened ring of a phone in the middle of the night.

"Isabelle." Marla's voice is so deep and throaty it sounds as if she's smoked a carton of cigarettes.

My mother answers the upstairs phone, not fully awake. "Where's that place we went?" she asks. Maybe she is halfway through the recurring dream she used to tell me about until she stopped talking about Henry. She and Henry are feeding the seals from the piers in San Francisco. Henry dives off the pier and disappears into the water. He has gone to live underwater and she must teach herself how to breathe in the underwater world, to learn to live underwater too, if she wants to be with him. Henry can't help her because now that he's gone he can't come back. She is frightened, standing on the pier alone. The barking seals frighten her, always waking her up before she has made a decision.

"David?" my mother says into the receiver. The name is so rarely spoken that I don't recognize it at first. David is my father.

"It's for me," I say. "Go back to sleep."

"I am asleep," she says, waking up.

"Then stay that way and hang up the phone." She does.

"Marla, it's the middle of the night," I say.

"So why are you answering the phone?"

"Just tell me what you want."

"I just checked my messages at the office."

"Do you ever sleep?"

"Isabelle, you've got to listen to me," Marla says, all desperate double agent. "The receptionist at the First Church of Jesus Christ fell into a ditch made by the construction around the old pizza place. She's a wreck. Not very stable to begin with, but the sprained ankle has sent her over the edge. I thought I had a girl lined up, but she just returned my call from a bar—left a message saying she was sick at home in bed. I could smell the liquor on her breath over the phone and there was loud music, *bar* music, in the background. Does the girl think I was born yesterday?"

"Marla," I start. I can see her in a frilly nightgown, fresh pillow creases lining her cheeks. The details of her job bully their way into her dreams and render the frantic little sleep she does get useless. She sits bolt upright in the middle of the night to make these calls. Her husband, accustomed by now to her middle-of-the-night frenzies, takes refuge under a pillow.

"It's a one-day emergency gig, Isabelle." With most people, the use of the first name as a selling tactic seems forced, but Marla pulls it off. After waking up in the backyard to a wrestling match with a homicidal cat, the way Marla says my first name is comforting, an invitation to evolve and join the human species.

"I don't know," I say, wanting to hear how much she needs me.

"Isabelle, you're all I've got," she says. "And besides, what else do you have going on tomorrow?" She's had my number all along. Her file on me is suspiciously thick and overflowing given the short time I've known her. She made the assumption the first time she appeared mysteriously out of the Temporama office mist that I have nothing better to do than whatever she wants.

"Aren't you supposed to counsel me? You're a temp *counselor.*"

"To a point," Marla says. "And then I'm as desperate as anybody else. You know I love you, Isabelle, but will you or won't you?"

Marla throws love around easily, like a pen from a ten-pack of pens exactly like it: Here, borrow mine, I don't need it back. Chew on it all you want. Use it to clean your ear.

"Of course I will," I say, already starting to wonder what a receptionist at a church wears and whether I have the wardrobe to accommodate such an outfit.

"Just remember," Marla says. "There are plenty of temps who would love a church job." She hangs up.

AFTER my mother's car disappears around the corner, I knock frantically at Raymond's door. When I saw him at his regular morning post at the kitchen window, watching my mother leave for work, I knew I could enlist him. A man who could dream up Tinseltown has to be good at costumes.

He comes to the door in his jeans and a rumpled T-shirt that says "I'm the stupid with you." Underneath these words is a big black arrow pointing to the left. His eyes are puffy and creased, but at least he's changed out of last night's sweatpants.

"Hey," I say. "I need some help."

Raymond considers this as he pats the door frame in the way that he often touches inanimate objects for comfort. He once told me that he is guided through his days by the furniture in his house. These objects call out to him. He claims that a chair once saved his life. The smooth wood of its arms kept him sitting as he ran his hands along the silky grain a few seconds longer on a day that there was a three-car pileup at a nearby intersection. Raymond says he was on his way to that very intersection for one of his highway strolls. Raymond doesn't have a car, but he occasionally gets out to the nearby supermarket for his microwavable dinners. On the day of the pileup the smooth wood of the chair's arm under his palm called out to him: *sit here a while*.

"What happened to the wig?" he asks. "I was just getting used to it." He pulls a stray bobby pin from my hair, and then another. I want to get an "I'm with stupid" T-shirt and stand beside him.

"Creampuff ran off with it," I say dismissively, not wanting to explain.

"That cat is nothing but trouble." There are no whys, whens, or hows with him. I shake off a crazy urge to take him in my arms.

"I need you to help me pick out an outfit," I say. "Put the Tinseltown dream to work. I need help dressing up as someone who holds a regular job as a secretary in a church. A famous churchy secretary."

"I don't have any churchy secretary clothes," he says.

"We're going to look through my mother's closet," I start to explain, but he just laughs.

"I was kidding," he snorts.

"Jesus Christ, are you going to fucking help me or what?" I'm annoyed at my own slowness. Why don't I get people's jokes anymore? Why does everything seem so unfunny all of a sudden? Maybe my mother, Dennis, Raymond, and Marla should all hold up signs that read: I'M BEING SARCASTIC NOW whenever it applies.

"How are you going to do this church job with a mouth like that?" Raymond says. He shuts his door behind him and turns me around to face my mother's house.

"I'll wait downstairs," Raymond says as we step into the front hall.

"Come upstairs," I say. "It'll be easier." But Raymond has already wandered into the living room, sliding into his usual seat on the couch.

"I'll stay here," Raymond says firmly. "Why don't you put outfits on and come downstairs and model them for me?"

I don't have time to argue so I run up the stairs to ransack my mother's closet. I begin the fashion show with a flowery summer dress with a high neckline and shoulder pads, and Raymond immediatcly nixes it.

"You look like a cross-dressing football player," he says. He's made himself at home on the couch, sinking deep in the pillows. He's enjoying his role as arbiter of taste.

"Too blousy," he says of the next shirt and slacks combination. "You look like you've got room for two in there."

"Too arrogant," he says of one of my mother's pantsuits.

"Too arrogant? How can clothes be too arrogant?" I am sweating from all the changing and racing up and down the stairs. "Raymond, I've got to choose *something*." I hold up a drab blue skirt, a white blouse with a ruffled tie in front, and a scarf with giant tulips.

"That's it," he says, jumping to his feet. "Do I get to help with the makeup?"

I hand over my mother's all-in-one makeup kit and Raymond gently dabs cover-up under my eyes and along my T-zone.

"How do you know how to do this?" I ask as he applies mascara and a dab of eyeliner in the outer corners of my eyes.

"Infomercials," he says.

He takes my chin gently in one hand as he prepares to dust me with blush and powder.

"Shut your eyes," he says. He puts the blush brush between his teeth, passing his hand lightly over my face like someone tenderly closing the eyes of a person who has just died. I don't open them again until he's done with me.

AT the First Church of Jesus Christ, nobody looks twice. I sit in a back office by myself, interrupted only once when the minister comes in to offer me magazines with lambs and flowers on the covers.

"Reading material?" he asks. The articles have titles like "Your First Fight with the Lord: Three Steps to Making Up" and "How to Dress for God."

"Thanks," I say. I'm interested to see how Raymond and I did in the dressing-for-God category.

"You'll be bored," the minister says definitively. His tone says he has been for years.

Everything in the windowless office smells like smoke. The receptionist's office seems to be the exception to the church's no smoking policy. The building was first a library, then a YMCA, and finally, the First Church of Jesus Christ. A "What to Do in Case of Fire" poster with yellowed, frayed edges from 1972, before any of the building's later incarnations, hangs on the wall. A sketchy house with stick figures climbing out of windows and running down flights of stairs illustrates the poster's main point: Get out fast. Every piece of paper in the office, including this one, is saturated with the injured receptionist's mentholated cigarettes. It's as if everything in the room had been breathed in and breathed out again, through yellow teeth and lips chapped from dry air trying to circulate.

Time passes in mysterious ways at a temp job—going to the bathroom takes two minutes but staring at a blank wall fills hours. With no one around, I make faces to myself. I try for the face of someone who might do something extraordinary, something unheard of, or only heard of in a story that someone tells tenth-hand in amazement—that temp who burned down the church, that girl who seduced a minister of God.

Until this summer, I hated acting—the trembly hands, the shaky voice. It was something I avoided at all costs. When I went to see the performance in which the carpenter/actor appeared in a loincloth, there was audience participation and I was dragged halfway to the stage by another actor in ancient Greek underwear. I began to cry when I saw him coming, and it wasn't until he saw that my tears were real that he let me go and found another victim. The very idea of performing makes me sweaty and hysterically tired; I want to lie down and fall asleep. I became narcoleptic when, on another date with a computer programmer/stand-up comic, I was forced to play charades. Before it was my turn, while someone from the other team jumped up and down, flexing her biceps, in an effort to act out Xena, Warrior Princess, I preemptively nodded off on the couch.

My mother says this fear started with my kindergarten class poetry recital. Nine classmates and I sat on the floor in a semi-circle in the Temporama building when it still had the cut-out alphabet animals in the window. Our parents sat on the floor in front of us, cross-legged and nervous. I could feel their nerves, jangly and electric. I would feel that anxious electricity again and again over the years—when I went off to college, when I didn't find a job, when I didn't get married. It wasn't that my mother disapproved. She was a supportive mother. It was more that she was terrified that I would see her worry. She was afraid that worry would seep out uncontrollably like poisonous gas into the atmosphere no matter what face she put on: What if Isabelle dies without a career? without children? without love? Those aren't the most important things, she thought, but what else is there? That evening, I recited an Emily Dickinson poem and before I finished the line "Are you nobody too?" I lost the ability to focus—the world became a kaleidoscope, everything moving all at once. I saw eight of the girl next to me and fell immediately asleep, drenched in sweat.

But with these mystery shops, I don't just escape life, I escape memory too. When I dress up as a churchy receptionist, the Xeroxing of my breasts in San Francisco is somebody else's humiliating story. Instead, I can choose other people's memories—my guest-spot on *The Honeymooners*, or Henry drawing a stick-figure picture on a napkin meant to be me in my bed, thinking of him.

Years or minutes later, the door flies open and air rushes into the stagnant room.

"Francine." The tallest boy I've ever seen looms, squinting, in front of my desk. He looks like a twelve-year-old trapped in a thirty-year-old man's body. Without waiting for a response, he continues, "Francine, I've seen you with him, that man on the motorcycle." Each word is carefully chosen. He speaks haltingly as if he were remembering his lines. He clearly has been practicing this all morning. There's no stopping him. "I've seen you riding with him, your arms around his waist, wearing a scarf tied around your neck that I've never seen you wear before—a wild scarf."

I touch my mother's wild scarf, covered in giant tulips. The man-boy leans over the desk so that his squinting face is close to mine. "You never wore a wild scarf with me. Never once," he says. His sad voice and his bad posture start to ring a distant bell.

"Francine?" he says, looking hard at my face for something familiar. It occurs to me that he can barely see me through those squinting eyes. I am an outline, a sketch of myself. He slumps into the stiff-backed chair by the door, designed to discourage guests.

"Who are you?" he asks accusingly. He picks up one of the lamb and flowers magazines and flips the pages distractedly as though he's been transported to a waiting room in another office and he couldn't care less who I am.

Now I remember him—he's the man-boy who skulked at his girlfriend's side, pushing the thick-lens glasses up the bridge of his nose as they cruised Walgreens that day looking for the church. He is the slouching man-boy, recognizable as a movie star, at Francine's side at the movies.

"What happened to your glasses?" I ask. I hold gnome-lady's leftover glass of water, covering the hole in the straw with my fingertip. The straw's tip is red with her lipstick. She found the church after all.

"I threw them at Francine and her motorcycle man yesterday. I missed them, and a car crushed them into tiny pieces," he says, without a trace of embarrassment. I admire his ability to revel in his own patheticness. He refuses to disappear.

"Who are you?" he says again. "Where's Francine?" When he sits up straight, he's twice his slouching size. He waits for me to tell him about a horrible motorcycle accident in which Francine's motorcycle man was killed and Francine sustained small but important injuries. He waits for me to tell him that she screamed his name as the motorcycle slid under a tractor trailer.

I can tell him anything I want. It's like that moment when the lights go down in the movie theater, that in-between darkness just before the previews start when you are anonymous, floating in the dark. You are part of the darkness, ready to receive any drama that comes your way.

"She didn't have a motorcycle accident, if that's what you were hoping for," I say, leaning across the desk like a judge on small-claims court TV. "Well, would you look at that," Raymond always says at the end of those shows. Every time, he is newly astonished at the way justice is served in half-hour portions. I think of Raymond's hand cupping my chin, his light touch brushing my eyes closed.

The man-boy's face drops with disappointment; he has nothing to hide. These faces just come to him.

"She saw a ghost," I say, jumping at the opportunity to make Star true. "She saw a ghost outside the pizza place where they're doing all that construction and she tripped and fell into a ditch." I imagine Francine stepping fierce and bold through the construction, her caterpillar eyebrows bunched, tumbling angrily into a hole.

"Star," the man-boy says with excitement. "She saw Star!"

"What?" I push Francine's water glass away from me in disgust. I'm the one who dreamed Star back to life—how could this slouching squinter know Star? I don't want him to ruin her, taint her with his reality.

Man-boy drops the lamb and flowers magazine on the linoleum floor that hasn't been swept since the building's library days. His eyes, unfocused to begin with, have gone dreamy with the mention of Star.

"So, Francine met Star," he says to himself, suddenly in control.

"She didn't *meet* her. She saw her *ghost*," I say. "Doesn't that seem a little strange?"

"Star was my first girlfriend," he says slowly, now that he has my attention. "An older woman. I helped her dye her hair orange the first time. We did it in the boy's bathroom at school. Dye her hair, I mean . . ."

"Did I mention the word 'ghost'?" I say, interrupting. I won't let him have Star without a fight. If I have to, I'm prepared to steal these memories. "As in, dead person come back to life."

"Look," man-boy says, turning his unsteady gaze on me. "How do you know ghosts aren't living people who have come back to death? How do you know I'm not a ghost?"

"Do ghosts need glasses?" I ask. But he's got a point.

"Star was a beautiful girl," he says, wanting to know her the most. He makes an elaborate production of getting to his feet, pushing with both hands off the arms of the chair. He stands with his arms in the air as if he has been healed. Hallelujah! The man-boy ghost walks! He's going for a big exit. He heads for the door on his way out to the street where he will fantasize about Star in all her orange-hair glory, come back to life, or to death, after all these years to seek out her one true love, her first kiss to steal back the part of her that is his luscious memory.

The minister appears in the doorway, as though he'd been waiting around the corner for a sign. "Beat it, Jake," he says wearily to the tall, slouching man-boy ghost. "Quit fooling around." This is not the first time, but it is the last straw. It's time to can Francine. The minister will scrub the office and set up a battalion of fans to revive the dead air. He will spray vanilla air freshener until the yellowed, smoky office is thick with the sweet scent. He rolls his eyes at me in apology, then puts his hand gently on Jake's shoulder, the way he would any lost cause, and guides him down the hallway.

Dear Francine, Jake loves you very much. He loves your wild scarves. If he could drive a motorcycle, he would take you anywhere. At the end of the day, I write this on a yellow sticky and stick it to Francine's water glass next to a glass container one-third full of hard-candy suckers. All of the candies are green, though once there was probably a rainbow of colors. The green candy has gone white and dusty around the edges. No one will ever eat them. They will be here forever unless Francine takes them with her to her next job—if the exasperated minister fires her—where they will remain untouched on her desk. She will never bring herself to throw them away because she is frugal and because she is unable to imagine a future beyond the green suckers. She will forever anticipate some unbearable fluorescent moment of office boredom when they might bring her some relief.

Every night for weeks after Star's alleged murder there were TV interviews with her elementary-school teachers and old baby-sitters. Her parents wouldn't talk to reporters and so remained frozen in Standardsville's collective imagination as the couple in the snapshot taken by Star herself that the news got a hold of and offered up every night—a weary looking pair even before the murder, standing side by side but not touching in front of the town line sign: WELCOME TO STANDARDS-VILLE. This picture was taken by Star when she was six, the day the family moved to town. As soon as the investigation was over, Star's parents crossed as many town lines as possible to make sure they left Standardsville behind.

The local newscasters asked questions that traveled backward: What do you remember best about Star? Are there any special memories you would like to share? The teachers and alleged baby-sitters pointed to moments when Star was the best student, the kindest child, the most considerate of young girls. There was no best friend to interview, but all of the kids she spoke to in the high school corridors gave themselves to the spotlight willingly.

"She always told the truth," the awkward football player was quoted as saying, missing the point of Star altogether, the way she helped script the chaos of teenage life, rein it in with TV and movie-speak. "She gave it to you straight," he said, helping the celebrity newscasters make her young life look filled with available facts.

The police had another suspect after Jay Delaney split town — a man remarkable in his utter blandness. With his spongy, long face and his dull blue eyes, he could have been the cashier who gave you change for gas at a convenience store or the waiter, all generic manners, at a restaurant where you ate a meal you would immediately forget. As soon as I saw him, I began to forget him. He seemed aware of his own blandness, stepping up to take the blame as though, like Jay, he realized that this might be the only thing he would succeed in doing, the only thing he would ever do well. But then he disappeared too, skipped town, before anyone even had time to form an opinion about him, to fit him into the story people were learning to tell about Star's untimely death. He vanished before anyone could make sense of the way a life ends suddenly, for no reason.

When I walk out of the stuffy mentholated church office into pillows of heat, Jake is sitting on the curb. The sun is still strong at five o'clock and he rubs sunblock on his skinny arms and naked chest. His long bones are waiting for the rest of his body to catch up. He will wait until tomorrow, until Francine is back in her rightful place, wearing red lipstick and sucking from the same old straw.

But when he sees me, he jumps to his feet, unfurling those long bones. He pulls something out of his pocket, and all of a sudden he's wearing his thick-lens glasses and his wandering eyes are focused again, magnified to three times their normal size. "Boo!" he shouts, triumphant.

"I thought . . ." I start, already feeling like a fool. "Francine and her motorcycle man . . ."

"I'm a ghost looking for a little trouble, not *catastrophe*—what would I break my glasses for?" Jake the man-boy ghost laughs wickedly, and I realize that he must have talked to the minister on the way into the church, found out that Francine was out with an injury, and decided to have a little fun with the temp. "And besides, who knew you'd play along? You're a better prop than broken glasses."

"You should be visiting Francine." It's the only comeback I can think of off-the-cuff.

"Where do you think I was all morning?" he says. "I've got to be back at her place in half an hour with dinner." He pulls a crumpled piece of paper out of his pocket.

"Grocery list," he says, waving it overhead.

"Did you even know Star?"

"Nope," he says. "I got shipped off to military school long before that happened."

"You're bad," I say. I'm going for authoritative and scolding, but it comes out childlike and awestruck. I'm impressed.

"Yeah, right," Jake says. "*Francine saw a ghost.* Look who's talking, sister." He sinks to the curb, reeling his long bones in again. He waves an exaggerated good-bye, a fake smile plastered on his face, as I drive away. He doesn't care what I think. He's used to seeing the characters in his own personal dramas recur.

8

My mother is on her hands and knees, gathering tiny tumbleweeds of dust from the corners of the living room with her fingers. She practices the Italian she knows while she waits for this evening's date with Salvatore, a restaurateur who recently opened a restaurant called Salvatore's, next to the Hotel Fugor.

"Do you want to use the vacuum?" I ask, knowing she'll refuse. A vacuum cleaner would mean a commitment to cleaning. She only uses the vacuum cleaner for special occasions, like drowning me out. Spontaneous last-minute spot cleaning is more satisfying than regularly scheduled full-scale cleaning because the expectations are lower, which means she's pleasantly surprised by the results. Surprise: A random corner of the house is spotless.

"*Lucertola*," she says. She moves her lips as though she were kissing. She won't dignify the vacuum cleaner question with a response.

"What's that?" I ask.

"Lizard," she says. "*Il pippistrello,*" she murmurs. "That's a bat."

"You're going to be a wonderful dinner companion." I mean this sincerely, but somehow everything I say to her these days comes out of my mouth laced with sarcasm.

"*Vafanculo,*" she says with exaggerated sweetness. "Or as we say in Standardsville: Go fuck yourself."

"Lovely," I say. "Please get off the floor. You're getting dust all over yourself."

She and Salvatore are going on a second date—a picnic in the woods behind the gated community going up next to the Super Cineplex. Salvatore said he wants to romance her under leafy trees because he wants her to enjoy the "shady side of summer."

"I *like* shady," she says, before I can think of a wise-ass comment.

"There's a grim man-made pond with a sad, lonely duck," I try. I follow her into the kitchen, where she flicks the tumbleweeds into the trash can, then back into the foyer, where she plants herself in front of the mirror.

"Going into the woods with a bottle of wine is like skipping to the fourth date." She continues to ignore me, so I pick lint off her skirt and fluff it so that it floats dreamily around her thighs. "Salvatore isn't even his real name. I read in the paper that his name was Fred before he opened his restaurant." The urge to ruin her good time rampages wildly and uncontrollably through me like a wild beast.

"So he's made some changes in his life. We could all stand to make some changes. And I appreciate a man who is willing to risk skipping to the fourth date. A guy who is willing to make a fool of himself to make me feel good." My mother has had enough of me.

"And plus, *nella vita non si sa mai.*" She watches herself laugh in the mirror, practicing for later. "In life, one never knows." She purses her lipsticked lips, sucks in her cheeks to create shadow.

The sound of the phone is like an alarm, a warning saving me from further humiliation.

"*Pronto,*" I say when I pick it up. My mother nods approvingly without taking her eyes from the mirror.

"Isabelle?" Marla whispers, low and breathy like a prank caller.

"Would you please speak in a normal voice?" I speak loudly, modeling appropriate phone voice volume.

"I need you to come to the office right away."

Salvatore appears, a chubby post-happily-ever-after fairy-tale prince, in the foyer. He is a tall man with womanly hips and the stiff posture of someone accustomed to wearing suits, but this afternoon he's going for an after-work, casual-wear look with belted madras shorts and tucked-in white polo shirt. My mother blows me a kiss, glad to avoid introductions.

"Have fun," I say, putting my hand over the mouthpiece like somebody's busybody mother. They're already out the door.

"Bring some dress-up clothes," Marla says impatiently.

"Dress-up clothes?"

"Pretend you're going to be in a play."

"What kind of play?"

"A play in which you play an adult." I can hear her long, beige nails—today is beige day—drumming the top of her desk.

"Marla, I *am* an adult." I try to say it with conviction.

"You know, an adult who dresses like a grown-up. A married grown-up, one with kids. Someone with a real job, like those women you see in magazines, the ones who wear mix-and-match suits," Marla says, exasperated. "Now are you coming or what?"

"I'm guessing 'or what' is not an option."

"Ha." She hangs up.

I open the front door to go to Raymond's, but he's already on his way over, headed my way as my mother and Salvatore turn out of the cul-de-sac.

"You've got to help me," I say. His face is comforting, like the sound of rain on the roof at night. "You need to help me dress like a grown-up."

"I think you look just fine the way you are," Raymond says. He heads straight for the couch, sweeping one hand through the air, up and down the length of my body, to indicate that the sweatpants and the T-shirt I'm wearing is just fine.

"I'm not fishing for a compliment," I say, though I'm touched. "I need to dress up for a temp job. A temp job where I have to pretend to be somebody I'm not, like the churchy secretary with less church."

Raymond doesn't know about the mystery shops, but he nods as if having a job where one would need to pretend to be somebody she's not is perfectly normal. This is one of Raymond's greatest qualities—his ability to make me feel that my life is normal, or at least okay by him.

"And who would that be?" he asks, taking his seat on the couch.

"A grown-up." I channel Marla.

"Oh, that." He runs his hand carefully, curiously, over his hair as if it had suddenly appeared on his head.

"You know, married with kids, a nice haircut, a routine."

"I see," Raymond says matter-of-factly.

A tiny bird thumps into the living room window. It trembles where it's fallen to the ground, then shakes itself off and flies tentatively away.

"Did you know scientists covered the eyes of homing pigeons with Ping-Pong balls and discovered they still found their way home? They respond to the earth's magnetic field." Raymond examines the hand he's been running over his hair—it too is astonishing.

"Maybe I'm a homing pigeon trapped in the body of a temp?"

"I saw this on a nature show about navigation," Raymond says. "There are two kinds—dead reckoning and piloting. A dead reckoner doesn't need anything to guide him. He just keeps track of where he's been. The pilot uses landmarks and familiar objects to keep going. That's me, a pilot, because, let's face it, I can't keep track of anything. And you, Isabelle, are one of my landmarks."

These words pierce the summer haze around my heart. I am not only on his life's path, I am a recognizable fixture. Take a left at the stoplight and turn right at Isabelle to get to Raymond. I kneel in front of him and look into his sad, sweet eyes to try once again to see what he sees.

"Raymond." When I say it, I can suddenly breathe more easily. Floating in the air between us, his name sounds like love. I lean over and kiss his dry lips. I run my hand across his rough cheek. He is completely still, except for the flicker of his eyes underneath closed lids.

He is the first to pull away, moving his head back so that I slip forward, pinning him to the couch.

"Sorry, sorry." I've got my face in his lap. "Oh my God, I'm so sorry, Raymond." I scramble to get up, but he's wriggling too, and we're both being swallowed by this couch that has been threatening to swallow us all summer. Finally, I'm on my feet.

"Isabelle," Raymond says. His hands hover at his lips. When he says my name, it's not love but something quieter, something that rings with the sadness of seeing beyond love. All this time, I thought I'd seen that far, but I was so wrong.

"This is just one summer in your life," Raymond whispers through trembling fingers.

"But Raymond, that's not what I meant." I grab words out of the air. "You're my landmark too. We could be each other's landmarks—like trees or signs. Lampposts. Let me be your lamppost. A shrub—I'll be your shrub."

"Let's find you an outfit," Raymond says, escorting me to the stairs, determinedly avuncular. "You're family, Isabelle." He pats my arm, escorting me as though he were my nurse, as we make our way up the stairs to my room. "You're my family. We take care of each other."

"That's just it." I start, but I can't continue. I want him to be my family, my own special version of family. A little shrub family. Something other than wives and husbands and children, beyond ritual and custom, where our loneliness can exist side by side, undisguised.

Raymond follows me into my room and sits on my bed while I riffle awkwardly through my closet, overflowing with piles of T-shirts, cutoffs, and sweatpants I haven't washed since coming home for the summer. I abandoned my phone-company clothes in San Francisco. The fanciest thing I own is a pair of black pants that Samantha thought I should have.

"These had better work," I'd said. "They better change my life and lend structure and meaning to my life—breakfast, lunch, and dinner, those elusive three square meals, some chitchat about some sport or current event at my job where people actually stand around a watercooler, a trip to the dry cleaner on the way home because I'll suddenly have clothes worthy of being dry-cleaned."

"You're lucky you're so creative," Samantha said, which meant she thought I dressed badly.

Raymond lies on my bed, looking out my window, the way I look out my window at night to watch him. His body has gone noodly. He would never tell me I was "creative." He wouldn't tell me to buy "essential" black pants. He appreciates the way I lurk around the edges of other people's lives, afraid someone will call out for audience participation, because he lurks too.

"There's really nothing here that is appropriate for anyone older than fifteen," I say, throwing a dirty T-shirt back into the closet. "Follow me." I head for my mother's room, but when I get to her closet and turn around, Raymond is frozen in the doorway, his body rigid as ever. My mother's drugstore perfume floats all around us. Raymond sneezes violently.

"I have been trying to make her switch for years," I say, waving my hand in the air. "Maybe you're allergic. I know I'm ready to be." But Raymond doesn't hear me. He's staring at the hat on top of my mother's dresser, the jaunty one she wears in Henry's picture, with the pigeons in the park.

"That's the one from the picture," I say. "She never wears it anymore."

"I can't stay," Raymond says. He heads for the stairs, moving faster than I've ever seen him move before. He slides his hand along the banister, begging it to speak to him.

"Raymond." I go to my window and call out to him as he runs across the street and into his house. He doesn't even stop to check his mail. "Raymond. Come back." I've ruined everything. "Raymond." I want his name to sound like love but it sounds more like panic, ringing in my ears as I hurry to dress alone.

WHEN I drive past the Hotel Fugor on my way to Temporama, a teenage boy in full knight regalia on a horse paces the small, worn patch of lawn out front. The knight, his face streaming with sweat, holds his helmet in one hand and a cigarette in the other, and when the horse jerks his head down to graze, both the helmet and the cigarette fall to the ground. The knight jumps off his steed and frantically stomps up and down on the cigarette, afraid that he'll set the Hotel Fugor's tiny, dry plot of land ablaze. People honk and wave from the highway. The hopping-up-and-down boy with the rented horse, risen from the highway ashes, is something miraculous to behold.

At Temporama, I sit in the lobby with a plastic bag filled with my mother's suit, her heels, and my wig, still slightly mussed from my struggle with Creampuff—stuff I hope will pass as grown-up equipment. As I sit next to piles of magazines for career women—women in navy suits, with haircuts that swing as they stride confidently through corporate America—three of Marla's colleagues gather around a menu at a nearby desk. They wear slacks belted above their waists and two of them hold their jackets slung over their shoulders like they just stepped out of one of the career-woman magazines. According to Marla, they claim to be vegans whose main topic of conversation at any given time of the day is the food they do or do not eat. Marla watches them order tiny amounts of food three or four times a day from the macrobiotic deli down the street, owned by the people who also own the dental equipment store next door.

"Fat-free, wheatless chocolate chip muffin," says the pixie blonde jacket-slinger to the sullen brunette writing down the order.

"Protein shake with soy milk," says the other jacket-slinger, a poofy-haired blonde.

When the sullen brunette says nothing, both jacket-slingers turn to her.

"What are you having, Annette?"

"I'm not sure," Annette says slowly, realizing her power.

"Maybe I won't have anything then," the pixie says.

"Me neither," the poofy blonde says, letting her jacket slide off her shoulder and drag on the ground.

A box of diet cookies sits unopened on top of the office fridge. I've looked inside that fridge before and seen the soy milk nobody actually drinks. Marla tells me they sneak across the street to the supermarket for whole milk. She particularly dislikes Annette. She claims it's because she doesn't process the time sheets correctly, but I once witnessed Annette walk away from a birthday cake as if it were a stapler or a file folder.

"Isabelle, ma belle." Marla emerges from the women's bathroom in a cloud of perfume that smells like a mixture of household cleaning products. The lobby crowd consists of a high school girl looking for summer work, and a man, his hair dyed a slippery jet-black to hide the gray, wearing new-smelling clothes. They sit in the postures of people signing up at a temp agency for the first and last times — the girl's back is rod-straight and the man slumps in a last-ditch hunch. They could be the beginning and the end of a poster depicting temp evolution.

When I stand to follow Marla, they both look up from their magazines in case Marla has come for them, then readjust themselves in the slippery, plastic chairs and return to their magazines when they realize she hasn't.

"Here we go." Marla races ahead of me, looking ready as ever to offer habits as remedies. Before sending me off to my first office job, she told me: Get up fifteen minutes earlier than you normally would so you can put together an appropriate outfit and have a relaxing cup of coffee, a quiet "me moment," before reporting to your assignment. Now she leads me into an abandoned back office filled with boxes and without chairs and closes the door behind us. I stand under the fluorescent lights, the plastic bag dangling from my wrist.

"You're ready for the big one," she says in her mafia growl whisper. I look around expectantly for it — the big one. "The movies were small potatoes, honey." She's beginning to sound like last week's movie-of-the-week heroine who, when faced with the choice of her husband or the search for her surrogate daughter, looked at her husband and said, "You're small potatoes, honey." Raymond called me "small potatoes" for the rest of the night—hey, small potatoes, are you from Idaho? Hey small potatoes, are you mashed or baked? He made potato jokes all night long, laughing so hard he cried.

"Marla." I say her name softly because she's starting to scare me. The light shines off her add-a-bead necklace and her eyes are glossy. "What's 'the big one'?"

"You're ready for real estate, Isabelle," she says. "Those movie mystery shops were a test. You made it a few yards down the field and now you're ready for a touchdown. This is the big time." She's more movie-of-the-week than the movie-of-the-week.

"Gated communities," Marla says in an excited voice that betrays her dull life—her husband sprawled in front of the TV, flipping channels as she tries to read to him from an article about how everyday chitchat can improve a relationship; regret for all the office birthday cake she wished she had never eaten; her hatred for the women at work; how she would rather kill herself than order from the same lunch menu one more time. The solitary duck bobs in the man-made pond outside the gated community half-built behind the Super Cineplex, near my mother and Salvatore's picnic blanket.

"Where the new American family lives," Marla continues. "Communities built for comfort and fortified from the outside world. No reason to leave. You got your view, your pool, your recreational facilities, your health-and-fitness center. Did I mention day care?" Marla takes a breath, twisting the chain of her necklace around her index finger. "These places are owned by people in Texas or Arizona, one of those dust bowls.

People who can't be bothered to leave their air-conditioned worlds to fly all the way to the Midwest to make sure that their people are doing the job for them. And that, kiddo, is where you come in."

"What do I need to do?" I try not to shout. Marla is on the verge of hyperventilating and the plastic bag is digging into my wrist. I bob my head in time to Marla's words, caught up in the physicality of her excitement, her breathlessness, and her fidgety hands. I'm horrified. I'm thrilled. Like one of those dreams where you are standing on the edge of a cliff, this is one of those moments when a force you didn't know existed inside you rises up and compels you to jump.

"We dress you up," she continues. "Give you a fake name, fake job, fake husband, fake life, and we send you in there to rent an apartment so we can see what goes on behind the iron gates." Marla looks around for chairs, realizes there are none, and leads me out of the mysterious room and back to her desk where we normally meet. She has a new scrap of paper taped to her desk, next to all the others: *When the rug is pulled out from under you, you must learn to dance on a shifting carpet.*

"Highway Psychic?" I ask. I decide not to tell her that Clifford says this to all the women who go to him for answers, that, in fact, he's the one pulling the rug.

"If this is your life-path, I'm on it," she says. I was never a big believer in destiny, but Marla is all over my life's path.

"Tell me what I need to do," I say.

Marla squeals with delight when I pull out the wig. Her range—from low and growly to high-pitched and adolescent—is impressive compared to the other temp counselors with their bored and hungry monotones. They all turn to stare as

Marla holds the wig up with two fingers like it's a dead animal she's found in a drawer. She looks at me very seriously, her big, made-up face a festival of color.

"It's a fabulous piece of head wear," she says, "but we've got to make it look real." I am Marla's shot at glory. She sits at her desk all day long, staring at her scraps of advice and wondering how to apply them to her life as she sends people out on temporary jobs. If I am a temporary, liminal being, then Marla is a fake god, a divine arranger of limbo. She looks me dead in the eye. "First on the list," she says, "is the Comfort Station, 'where everyday is a rest stop on the road of life.' "

She pushes me toward the bathroom. Lipstick, eye shadow, mascara, and blush are scattered across the bathroom counter, next to the rain forest potpourri. I go into one of the stalls to change into my mother's business suit and her high heels.

"I pointed out to the manager at Comfort Station that the name sounds like a highway restroom," Marla tells me while I shimmy out of my jeans. "He told me that was his intention all along. As if highway toilets were real-estate-paradise. I gave him a look and he just said, 'Irony, Marla, irony.' That's the weirdest irony I've ever heard of. That's an *ironic* irony." I come out of the stall and we stand under the office cleaning schedule as Marla begins the makeover. The banner above the chore wheel reads PRIZE FOR CLEANEST CLEANER!

"Look up," Marla says, doing my lashes.

I stood in front of my bathroom mirror like this on prom night, learning for the first time how to apply mascara, having barely mastered lip gloss. "I bet Dennis won't even notice," I'd said when I finally emerged—afraid of my own newly discovered cleavage and raccoon eyes—to show my mother what I'd done to myself.

"They never do," my mother said matter-of-factly.

"Then what's the point?" I demanded.

"The point is not to recognize yourself."

Teetering in my mother's heels, transformed, I fully grasp what she was talking about. Travel, sex, and higher education never made me feel this focused, this significant.

"Are the lobby refreshments in clear view or are they stashed stingily in a cupboard? Does the person in the front office stand when you walk in the door? Does he or she use your name in conversation? Are there awkward pauses?" Marla quizzes me while she uses her fingers to subtly blend the two types of blush she's chosen for my cheeks.

She hands me the questionnaire. "Memorize this. You won't be able to take it in there with you." *Did the agent use tie-down questions after the tour, like "What do you think?" "How do you like this?" Was a positive sense of urgency created?*

In the mirror, I become the grown-up Marla has invented— a graphic designer, $100,000 a year, at Prints Charming downtown, where all the buildings are made of glass and shiny steel. A graphic designer with no pets who has moved here specifically for the job. And to be closer to her mother. This added detail makes me loyal, the sort of renter with family ties, the kind who will stick around. And, as Marla points out, any great actress can use the similarities between the character she's playing and herself to go deeper.

"I took a few acting classes back in the day," Marla says. "Now, do you remember who you are?" She uses her pinky to smooth my unruly eyebrows. "Don't get carried away or they'll suspect something. Your husband's a lawyer, doctor, or runs his own Internet company. Entirely up to you. Now pucker." She dots my lips with pink lipstick the color of the wallpaper in the bathroom. "Lips together." She hands me a wad of toilet paper. "Now kiss." After she pins my real hair up, I slide the wig on. "Amazing," Marla says, impressed. "You could be your own sister."

We stand back to get a better look at Marla's creation. She puts her hands on my shoulders and squeezes gently so as not to wreck her work. "Perfect," she says to my reflection—a woman with a full date book, places to go, and lunch engagements that she squeezes into her busy workday. This woman has a husband and a child who consider her competent, capable of whipping something up in the kitchen when there seems to be no food in the refrigerator. This woman knows that the trash goes out on Tuesday and Thursday nights, and the recycling goes out on Mondays. Her closet is filled with clothes that go together, cultivated and honed over the years. She knows that hairspray gets out ink stains (she keeps a bottle of it in her desk at work) and club soda gets out everything else.

"Delilah?" Marla says. "That's a very grown-up name."

"Priscilla?" I offer. Priscilla sounds like a sensible woman who had a little fun—a few carefully selected but wild affairs in her twenties (when she called herself Prissy)—before she settled down with her husband.

"All right," Marla says, shoving me toward the door with football bravado. "Remember: Winning isn't a sometimes thing!"

I tuck the sprung foam back into the cracks in the Chevy's bench seat's vinyl and sit on a towel I dig out of the back so as not to muss my outfit. When I pass the Hotel Fugor, the teenage knight has company. Outside the cul-de-sac, Raymond looks like a cutout pasted onto the landscape. But there he is, in the flesh, on one of his highway strolls, stroking the long face of the knight's horse. The knight sits cross-legged on the grass, his helmet in his lap, a fresh cigarette dangling from his lips. He looks at Raymond in wonder, as if Raymond were a part of a museum exhibit on prehistoric man. I can picture Raymond on his parents' farm, speaking to the animals about his dreams for Tinseltown. "And you," he'd whisper in the ear of a particularly seductive sheep, "can be Mae West."

I slow the Chevy down to a crawl as I drive by and it bucks a little, threatening to stall out. The knight puts his helmet back on, wets his fingers to pinch the lit end of his cigarette, and stubs it out vigorously to once again prevent a medieval forest fire. He pulls the horse's head away from Raymond and says something that causes Raymond to brush his hands on his pants legs, like he's packing it in. I swear Raymond sees me because he looks straight into my eyes, but he chooses not to recognize me, eyeing the interior of the car as it rolls by as if it were a dark cave. He kicks up highway dirt that rises up in a sparkling cloud all around him. Walking slowly away through his own tiny dust storm, he is a wizard banishing me from his domain.

A lady in an SUV filled with children leans on her horn behind me. She drives by and rolls down the automatic window on the passenger side to shout something I can't hear because my windows are up, sealing in the feeble air-conditioning. Her face contorts with rage as her children look at me blankly. One of them sticks out his tongue.

Following Marla's directions, I continue on. Eventually I pass a pool hall that used to be a restaurant where my family ate when I was very little. The wallpaper was made out of maps of the United States—maps of different regions, maps of every state, detailed maps of cities. My mother, my father, and I always sat in a booth under a map of Standardsville when it was still uncharted territory—rivers and bare terrain. Every time we ate there my father pinpointed the place on the map where our house would someday be located in the vast expanse of space. Now it's as though he was predicting our future, divining something from a landscape oblivious of its own potential.

In San Francisco, I searched for myself in the cable installation maps that I fed through the giant copy machine for the phone company, studying the intricate lines that marked the north, south, east, west, and interior walls. The lines converged in darker intersections called splice closures, which always sounded like something good to eat. The vocabulary of the maps had a pleasantly mysterious sound like big words you hear as a child in adult conversations: "aerial," "allowable consumption rate," "proposed compressor." Day after day, I located myself in between the lines. It helped me feel like a part of something, imagining myself, tucked deep inside a fire-retardant duct.

The restaurant-turned–pool hall has its doors wide open revealing a poster of a Harley, but there's nobody inside. My heart drops at the passage of time. It's the feeling of hitting a bump in the road and rising up for a minute only to hit the ground again, disappointed that you didn't rise and rise and fly away. I wonder if, sitting in that booth navigating uncharted territory, my father predicted the way he would walk off our map or the way I would leave and return.

There is still countryside along the highway and up ahead, Comfort Station stands alone surrounded by pastures filled with unsuspecting cows. One corner of the complex is under construction as if it were undergoing plastic surgery. The red earth is turned up expectantly, waiting for the beautifying change.

What kind of people live here? Is there crime in the area? I practice the questions from the questionnaire. I say them to myself in the car once I've turned off the engine. *What kind of people live here?* I ask the Chevy's huge steering wheel. According to real-estate law, Marla says, the appropriate answer is "all kinds" or "diverse."

"And what if they have another answer?" I asked.

"Then the boys in Texas or Arizona or Timbuktu will take care of them," Marla informed me with a creepy smile that suggested she'd like to see this happen.

In the lobby of Comfort Station there are brown-and-purple patterned couches, an Easterner's notion of the colors of the desert. On the glass table in front of me as I sink into one of the soft couches is a fake rock with the engraved words: *Some people make things happen. Other people watch things happen. Still others wonder what happened.* In a room sectioned off by a glass wall, people with terry-cloth headbands pedal furiously on stationary bikes in a room done all in whites.

"Are you looking to rent?" a radio announcer voice booms behind me.

When I turn around, a man in a seersucker suit takes my hand between two clammy palms.

"Sure," I mumble. Then, "Yes," the clear-voiced way I imagine Priscilla would.

"My name's Marv." His voice is squeaky, his words scrambling over each other to get out of his throat.

"I don't have any pets." I panic, my head full of Marla's sound bites. "My husband's busy at work. At the new company. Web company. Design."

"Whoa," Marv says. "Slow down." His words slow down too as they fall into line, marching out of his mouth in an orderly fashion as he leads me over to the counter where cookies and lemonade are displayed *in plain sight*. "Lemonade?"

"No, thanks." Priscilla's voice comes more easily, the kind that hisses its Ss in an effort to be precise. Still, I jump when Marv grasps my elbow, leading me through the brown-and-purple lobby out onto the grounds where the sun pounds down on new pavement. He gentles his clench as we pass the fenced-in pool where a woman sprawls on a beach towel. Her bikini top is untied and she serves up the naked expanse of her fleshy back to the sun's rays.

Marla instructed me to point out one aspect of the complex that doesn't meet Priscilla's standards so that the agent has to prove himself. "Why the fence around the pool?" I ask. Surrounded by this scenery, it's easier to be the sort of person who cares about these things. Like a movie set, everything—the hot, yellow sun, the woman's reddening back, Marv's clipboard, the pen tucked behind his ear—is designed to encourage real-life amnesia.

"Residents only, Priscilla." This is something Marv has memorized from the employee handbook. He waves a hand to point out a twin set of muddy man-made ponds without ducks.

Soon this town will be submerged. Muddy water everywhere, it will revert back to primitive sludge.

"There was a small, insignificant mud slide last night," Marv says, his voice scrambly again when he sees me looking at the unattended dirt-filled dump truck at the edge of the pond, a prehistoric beast that has just crawled onto dry land to adapt and evolve.

We walk toward one of two apartment towers as Marv describes the cozy community at Comfort Station, how a girl would have neighbors she could trust, people from whom her future children could borrow a cup of milk, their children people from whom her future children could borrow a cup of milk. "What I'm talking about," Marv says, finding the deepest version of his voice, "is lasting relationships." As we climb the stairs, I look out over the endlessly flat fields that surround us. There is nothing for miles, like the map of Standardsville before there was Standardsville, when the land was its purest self.

Marv walks me through a one-bedroom apartment, opening kitchen drawers, turning on faucets, sliding open closet doors, switching on and off the gas stove, using words like "convenient," and "modern."

"And there's always the opportunity to move up to the deluxe family condo. You know, in case you and your husband start baking something in there." Marv looks at my stomach.

"Oven's ready," I say, patting my belly. I'm suddenly speaking Marv's language. It comes easily. "Just a matter of pounding that dough."

"You're a quick one, Priscilla." Marv chuckles. "I better watch my step." We venture out onto the deck overlooking the duckless pond. From this vantage point, I can see bits of trash floating on the dark surface.

Marv turns to me. "What do you really want out of an apartment, Priscilla?" as if now, at last, we can really get down to business. At this point, according to the questionnaire, I should be studying the way he moves in for the "clencher moment." *Does the agent sound sincere? Does the agent use effective body language without seeming aggressive?* Marv squats on the deck like a camp counselor trying to make himself the same size as his campers. Puzzled, I hitch up my slacks and squat too.

"I work at Prints Charming. It's a graphic design firm," I offer. I imagine myself there surrounded by useful tools— computers and brilliant ideas with practical applications. It's the kind of office where there are affectionate fights over who gets to use the beautiful royal-blue coffee mug with tiny flowers that somebody's daughter made in pottery class.

"I'm happy at my job. I'd like to be happy in my apartment too," I say. I'd savor an after-dinner cigarette out on this porch after a long day of hard but satisfying work.

"Priscilla, does anyone ever call you P? As in little P. Hey little P." His voice squeaks, and he drops it back down an octave as he looks out vaguely at the big blue sky.

"Not until right now," I say. I'm game for anything. Bring it on, Marv.

"Do you know what they do to geese to make pâté?"

"No, but I can tell by your tone of voice that it must be really interesting." I'm impressed by the sincere tone I achieve. I check my look in the sliding glass door. I could just disappear. Just walk off to somewhere else in the world looking like this.

Like those people on talk shows who just walk out on their families; go to work; see you later, honey; and never come back. They make a new life for themselves, like my father. It suddenly seems so easy, so tempting.

"Force-feedings," Marv says. He licks a finger to wipe something off his scuffed wing tips. I nod, my head bobbing up and down like the pond trash. "They insert a funnel and pour grain down their throats." He looks at me with the middle-distance stare of Clifford, the Highway Psychic. "But that's not the worst part."

"What is the worst part?" I ask, trying to imagine what Priscilla would do in this situation. We're still squatting. Priscilla would not squat. She would know not to squat.

"If they take the funnel out of the goose's mouth, he chases after it. *He can't help himself.* Instinct," Marv says, staring into my eyes so deeply that I fear he will damage them. "Priscilla, I'm like that goose."

I stand up. "Huh," I say. "Uh-huh."

Marv stands too. "Priscilla, I can't stand here and try to rent you this apartment." My breasts fill my blouse, suddenly as proplike as the pen behind Marv's ear. I toss my hair. I smooth my skirt.

"I'm like a goose." Marv noodles me up against the deck railing. He seems boneless, like he's made of pure rubber—chewy and pink. When I put my hand out to catch myself, the rough wood scratches the skin but the sensation is delayed, a feeling echo. "Force-fed by the real-estate establishment to force-feed you," Marv says, his Bianca Blast–enhanced breath in my ear.

Priscilla, in a moment of living on the edge, in a month

when she's had it up to here with family life, with words like "security" and "responsibility," suddenly takes over. Careful what you wish for, Marv. She leans in and kisses him wetly. Her tongue fills his mouth, expanding. She thinks she might choke, but choking feels better than hunger.

"My goodness," Priscilla says, pulling away and looking Marv up and down. The power of faking it floods my system. I laugh loudly, louder than I've ever laughed before. My body is more flexible and I stretch my arms above my head like I'm just waking up. I wonder if I could do gymnastics, if Priscilla ever took a class in high school.

"My gracious," Marv says, baffled. He wipes his mouth with the back of his hand. He's a relentless flirt, but the clients don't usually go for it. They certainly don't respond like *this*.

"Thanks," I say, and Priscilla walks me gracefully down the stairs. "I'll call you about the apartment." Marv leans against the railing, dumbfounded. Then he waves a quick overanxious wave greedy for my attention. He's still there, waving his greedy wave when I climb into the Chevy. He's so small it's as if I were seeing him from a plane. I slam the car into reverse. He's a dot against the expanse of Comfort Station as I back out onto the highway and drive away.

I pull into the parking lot of the deserted pool hall to slide the wig off and pull out the bobby pins. The pool-hall door is still swung wide open, inviting anyone into its emptiness. With a pencil I fill out the questionnaire. *Good conversationalist: yes. Overcame your objection to the facilities: yes. Helped you to feel comfortable with the possibility of your new life: yes.* Marv *has* helped me. This last question is the point. I've been willing to go this far from the moment Marla first uttered those magical words "mystery shop."

A man and his two young children—a boy and a girl who is much older than the way she's dressed, the bow in her hair sad and out of place, the sash of her flowery dress undone—come out of the pool hall. At first, the girl laughs, throwing her head back in the way people do when laughter takes over. But neither her father nor her brother are laughing. Their mouths are firm lines that have endured this for years. The boy, younger than the girl but clearly in charge, puts his arm around her when she slumps into him and begins to cry. Her father gets down on his knees in the gravel, looking for something. He digs, throwing up stones and dust that quickly cover his clothes, fleck his hair. The dust covers the boy and girl. The girl stops crying and laughs and laughs. They don't seem to notice me, though my car is the only one in the pool-hall parking lot. The father throws stones in every direction, digging for whatever he's lost.

One of the flying stones hits my windshield as I give Marv a high score. The man and the boy look up and the girl begins to cry. The girl crying looks the same as the girl laughing. It doesn't seem to matter whether she cries or laughs. The idea is to break the air with a sound, to stretch the muscles in her face in any direction.

When I lurch into the cul-de-sac, "Fernando" at top volume, my mother is walking down our street. She walks slowly and stares at the ground. At first glance, she looks older than she's ever looked close-up, and that unexpected glimpse at the inevitability of her death cuts at my heart.

"There was something in the air that night," I belt out the window. "The stars were bright, Fernando." She's not amused.

"It's not enough," she says, when I get out of the car. She's continuing a conversation she's been having with herself the whole way home. I wait for her to tell me a story, how the duck waddled over and quacked at their picnic, how her skirt got caught on a branch and instead of bothering to untangle it, she stepped out of her skirt altogether. Instead, she stares at her feet intensely, as though they've just appeared at the end of her legs.

"Where's Salvatore?" I ask stupidly. I step aside like someone useless at the scene of an emergency as my mother stomps into the living room and flings herself onto the couch.

"Back in the woods somewhere," she says and gestures out into the world behind her. "Where he belongs."

"Where he belongs." I've moved from stupidity to a mimic's desperate echo.

I go to the kitchen to get her a glass of white wine and bring it to her on the sofa. She runs her fingers through her hair before taking the wine from me. She's her own sweetest comfort.

"I expect too much," she says. "I want to fall in love. I want love to make everything else make sense."

I take a sip of her wine. "You deserve that," I say. I sit down next to her and put my arm around her.

"He's not ready to commit. He's dating around. He used that expression—'dating around,' " she says, resting her head on my shoulder. "At his age?"

"He didn't offer you a ride home?"

"I threw his keys in the duck pond. He's still trying to fish them out."

There have been days this summer when it seemed like my life was so random it could be taking place anywhere. I might still be in San Francisco or lingering in my small, Midwestern college town. But with my mother's head on my shoulder, and the fading light catching sparkling specks of sparkling dust, making the room look abandoned even with us in it, this moment has been waiting for me all my life.

9

~

THE temperature has broken one hundred every day for the past week. The DJs in their cool booths celebrate while everyone else stays inside or scuttles from air-conditioned offices to air-conditioned grocery stores. People linger in the fruit and vegetable aisles, waiting for the spray to turn on.

Marla told me to give Marv her direct line at Temporama and when he made his follow-up call, she would pretend to be my mother. I told Marv my husband and I were staying with her until we found a permanent home. When Marv called, he told Marla that she had "quite a daughter" and that "Comfort Station would love to have Priscilla and her family join our community. We don't extend this offer to just *anyone*." Because of my success at Comfort Station, Marla has promised to keep me busy.

"I knew you were the one," she tells me. "You've got a gift."

Yesterday, Priscilla shopped Looks Like We Made It, where Kent—a self-described "major Barry Manilow fan"—demonstrated the Lifecycle in the community's fitness center. I cried, but without tears so my makeup wouldn't smudge, and told Kent that stationary bikes always reminded me of my husband who ran off with his personal trainer. It was a moment of inspiration—I wanted to try out Priscilla's vulnerable side. "The stationary bike was the cardiovascular segment of his workout," I whimpered.

Several community members turned to look at me as they skied and climbed in place. Kent jumped off the bike mid-mountain climb, rushed over to a paper towel dispenser, and ratcheted out several sheets.

"I *bought* him that gym membership," I said, blowing my nose into the coarse brown paper.

"Priscilla," he said. "We've been thinking about hiring an in-house counselor for just this sort of thing." He gestured toward what could be my new life—the blue sky, the rose-colored walkways. His gesture took in the clean, new-smelling apartments stacked floor upon floor. Somewhere in that stack was the "solo" apartment he'd shown me, "solo" like an adventure, a "solo" flight, "solo" living as a sport, as if you had to be in good shape to live alone, up to the physical challenge. He brushed Priscilla's hair from my face as he escorted me out of the fitness center.

"There's a lot to be said for living in a controlled environment," Kent said gently. With his arm around her, speaking in his steady, perfectly modulated voice, he almost had Priscilla convinced.

"I always knew your good penmanship would pay off," my mother says distractedly, on her way up the stairs to change yet again for tonight's date. She continues to believe I'm the graphic design firm's down-home calligrapher. She appears at the top of the stairs, pulling at the bottom of her dress. "Is this too short? It's too short, right? I'm changing." She walks back into her bedroom, pulling the dress over her head, before I have a chance to answer. Ever since Salvatore told her he wanted to date around she's been dating around with a vengeance. She goes to the movies a lot because the theaters have the best air-conditioning. I impress her dates by telling them which theaters have the most leg room, the cleanest bathrooms, the friendliest ushers, the biggest screens.

On her way down the stairs, back in the dress up for question, she runs a rag reeking of furniture polish along the banister.

"I've decided this dress isn't too short after all," she says. "What do you think?"

The combination of the furniture polish, her drugstore perfume, and her relentless, transparent optimism is too much.

"I'm going out," I say. "I'm going to go regress somewhere."

"That's nice, honey," she says. She continues to rub the rag along the banister, staring intently at her hand in motion. As I'm walking out the door, she calls after me. "Just make sure not to tell me about it later."

THE bar is a long dark hallway with a small alcove in front where the cover band, Hot Steal, is about to play. The drummer, George, who calls himself Yo, is a friend of Dennis's. I twirl Priscilla's hair between my fingers. I slipped the wig on in the bathroom at the Chinese restaurant where my mother went with a date and brought home colorful parasol swizzle sticks. I called Dennis from a pay phone and told him to meet me there. After some practice sessions in front of my bedroom mirror, I can now put the wig on easily by myself. I've grown skillful at adjusting it so it looks natural. The wig is the only part of Priscilla that I wear tonight. Instead of my mother's business suit I wear my usual jeans and a T-shirt. Priscilla on the skids.

"What is up with your hair?" Dennis finally asked at dinner, halfway through his sweet-and-sour pork at the dimly lit restaurant. "There's something different about it. Did you cut it?"

"I did," I said. "Just for you."

"You are whacked." He made cuckoo circles around his ear with his chopsticks to show me just how whacked.

As Hot Steal gets ready to rock, Dennis brings two beers to the table. "So basically you think you can call me up at the last minute and I'll drop everything to meet you." He's become indignant lately.

"Well . . ." I say, shrugging.

"Bite me," Dennis says. He smiles and gulps his beer.

The lead singer pushes his hair out of his face, strums a few dull notes, then leans into the mike dramatically even though his audience is me and Dennis and the bartender, who is smoking and holding his solar calculator up to the lamp beside the broken antique cash register.

"This one's by Cyndi Lauper," the lead singer says from behind his hair, which has fallen across his face again. He pauses to remember which one. He looks at me and winks. " 'Cause girls just wanna have fun," he says. The band breaks into "When You Were Mine."

"Who are these guys? That's a Prince song," I protest. I have to lean over, my mouth moving against his ear, so that Dennis can hear me. He's already tapping the beat out with his feet. The table's shaky leg is propped up with a pile of napkins, and every time he taps our beers slosh dangerously in their dusty glasses.

"She's so feisty." Dennis pinches my cheek.

I swat his hand away. "Why don't you . . ." I can't think of anything clever. ". . . get a life or something?" I'm reduced to this.

"Aw man, she told me to get a life," Dennis says, talking to an imaginary person at the empty table next to us. "Did you hear that? This girl is out of control. Don't mess with her."

"Screw you." I am sixteen years old again. The terrifying truth is, you can go home again. You can go home, age backward, and get stuck at sixteen the way your mother said your eyes would get stuck if you kept crossing them. You can go home and never, ever find your way back again. "Where's Peoria tonight anyway?" I ask, in an effort to bring us back to the present.

"She couldn't get a baby-sitter," Dennis says. "What do you care where she is anyway?" He jumps at the opportunity for a little power.

"I don't," I say, too quickly.

At dinner, my fortune-cookie fortune read, "The fool is like a person with integrity. His mouth and heart are equal." During one of his "transitional periods," Dennis decided to be an Emergency Medical Technician. He was required to take an anatomy class and I was home on spring break from college the week the class studied female anatomy. I lay on the end of his bed while he finished a chapter in his textbook. Its cover was the shadowy profile of a naked man and woman facing each other. They looked ready to wrestle. Dennis handed me a list of vocabulary words from class that day, proof that he was finally doing something serious.

He'd forgotten that he'd written his own class jokes in the margin. Next to "perineum—the space between the vagina and the anus," was Dennis's boyish scrawl: *chin rest*. He grabbed the paper from me when he saw me smile, claiming someone next to him had written it, but I recognized his handwriting from love letters he'd sent me in high school, letters filled with vocabulary words from that week's English quiz. "I know that my behavior is sometimes *heinous*, but don't be *maudlin* because I have the *tenacity* to see this through." He insisted that *chin rest* was written by someone else, not understanding that I was touched by the way he thought I was someone who'd gone out into the world and come back sophisticated and above it all, when really I thought *chin rest* was funny.

Dennis and I are the sum of our shared history—the mostly physical sequence of being in the same places at the same times over a number of years. There are days when all I want is to sit next to Dennis, in a dark bar like this one, his solid body filling the space beside me the way it did as we drove the back roads through high school. Earlier tonight he ordered vanilla in a gourmet ice cream shop boasting fifty flavors, and I was grateful.

Now Dennis puts one of his hands on my knee under the table and continues to keep the beat with the other. The weight of his hand presses down, painfully sweet.

"I remember where I was when Lennon died," the lead

singer shouts. "Do you?" He points out into the empty bar.
The band kicks into "Twist and Shout," and the microphone
makes a screeching sound. At the bar, the bartender has given
up on the solar calculator and scribbles on a napkin with a
pencil.

"Are these guys for real?" I ask.

"They're dumb on purpose," Dennis explains. He bounces
up and down in his chair. "The Isley Brothers," he says. "This
song's by the Isley Brothers."

The microphone screeches again.

"That noise is fucking with my teeth," Dennis says, his hand
still on my knee.

Dennis tells me everything, down to the way his teeth feel;
I tell him nothing true. I make up details about my make-
believe job as a sales rep at the phone company back in San Francisco where I claim to have a corner window office with a view of
the Bay. I tell him I have a picture on my desk of Sebastian and
me on vacation at the Grand Canyon. I told Dennis that Sebastian said he wanted to throw himself in, it moved him that much.

"How *sensitive*," Dennis said, pretending to vomit. I told
him Sebastian would visit again as soon as he was done with
his big account. "He's an ad guy," I tell him. I have only the
vaguest idea what an ad guy does, or what a big account might
involve, but these terms seem legitimate in a corporate jargony
sort of way. They satisfy Dennis, who doesn't ask or seem to
want to know about my real life anyway.

I told Dennis about another picture I have in my office—
one of me as a baby, bald as a billiard ball, perched on my
mother's knee. It's a picture that really exists, but I embel-
lished. My mother sits in a tattered armchair. My father kneels

beside her pointing to me like my balancing act is a magic trick. What would I do next? my parents seem to be asking. I told Dennis that I buy flowers every week as a present to myself and put them in a blue vase next to the picture. "It's a little routine I have," I said, enjoying the fantasy of myself as someone with routines.

"We're going to take a break," the lead singer whispers, to keep the microphone from squealing again. "Y'all have been awesome," he says. He holds up his rock-and-roll fingers.

"I hope for their sake that they're not being dumb by accident," I say, but when I turn to look at Dennis, he is staring at the door with horror.

"Let's go," he says abruptly. He takes his hand off my knee. Its warmth hovers after its gone—phantom tenderness.

I follow his frozen look to the door and there is Peoria, kissing Yo hello on the cheek.

"I guess she found a baby-sitter," I say, transfixed too.

"Okay, be cool," Dennis instructs. "This is bad. I haven't told her you're in town. This is really bad. You're my ex-girlfriend. Why wouldn't I tell her you're in town? I'm so fucked." He sinks in his seat, as if he had a chance of hiding in a bar where we are the only two customers.

"How about this: I'm your friend from out of town. No, I'm related—even better. Your cousin. Cousin Priscilla." I regret Dennis's equal heart and mouth as the inevitable moment when Peoria will expose me to Dennis as the gender-bending actress, researcher of highway psychics, spying ex-girlfriend, exposer of sexual secrets, approaches.

When she sees us Peoria heads for our table.

Dennis can't control himself. Even before the look of confused recognition crosses Peoria's face, even before she reaches our table, Dennis is on his feet explaining.

"Peoria, this is Isabelle," he says. "I've been meaning to tell you she was in town, but I thought you'd get mad. I thought you'd be jealous because she was my first love. Not *love* love. First girlfriend love." He looks at me, says "No offense," then, "Peoria, not telling you Isabelle was in town was definitely the wrong move. But now I'm telling you and here she is and here you are and here I am." He pauses to catch his breath, then slumps down in his chair.

I finish the rest of my beer quickly as Peoria looks me up and down. I brace myself for her next move. But instead of letting me have it for my double-crossing behavior, she begins to smile slow, the kind of growing smile that betrays her gradual realization of the upper hand. She is beyond the pettiness of words. She is that much more mature than I am. I imagine her mind as a sitcom in reverse as she scans back over the details of our initial meeting, attaching them to the name Isabelle and the woman sitting before her now. I twirl my empty beer glass in its ring of condensation on the tabletop covered with other stains. I study the stain collage intensely.

"I like your hair," Peoria says finally. She continues to smile. Her smile has reached its outer limits, achingly huge. I touch my neck where the deep, hot blush begins. I hadn't admitted even to myself that her confession in Wigged Out that Dennis likes her in a wig is the reason I slipped this one on in the restaurant bathroom before Dennis arrived. My effort to seduce is painfully obvious. It's sitting on top of my head. My whole body pulses with heat. But Peoria isn't going to tell Dennis that she's met me before, not yet. She's going to let me burn with shame. To come clean is my responsibility. To tell Dennis everything right now would be to save me from myself and she doesn't want to save me. She lets me imagine the conversation she will have with Dennis, privately and out of my control, the way the sexual power of *Star Trek* and the Dr. Crusher wig will only grow as a result of what I've done.

"Thanks," I say. I try to speak back to her in code. I use my eyes to ask her forgiveness, but she turns away toward Dennis, rising above.

"Don't you like her hair, Dennis?"

"Why are we talking about her hair?" Dennis knocks the shaky table with the knee that bounces when he's nervous, and his glass slides toward the edge. He catches the glass just before it goes over, but not before beer soaks his lap. He bends to pull a napkin from the stack keeping the table's bad leg barely steady and both glasses slide off the table, shattering on the ground by Dennis's foot. The bartender glares at us, then returns to his calculations.

"Looks like they're getting ready for their second set," Peoria says. She takes a seat at the adjacent table and runs her delicate fingers through her own lush, long authentic hair, shaking it out in all its glory.

"I thought you couldn't get a baby-sitter," Dennis says. He pushes a shard of broken glass around with the toe of his sneaker.

Peoria and I just stare at him for a minute. "What?" he asks indignantly, the victim of his own crime.

"Someone came through at the last minute," Peoria says. "I'm going to get a broom and a beer."

"I should go home," I say.

"Nice to meet you, Isabelle," Peoria says on her way to the bar. The final blow of killing kindness. She doesn't wait for a response.

"I'll walk you to your car," Dennis says to me.

Once we're outside, the color returns to Dennis's face. The blood pounds at my temples. Behind us, the band starts up again and when I turn around, the lead singer is reaching a fist into the air.

"It's time for the Queen of Soul," he shouts. The band launches into "Respect."

"Hey, that's Otis, you loser," Dennis shouts.

The band cranks it up a notch in response.

"I'm losing it, man," Dennis says.

I close my eyes as we walk, focusing on his smell. The smoking baby smell is particularly strong tonight, familiar as the smell of my own skin. Maybe this is what love is all about—familiar odors. The taste of someone's skin. The things that fill the senses, not the mind. Not the words a person speaks, but the sound of the words in his mouth surrounded by his voice. Blindfolded, I would recognize the way Dennis clears his throat or the sound he makes before he cries. I want to be a fool, my heart and mouth finally equal. But this connection mystifies me like the math I never understood in high school, a curve on a chart on a blackboard waiting to be solved.

When we are out of sight of the bar Dennis slides his arm through mine, letting me know he is there, just like that. I spent the entire year in San Francisco trying to let myself know I was there. When I left the Midwest a year ago, I left a sure-thing life with a nice man and an interesting job, hoping that my existence, floating weightless above the earth, might finally touch down and make an impression. A footprint in wet cement, graffiti on a bridge, my name scratched into a desk. I didn't go to San Francisco looking to do anything great. I had no extraordinary expectations. I only wanted to leave something behind as proof.

There was a woman who sometimes stopped for a glass of wine at the bar down the street from my San Francisco apartment. She was beautiful and self-assured, alone because she chose to be. One balmy night, after she uncurled her hand from her wineglass and left the bar, I followed her down a steep street to her apartment, which turned out to be the second floor of a Victorian painted blue and purple like a glorious bruise. From the street, I watched as she stood in her window making a phone call. When she looked out her window, as people sometimes do to provide scenery for their phone conversations, and her eyes passed over me, I waved. She looked closer to see if I was anyone she knew and when I wasn't, she drew back. Suddenly, all I wanted was for her to remember me. When she peered out again, I lifted my shirt. I had my dating bra on, red and lacy. Earlier that night, I'd been out with a sound engineer who was also writing a one-man show. I wanted to stamp myself indelibly into her memory, for her to tell the story of me to a friend. In her story, the bra would be black, or maybe there would be no bra, maybe I streaked by. She pulled her shade down, but when I walked home, this secret moment of exhibitionism was stored inside me, powerful like a book waiting to be read.

"I'm sorry my life is such a mess," Dennis says when we reach the car, as though I'd always thought of him as someone who had it all together and now his reputation was shot.

Dennis has had anxiety attacks since high school. The first time he kissed me on the playground, where everyone went to cut class, smoke cigarettes, and wait to someday be kissed, he excused himself to run behind a clump of trees and throw up.

"Your life isn't a mess," I say. Relatively speaking, it's true. I climb into the Chevy and fasten my seat belt. Dennis has no idea how much he is helping me. His falling apart means I don't have to, like the time I was on a plane with horrible turbulence and the person beside me started screaming. I was able to remain calm because my terror had found another vessel.

Dennis leans against the Chevy, his arms on the hood, staring in at me. The longing in his eyes is ghostly, reaching me like a star's light-years after the fact.

"I should go." It would be so easy to lean into him right now, to let my lips collapse into his.

"I'm glad you're back in my life," Dennis says. He pats the Chevy's vinyl roof and it undulates.

"I liked this night too," I say—translating badly from the foreign language of tenderness—and drive away.

I drive past the lit-up shopping malls and their vast empty parking lots. A few gangly teens smoke cigarettes desperately in a far corner under the yellow glare of parking lamps.

There's a sign up at the new pizza place: MODERN PIZZA: MATURE PIZZA FOR A MATURE WORLD. I wish hard enough, and Star calls to me from her home in the half-built wood and stone—pieces of her embedded in the new walls, her chipped bones lodged in the foundation. Her voice is older than the voice of the fifteen-year-old girl she was when she was killed.

Her mind has aged though her body is gone. *What does life feel like?* she asks in her woman's voice. I know she means how does life taste, what does it smell like, what is its texture because sensation is what she's lost, her skin a pile of dust blown away on a windy day. But the touch of it hurts me—Dennis's hand on my knee could kill me with its sweetness. The other day I was caught in a surprise summer shower, raindrops pelted me like bullets, sinking deep into my skin, seeking out my most tender parts. Star would be willing to die again to feel pain like this.

At home, Samantha and my mother are draped like cats over the living room furniture. In this weather that turns grass brown, they drink hot tea from giant mugs because one of their magazines has told them tea is comforting no matter what the season.

"She's back," my mother says. She lifts her mug to me.

"I'm here for an emergency consultation," Samantha says, lilting and slow, one hand dangling to the floor, fishing for something. In other words, I wasn't available.

"What did I expect?" my mother continues where she left off with the story before I interrupted her. "The guy owns a pet store called Let's Pet." I slouch down in the big armchair between them and studiously pull a long hair off my shirt to show I'm not interested.

"It was like some Dr. Doolittle nightmare. He's trained his parrot to say, 'No means yes.' "

"Oh, come on," I say. "He did not."

" 'No means yes.' I swear that's what the parrot said. You can teach them anything, you know, it's just a matter of patience," my mother says defensively. Samantha looks at me severely.

I'm a bad daughter for not letting my mother exaggerate at a time like this.

"Why do you bother with these jerks?" I throw it out there like a punch.

My mother ignores me completely. "The problem with love," she says, turning to Samantha as if I didn't exist, "is that the whole idea is to be as close as possible, but it's disgusting to be that close to another person. Being close to someone is a dirty business. The mean trick of love is that in order to keep it clean you have to stay a little distant."

"But then you always want to know more," Samantha says. She's eager to say anything that will make this seem like a normal conversation. Over Samantha's shoulder, through the window, I see the top of Raymond's head poking out of the bushes.

My mother watches me and I want to shout at her that she's right, being close to someone *is* a dirty business. She is disgusting right now with her eyes like hands pressing on my body. But instead I look at Samantha sprawled, her batik tank top riding up to expose a sliver of pale stomach, her ankles circling the air inquisitively. Her seductively lazy pose makes me want to scream.

"Maybe you all shouldn't take this so seriously," I say. Too late to stop now, let Raymond bear witness.

"Well, that's an interesting idea, Isabelle." My mother's voice starts low, leaving room to build. Samantha's loose muscles snap to attention as she realizes what's about to happen.

"Actually, it's a fascinating idea," my mother continues, gathering speed and volume. "So what do you suggest? Maybe

Samantha and I should be like you and not try at all?" She's on her feet.

"See you girls later." Samantha puts her cup in the kitchen sink, grabs her purse, and shuts the front door quietly behind her. Raymond's head sinks deeper into the bushes so that she won't see him on the way out.

"What are you doing, Isabelle?" The question encompasses everything—my nastiness just now, living at home again, hanging out with Dennis. It even covers the things my mother doesn't know about—the mystery shopping, the way I double-crossed Peoria, how some nights all I want is to crawl into bed with Raymond and stay there safely in his arms for the rest of my life. I feel a fight scratch its way up my throat like a small, furious animal.

"What am I *doing*?" I act as incredulous as possible. I gesture wildly, using my own sign language to show Raymond how I feel, to show him that my mother isn't worthy of his flustered attention. "*You* never told me what to do." I can't stop now. *Watch this*, I say with accusing hands. "Why didn't you tell me what to do? Why didn't you remind me to get married? Why didn't you tell me to aim for babies? Shoot for a career? *What am I doing?* I don't know the rules. You and your stories about Henry, your stories about the glorious tragic days of yesteryear. You were so busy telling me about your past, wallowing in it all those years after your husband left you. You didn't bother to tell me there was the future to deal with. I have no fucking idea what I'm doing. That's what I'm doing: having no fucking idea."

My mother circles the living room laying her hands on the

furniture as though she's checking to make sure it's really there. It's similar to the way she used to walk around my bedroom telling stories, but this time she's making contact with the real world. She stops with her back to the window. Behind her, Raymond slinks back across the street. Even he has limits.

"I thought you enjoyed those stories." Her voice is low and steady again. "I didn't want to demand accomplishment. What's the point? I thought you wanted a little mystery. I thought you wanted the truth. Life is how you tell it, Isabelle." She heads for the stairs and climbs them slowly, graceful in her sadness. My father must have walked behind her some nights just to appreciate each careful step of those strong legs.

In the middle of the night, I hear the rattle of pots and pans in the kitchen and think it must be Raymond, finally breaking into our house to demand our attention. But when I go downstairs my mother is sitting at the kitchen table doing a paraffin treatment for her hands. With a wooden spoon she ladles oil over every inch of one hand up to the wrist. When she sees me, she takes the hand out of the hot pot and the oil hardens into a pink wax glove.

I sit down next to her and without saying a word, she takes one of my hands to dip it. The oil is burning hot at first, but, then it tingles as if it were electric.

"I'm sorry," I say. I help her dip her other hand.

"We're both pretty sorry," she says, smiling. "Do you think your father is happy wherever he is?" It's the first time she's mentioned him outside of sleeptalking since the time she wanted to get her Curtis Mayfield albums back.

"I don't know," I say. We sit quietly at the kitchen table looking at our hands, fossils in pink soap, until there is a knock at the door.

"That's got to be Raymond," I say, hopeful.

"Raymond? Why would that be Raymond?"

"In case you hadn't noticed, he has a big crush on you, so he comes over here to breathe your recycled air."

"That's awful," she says.

"It's not that awful," I say. "He'll survive. People do."

My mother holds up her wax hands. "How will I open it?"

"It's unlocked," I remind her. "Just push, Raymond, I call out."

When he finally pushes the door open and sees my mother and me sitting at the kitchen table, Raymond stands horrified on the front stoop. "I saw a light on," he says. "I thought Isabelle was watching TV." He gestures broadly with his hands, sweeping the night for justification. "There's a late movie, isn't there?" He looks to me to back up his story and then turns to go, but my mother walks over to him and puts her pink club hand in the air by his shoulder, inviting him to the kitchen table.

"Please, Raymond," she says gently. "Come in."

"Wax dip?" I ask.

"The last thing I need is soft hands," he says. We all smile instead of laugh because it is so quiet with the three of us sitting around the hot pot. Outside the sky goes grayish pink as it lightens slowly all around the neighborhood, all around town.

"I should go," Raymond says, minutes, hours, maybe days, later. "I forgot what I came for." My mother walks him to the door. She tells him to come by anytime as if he hasn't already. Through the window I watch him safely across the street. He limps slightly, wounded from all our attention.

When my mother returns, we slide the wax gloves off whole. Our hands are left greasy and the wax husks sit empty on the table between us, each with its distinct imprint of veins, knuckles, age, and time.

10

⌇

IN the display window of Wigged Out, the mannequin's fallen ear has been glued back on to her head. It dangles slightly, threatening to fall again. All of the heads have been dusted with white face powder, even the dark brown and black heads. The powder looks like a disease, splotches of pigmentation deficiencies.

When I walk in, Peoria is helping a customer, an old woman whose pink scalp shines through thin wisps of white hair. Peoria has flopped two wigs out on the counter in front of her, like fresh scalps she's taken herself.

"These wigs contain real human hair," she explains. "We have a buyer who flies to different countries."

The little boy sits at the old woman's feet, singing to himself. He sings louder, signaling, when he sees me. Peoria glances up and immediately returns to the mass of hair on the counter in front of her. I'm beginning to regret my decision to apologize.

The old woman turns and shakes a trembling fist at me. "Is

real human hair supposed to be a good thing?" she asks. "Maybe I'll reconsider." She walks out of the store, still shaking her fist in the air.

"Did you come to find out more about your ex-boyfriend's fetishes?" Peoria asks. She clenches a wig in each hand.

"Could you put those down so we can talk?" I ask.

"I'm not really in the mood to talk to you," she says, letting the wigs fall onto the counter in a swirling mass of hair. "I've chosen to be flattered that you would find me worthy of investigation. Now leave me alone."

"I was way out of line," I say. "I should have told you who I was when I came in here before." I slip the orange wig off the mannequin head in the display window and the ear falls off again. I try to stick it back on, but it won't stay.

"If you're here to apologize, don't bother," Peoria says. "You don't really want to be my friend, do you?"

The little boy has stopped singing. He stares at the bright orange wig in my hand.

"Why are you so weird?" he asks.

I take my wallet out to pay for the wig, but Peoria waves it away.

"Just take it," she says. She walks out from behind the counter, scoops the boy onto her hip, and carries him toward the back, through the sea of mannequin heads smiling and pouting and pooching their lips to no one in particular.

TONIGHT my mother is going out with one of my high school teachers, a substitute named Mr. Jones. He was a gym teacher who was called in on an emergency basis to fill in for my English teacher, a woman so shy she couldn't look the students in the eye and who ultimately "went on vacation." Mr. Jones subbed for the rest of the year, and ended up staying for the next twenty. All the students liked him because he told long stories about his Navy days instead of discussing great literature. The only book he liked was *Billy Budd* even though he thought Billy was a wuss. When a student came to class smelling of cigarettes, he would tell the story of how his captain got him to quit by forcing him to smoke pack after pack while standing on deck one particularly stormy day.

"It wasn't pretty, folks," Mr. Jones would say, his squinty eyes disappearing into the folds of his craggy, seafaring face. "But it did the job."

"Still here," I say, seventeen years later, when I answer the door. I shrug the same shrug I gave him when I walked into English reeking of cigarettes.

"So you are." He claps me on the arm like I'm an old Navy buddy. His personal ad said that after a stint in the Navy and twenty years of teaching high school English (a job not unlike the Navy), he'd started his own construction business, lives a simple life, and wants a companion. "No Twinkle Toes, no Let's Pet," my mother said approvingly when she read it. "A straight shooter. He is what he is."

Mr. Jones looks up just in time to see my mother coming down the stairs, the way she planned it all along, shimmering in her outfit through a fog of eau de Walgreens.

They are going to see a movie about love in a foreign land during wartime. "The popcorn is the best in town," I say. "But if I were you, I wouldn't use the men's room."

"Isabelle's something of a movie theater expert," my mother says briskly. This is her moment. She looks at me as if I were a weirdo at a party who traps people in corners and spews odd facts.

Earlier this evening, in a reconciliatory gesture, I told her about a San Francisco date during which I went on at length and with conviction about the magenta candles at the restaurant table. "How long they are," I'd said. "How waxy."

"It didn't matter that each date was a different one," I explained, sitting on her bed as she rejected outfit after outfit, shedding blouses, dresses, skirts into a pile on her bedroom floor. "What I was offering myself was better than full-blown love. It was the potential for love, which is much less disappointing because there is always the possibility."

She turned to me, wielding a hairbrush. "Now, Isabelle, is not the time to wax philosophical. I just want to know what to wear."

I stand on the top of the porch stairs, a sea widow, as my mother and Mr. Jones drift away, disappearing into the Standardsville evening. Across the street, Raymond lurks in windows and corners like a spider. Even after their car is long gone, he makes no move to come over.

I've decided to cross the street to show Raymond the new wig—I'm sure he'll like this one better than the first—when Dennis's car rumbles up out of the night. It startles me and I trip on my way down the stairs, landing facedown in the yard.

"Jesus, Isabelle," Dennis says.

I scramble to my feet and go to the passenger window, hiding the wig behind my back. He's all staged bad boy, smoking a cigarette with half of a six-pack still in its plastic rings on the seat beside him. "What's with the rebel-without-a-cause act?"

"Wouldn't you like to know," Dennis says, scrutinizing me with squinted eyes.

"I don't have time for this," I say, brushing dirt from my knees.

"Oh, right. You must be really busy with all that *business* you've been doing. All that *traveling* and *representing*," Dennis says. "You always were a horrible actor. I've known since the Fourth of July that you're living with your mother." He pauses for a reaction, but I won't give him that pleasure. "And I saw the Temporama time sheets on the floor of the Chevy. You're a *temp*, Isabelle."

The word thuds out like a curse word. Temp you. Go temp yourself. Your mother is a temp. Peoria must have talked to him as soon as I left Wigged Out. Whatever she said, it's gone to his head.

"I bet that limey Sebastian doesn't even exist."

"You've got no proof there, Columbo." Bad enough that he's known all along that I'm living at home and temping, but now he's gone too far. Challenging my fake boyfriend is crossing the line. "Do you expect me to congratulate you for exposing my miserable life to me? I already know all about it, remember? I'm living it," I say. "And, by the way, if Sebastian did exist, he'd kick your ass."

I put on the wig, hoping for some of Star's wiliness and courage, counting on her to guide me through my next moves. I get into his car and pop open a beer. "You've been gathering evidence and now you've come over here just for this?"

The light in Raymond's kitchen goes off.

"You're a weird, weird girl, Isabelle," Dennis says, looking at my flaming orange head as though it were actually on fire. "You know, Peoria told me . . ."

"This wig has nothing to do with turning you on. Let's get that straight right now," I say.

He shakes his head and looks straight ahead into the dark. *"He Said, She Said, He Said. Right.* How's the highway psychic book coming along, red?"

"Just drive, asshole." I adjust my wig.

"Whatever."

Dennis punches the gas and we peel out, leaving Raymond's dark house behind. This is what our reunion has been headed for all along—a return to the indifferent smell of burnt rubber and the fizzy taste of cheap beer, the headlong feeling of going nowhere with a vengeance.

We don't even play the radio. We tunnel through the night, rocketing bodies in a dark machine. The sound of the engine and wind through cracked windows mask the sound of my heart and my breathing, the terrifying sounds of being human.

Dennis throws his cigarette out the window and it disappears behind us, a tiny red comet. We drive and drive, out of Standardsville and into the country until there is no light except for our burrowing headlights. We twist and wind through back roads, hugging corners as if our lives depended on this one trip on this particular night. At this speed, it's as though time were amounting to something.

Light years away, Dennis pulls into a driveway that ends abruptly in a pasture with dug-up pockets of land. A sign sticks out of the earth: UNDER CONSTRUCTION. TWILIGHT: WHERE GROWING OLD IS AS GLORIOUS AS THE SETTING SUN. START DATE: 2001.

"Here's to it. May we die during the magic hour." I hand Dennis a beer and open another for myself. He turns off the headlights and, after my eyes adjust, I see a house in the middle of the pasture with a light on in the second-floor window. The shapes of a man and a woman emerge from the blur, two distinct forms pacing in opposite directions.

Dennis looks at me, then looks at the man and woman in the window. "Check it out?" he asks.

We get out of the car, beers in hand, and head toward the house.

"Do you think they're fighting?" Dennis is hopeful. He takes my hand and the last fifteen years shrink into the space between our clasped palms as we stumble through crumbling dirt. We collapse on the small slope outside the house. From where we sit, the man and woman have no features. They gesture, faceless bodies in a room with a couch and a table and a lamp. On the wall is a painting, giant blotches of bold color. I lie back to look at the wide open sky, wishing something as big as the sky would swallow me up, take me in, and let me be a small, useful part of it, an utterly necessary patch of black.

"They've been fighting all night," Dennis says authoritatively. Dennis and I played this game in high school — sitting in his car in the parking lots of supermarkets or fast-food restaurants, we'd watch people and make up stories about them. This man loves his son's wife, that woman makes love to her tropical fish. That man cries himself to sleep every night, but he doesn't know why until a psychic reveals that he sold his child for some land in a former life. This woman has just discovered that she has an inheritance that will allow her to travel around the world. When we were through with other people, we would pretend that someone was watching, attributing drama and bittersweet tragedy to us as we had sex in some abandoned construction site. The man and woman in the window stop pacing and sit down on the couch together.

"This house is so isolated," I say. "Maybe they're agoraphobic and have to order supplies from the outside world. They're afraid of everyone except each other so they have the supplies dropped off on their front porch."

"You could have told me that things didn't work out for you in San Francisco," Dennis says suddenly. He pulls the wig off my head and puts it on the ground between us. It is a flash of color in the dark, an emergency highway cone. "I would have understood. I would have understood more than anybody." The denim of his jeans brushes against my bare leg, a question.

I don't want to talk about the ways I've failed myself. "Let's just enjoy the show." The man and the woman move into a long embrace, a postfight clench of relief.

"I admired you so much for leaving, for everything you tried," Dennis says quietly.

When the couple begin to kiss, I follow their lead. I lean over the flash of orange hair to Dennis and put my mouth on his in a long, deep kiss that searches the back of our throats to years and years ago. Our faces push into each other, fighting the limits of our bodies to be as close as we can be. As the couple begin to undress so do we, in a game of how precisely we can imitate their gestures. When I pull off Dennis's jeans and slide his T-shirt over his head, his body is as familiar to me as my mother's house. When the couple sink to the floor, disappearing below the windowsill, Dennis and I are naked in the dirt.

"I don't want you to think that I carry condoms around in

my pocket," Dennis says, reaching for his jeans. "Like I came over just for that."

"But you did?" I offer. Here on this hill in unfinished Twilight, we can help each other.

When the couple turn their lights off, the only difference between earth and sky are tiny star punctures. For a moment, Dennis and I are swallowed whole by the darkness all around us. We move together, necessary patches of sky and earth. Dennis's features move from solid to shadow to liquid. When he puts his cheek against mine, a tiny fluttering inside me flies up to meet his tenderness.

"What?" Dennis whispers, though I didn't say anything. His question is lost in the flood of light that suddenly streams from the couple's house.

"Who the fuck are you?" The woman's voice is a screech, not the low, sultry voice I had assigned to her. Behind her, the man skulks, wrapped in a blanket.

"Get out of here," the man says, not very convincingly, standing behind the woman. She is coming down off the porch, wielding a flashlight, but Dennis and I are already running, naked, kicking up clumps of earth with our bare heels.

"Who the fuck are you?" the woman keeps asking, as if knowing the answer to this question would solve everything. She stands in the same spot outside the house, pointing the flashlight at Dennis's car as we drive away. The man lingers fearfully in the doorway. We are still naked in our seats, our clothes and Star's tangled hair in a pile at my feet.

"Let's drive around nude," Dennis says.

"Exactly what I was thinking," I say.

We make the rounds naked, our seat belts on—we've

learned that much over the years. It's not midnight yet so there are still lights on in houses and cars on the road, but nobody notices us. No one expects naked people in a car. We coast through dimly lit residential streets, past the house of the guy who was Dennis's drug connection in high school, then the house of the boy who first broke my heart, now divorced and working at the record store at one of the malls. Dennis knows where everybody lives. He keeps up with people by adding them to the Super Cineplex mailing list when they go to the movies.

We drive by the house of an elementary school friend of mine who now runs the Hallmark store next to my first love's record store.

"What do you think Jean would say if she happened to look out her window and see us?" Dennis asks. I can tell he already has an answer planned by the way he asks the question so quickly. "For the love of someone special, put some clothes on!" He laughs his wild-bird laugh.

The incongruity of being naked and upright in a car makes the whole world magically silly. Stoplights glimmer—tiny, beautiful pools of green, red, and yellow in the dark. Every house is a cartoon house, filled with cartoon families who hit each other painlessly over the heads with frying pans and eat huge mutton chops with reckless abandon.

We pull up to a red light next to two teenagers in a jacked-up truck. Their hair is frizzed post-make-out session and their eyes red and bleary like they are either drunk or in love. From the passenger seat, the girl notices us, then calmly turns to her boyfriend to explain. They look over nonchalantly. Dennis smiles and waves.

"Do you all know that you don't have any clothes on?" She could be asking for directions.

Dennis slowly pans down his own body, then gasps and slowly turns to the teenage girl, horrified. "Jesus, Mary, and Joseph!" he screams. "Let's get the hell out of here!" He hits the gas and we screech away, a story that the teenagers will tell to their friends later to prove their drunkenness or love.

We drive by Dennis's house with its slanted porch, where his roommates, Stan and Kevin, sit on the porch swing drinking beer. They are friends of his from high school who spent most of their time parked in the school parking lot, the windows of their red Mustang rolled up to enhance their high. I once asked them why they didn't drive the Mustang somewhere with a view instead of sitting in the concrete parking lot, staring at the prisonlike high school. They just laughed their stoned laughs. But I knew that way out in the countryside, no one would know they existed. In the high school parking lot, there was a chance someone would find them before they vanished in a cloud of smoke.

When we get to my street, I undo my seat belt and fish my underwear out of the pile of clothes at my feet.

"That's dangerous you know," Dennis says.

"Getting dressed?"

"Not being naked anymore," he says.

By the time Dennis pulls up in front of my mother's house, I've wriggled into my underwear and slipped on my tank top. I dropped my bra in the upturned earth of Twilight, my own private time capsule.

Dennis and I sit in the car—him naked and me half dressed—kissing with raw lips. With the porch light shining in on us, the magic of the night has faded and we're headed for the hard light of day.

Through the window I can see my mother at the dining room table with her head in her hands, alluringly tragic. Raymond crouches in the bushes, peering in at her.

"You guys should get a restraining order," Dennis says when he notices Raymond too. Dennis caught Raymond spying on the way out to his car after the Fourth of July barbecue. When Dennis asked him what he was doing, Raymond used my trick and told him he'd lost something in the bushes. I live right there, he'd said, pointing to his house as if this would explain everything. Dennis called Hugo at the Hotel Fugor the next day and left a message for me saying he was concerned about my mother's neighbor.

"He lives across the street," I said when I called him back.

"I'm a neighbor," Dennis said. "You're a neighbor. We're all, in one way or another, neighbors. That doesn't mean I go sneaking around in people's bushes."

"He was looking for something he lost," I offered, ready to fight for Raymond's right to spy if necessary.

"It's not very neighborly." Dennis wouldn't give it up. "In the dictionary under 'neighbor' there's not a picture of someone creeping around in the bushes."

"Leave Raymond alone," I say now.

"I'm not going to be here forever, you know," Dennis says softly.

"None of us are," I say, sliding out of the car. I don't return Dennis's woozy gaze. I'm distracted by Raymond. "Good night, Dennis. "

"Oooo, she's so cool," he says. "Careful what you wish for,

Isabelle. You'll end up all alone." He pulls the passenger door shut behind me and it jiggles on its hinges. Cranking the radio, he takes off out of the driveway, leaving me and my meanness to stand awkwardly in the driveway. The background gospel singers build to a fevered pitch as Dennis fades down the street.

The truth is, I loved this night, the stir of something beyond my control. It's the end that is unbearable. My mother and I in the same house, our sadness echoing through the quiet rooms. We could go on and on like this forever; this could be all there is. It makes night after night of Jell-O look like paradise.

"Raymond," I say. It's a request. Standing there in my underwear, I want him to tell me what he knows. I want his wisdom from having lived longer so I can get a headstart, build from there, and make a life better than this. He turns and looks at me the way he would look at a complete stranger. Catching him in the act, I've broken our pact. He gets up from his knees and begins to shuffle quickly across the street to his house.

"Raymond," I say again. "Don't leave. I need you."

He doesn't even turn around. He opens his mailbox, slamming it shut after his requisite grope. The mailbox door falls open, gaping at me.

I start softly, but soon I am pounding on the front door he's slammed behind him.

"Raymond, let me in." He turns out all of his lights. The darkness is stern and scolding, not the inviting wide-open darkness of the Twilight sky. It's the kind of darkness that could swallow a person whole.

"What's going on out here?" My mother opens the door

just as I'm shimmying into my mud-covered shorts in the middle of the street. "Never mind. Don't tell me. I don't want to hear it."

"Maybe I don't feel like telling it," I say in a singsong copycat child's voice. She doesn't deserve to know, the same way she doesn't deserve the attention Raymond lavishes on her.

"I'd really prefer not to hear it," she says again, as if she hadn't heard what I just said. She returns to her vodka tonic sweating on the dining room table.

I stash the wig—muddy from Twilight, sprinkled with loose dirt and twigs from the car floor littered with old candy wrappers and parking tickets—in the bushes outside my mother's house. Then I follow my mother inside and make a drink of my own, slouching sloppily against the kitchen counter, doing my best to look like I don't care.

My mother sighs, sipping from her sweaty glass. "Don't track mud everywhere," she says, eyeing the dirt I've brushed from my shorts onto the kitchen floor.

"What's wrong with you?" I can only pretend with her for so long. I brush the dirt into a small pile with my hand and throw it into the sink.

"I really like him," she says, putting her head back in her hands.

"Raymond?" I ask.

"What?" she says.

"Mr. Jones?" I remember him, his mouthful of chewing tobacco, spitting juice out of the side of his mouth as he patroled the parking lot before school for early-morning pot smokers, thrill-seekers rushing the speed bumps in their parents' cars.

"I drove your father out of here," she says. "I don't want that to happen again. I don't want to drive anyone else away." The night suddenly changes course. The kitchen pulses with light. Outside, the sky is blacker than night. I don't want to be alone with this. I wish Raymond was in the bushes, but his house is blind with darkness.

"Mom," I say. An incantation, the most holy word.

"I didn't pay him enough attention." She holds up her drink with one hand and with the other, she draws squiggly lines on the sides of the glass.

"That was years ago," I offer.

"But as much as I'm afraid to lose someone, I want to fall in love," she says. "I want love to make years ago better." How did she come up with this plan? It seems like such a good idea.

"You will." I want it to sound like a prediction. I want to be that powerful in her life.

"Once you were born, I loved only you." She's telling stories again, but this one is different from all the others—raw and unformed. Weary with what she is about to tell me, she pours the rest of her drink out in the sink.

"And when you were old enough to talk to, I only talked to you. Your father couldn't fault me for that. You were my child." She cuts corners to make up for what she can't say. He faulted both of us; he ran away to escape us and the way he felt like nobody in this house.

We switch places. I pace while she slouches against the kitchen counter. It's not her job to love me that much anymore. I think of her pacing my room, telling her San Francisco stories, making up the world for me. It felt like passion that drove her storytelling, but now I see clearly the cold stone at the heart of it. She left my father to dream in bed alone.

"You can't stay here forever, Isabelle." The sentence has been hiding around the house all summer — in the man-eating couch, in the legion of wineglasses underneath my bed, in the way my mother came glimmering down the stairs tonight. Spoken, it is hard and rough as concrete.

"You can stay until the end of the summer," she's saying. "That gives us a month." She loves me and she will love me wherever I go, she says. She will send her love to me, Federal Express. It will surround me like weather.

I have to get out of here.

"I'll be back." I walk out in my muddy clothes, retrieve the dirty wig from the bushes, get into the Chevy, and drive. I force Dennis's ABBA tape out of the tape deck, snagging the ribbon so it unspools wildly like a wild snake tongue. I drive past the teenagers hanging out in the mall parking lots, smoking themselves somewhere else, underneath a new antismoking campaign poster: WE'RE GOING TO MAKE SMOKING HISTORY. Hugo stands in front of the hotel's giant oak door in his Three Musketeers outfit, laughing gently to himself. His giant shoulder pads bob up and down.

I circle back to Modern Pizza, finally open for business — but not at this hour. I press my nose against the windows, searching the darkness for some trace of Star. I hold the wig, the spectacle of it, in my hands, an offering. I want her to talk to me again, to shame me into figuring out something I can use. Something that she knows from having lived so briefly and from dying in a way that retold her whole life. I pull the door, knowing that it will be locked but counting on Star's magic to let me in.

The police car's headlights illuminate the square tables with the precarious upside-down chairs perched on top and the enormous brick oven. When I turn around, the police officer walks slowly toward me, his hand on his holster, just in case.

"Is everything okay?" he asks sternly.

"Do you really want me to answer that?" My hand is still on the door.

The officer creeps closer. "Have you been drinking?"

"I had a beer awhile ago." My words are slurred. Now that I'm finally telling the truth it sounds like I'm lying.

"What's your name?"

"Jane Smith?" My capacity for storytelling has taken a nosedive.

The officer puts his hand on my elbow with such gentleness that I whimper. *Remember this: A stranger touching you kindly.* Star's grown-woman voice whispers in my ear. I am ashamed—Star's young-girl underwear hangs from a tree branch. That was no kind stranger. *What more do you expect to learn from me except the brutality of random events? The way life can change in an instant and turn into something else, something unrecognizable, inexplicable. And, for the record, I never wore my hair in a stupid bob.* Then she disappears.

"I'm sorry," I say to Star.

"Don't worry about it," the officer says. "This kind of thing happens to everybody. What is that you've got in your hand?"

The officer takes the mud-caked wig from me. "This looks about finished." He opens the lid of the Dumpster and throws it inside. "Why don't I give you a lift home. I'm sure your husband, John Doe, is concerned about you."

"Actually, I'm not married," I whimper, as if he were being serious. "I'm a temp, and I'm living with my mother who dates more than I do." I attempt a laugh but hiccup instead.

"Why don't you leave your car here?" the officer says. "Come back and get it tomorrow."

On the ride home, I tell him about my mother dating my high school English teacher. He listens silently. "My *high school English teacher*," I repeat. He nods.

"Take care of yourself," he says when he drops me off.

"Good night." I lean over and kiss him on the cheek like we've been on a date. It feels like we've been through a lot together.

The house is dark, but I know my way around by heart. When I walk by my mother's room, she says my name hopefully. She lies there, a survivor of inexplicable randomness.

"Everything's fine," I tell her. Language is the signal I send her, the flashing light across the vast and stormy sea.

I dream again of Star. We are young girls in giants' bodies, walking with our arms linked, down the middle of the highway, from Twilight all the way into town. Each of our feet fills an entire lane. Star turns to me, stopping me in my plodding, giant tracks with her hand on my elbow. She assures me that inside this body there's a dead girl waiting to get out.

11

At this point, my mother sleeps through Marla's wake-up calls. "That temp agency keeps the strangest hours," she said once, leaving it at that. Now when the phone rings as the birds are just beginning to chirp she does what she does this morning—lets it ring and ring until I pick it up.

"Come on, champ," Marla says. She's my coach, shouting me to the finish line from the sidelines—go, Isabelle, go. "They're expecting you, so get up and go work that magic. Our Priscilla is on a roll."

But our Priscilla has had it. She wore herself out crying over her lost Lifecycling husband at Looks Like We Made It. She's decided solo living is not for her. She's quitting her job at Prints Charming and moving to the East Coast, near the ocean, where she and a recently divorced college roommate will live—two single women happy to stay that way for a while—and run a bed and breakfast they will start with money borrowed from their rolled-over 401(k) plans.

"Sure, sure," I say, hurrying Marla off the phone. I've got other plans. I grab the hair dye I bought during a recent tour of Walgreens, inspired by the instructions on the box: Change your hair color. Change your life. Be sure you are not allergic. When I look in on my mother, she is sleeping on her back, arms tucked behind her head as though observing something wryly. Her breath is soft and steady. Her eyes flutter as she speaks half words—*sho, let, ba*—dreaming deep morning dreams. Through with the story of her San Francisco days, she dreams instead the stories she will tell ten years from now, the ones about the way she and Mr. Jones met through the classifieds, the summer her grown-up daughter floated through the rooms of her house like a ghost who'd recently shed its body.

"So," she says in her sleep, giggling. She dreams me gone, sending me to a place where she can know peripherally that I am happy and content. We will write occasionally, call on the weekends, behave like a mother and daughter should. I head across the street. Raymond's up already because I saw him open his living room curtains before he sat down in front of his TV and began to eat what looked like canned peaches out of a can.

"Who is it?" he asks when I knock, as if I weren't the only person who ever darkened his doorstep.

"Raymond, come on."

When he opens the door, I hold the box of Cherry Persian hair dye next to my face, smiling seductively like the woman on the box.

"Do you need my help *again*?" he asks. His annoyed tone belies his hope.

In the bathroom, Raymond sits on the edge of the tub, his hands curled around the rim. The shower curtain hanging behind him is covered with movie-star Scientologists, ordered from a late-night Scientology seminar on TV. Raymond's not a Scientologist himself, he just liked the movie-star shower curtain. "Who knew L. Ron Hubbard was so glamorous? And he's one. And she's one," he said, showing me all of the movie-star converts one by one. I pull the plastic gloves away from the instruction sheet and, according to the instructions, use the tip of the applicator bottle to make parts in my hair, squirting the creamy mixture along the bone-white strips.

"Get ready! Get set! Go!" Raymond reads from the discarded box. "We want your hair to be exactly the way you want it to be. If the color is too light, too dark, streaked, or in any way undesirable, please call our hotline."

"I'm sorry about the other day," I say. I count on the forced intimacy of the bathroom to make an apology easier. With all of the apologizing I've been doing over the past couple of days I'm starting to feel like I'm in a twelve-step program, though I'm not sure exactly what I'm stepping toward.

"You mean pounding on my door?" Raymond asks.

"No," I say, embarrassed. "You know. The couch. The kiss."

"Oh that," Raymond says.

"It must have had quite an effect on you," I say, even more embarrassed. My hand slips and I squirt dye on my tank top. It immediately leaves a huge white blotch. "Oh terrific," I say. "I hope this is no indication of what my hair is going to look like."

"Don't be sorry about the couch kiss," Raymond says, handing me some toilet paper, which I rub into the stain until it's covered with crumbled pieces of toilet paper.

"Let me do your hair for you," Raymond says. He sits me down on the closed toilet seat and takes the applicator bottle away from me like it's a loaded gun I've got pointed at my head. "You have to be careful with these things."

"Never use hair color on eyebrows, eyelashes, or other tender areas," I read from the box. Every inch of my body feels like a tender area. Raymond dabs at the tears that roll down my nose with the same wad of toilet paper he's using to stop the dye from running down my temples.

"Stop being sorry," he says severely. "Sorry isn't the point. I wasn't upset that you kissed me. God no—an old guy like me, a young girl like you. That's not why I left. There's a lot that you don't know. Just remember that. You don't know everything."

I close my eyes as he draws the applicator down the final strip of scalp. "Raymond," I say. His name is love this time.

"You have to be patient. The color takes time," he says impatiently, before I can continue. He throws the empty applicator bottle into the trash can. "Just wait."

EVEN this early in the morning, the sun is heavy, pushing down on me, making it hard to walk. The air is too hot to breathe deeply. My new brassy red hair is dry by the time I get to Modern Pizza.

The Chevy is not alone in the parking lot. A battered blue VW bug, covered with bumper stickers that suggest the earth and all of its creatures are worth saving, is parked at a sloppy angle next to it. Two oversize red dice hang from the rearview mirror, and there's a squashed beer can jammed into the dashboard. As I jiggle the key in the lock of the Chevy, the door to Modern Pizza swings open. For a second, I think that it's Star, resurrected. Instead, a bone-thin teenage boy saunters out wearing an apron splattered with tomato sauce; his apron strings fluttering like ribbons behind him.

He fishes a pack of cigarettes from the VW bug and then, looking me up and down, says lazily, "I was about to have your car towed." He cups a match with his hand as he lights a cigarette though the air is still. "I open by myself and my boss will throw a shit about customer parking only." Today's our grand opening. As an afterthought, he extends the pack to me.

"I'm glad you didn't," I say. I enjoy holding the cigarette—the bend of my elbow, the way my body relaxes into a smoking posture, my elbow resting on my hip as I lean against the Chevy.

"Nice car," he says, gesturing with his pointy head. I turn to look at the rusting mint-green Chevy. But the boy has the pure intonation of someone still too young for irony. He means it.

"Thanks," I say. I throw the rest of my cigarette on the ground, grinding it into the pebbles and concrete with my heel. "Hey, do you know the story of the girl buried underneath this building?"

"I heard she was a slut," he says, laughing. He digs at the gravel with the toe of one of his cowboy boots. The sun has melted its own edges. It is a blur expanding to fill the sky, threatening to incinerate us all into parking-lot ash.

"She was someone I knew," I say, looking at his eyes looking down. My lie feels especially mean. I could tell him anything and he would believe it.

He looks up to see if I'm kidding, but I'm not smiling. He considers my face for a minute, like a lover locating your lips before kissing you. "You're a lot older than you look," he says, eyeing my cutoffs and tank top. "Up close you've got lines around your eyes," he says, examining my face. "And . . ."

"I get the point." I interrupt him before he can do significant damage. My lie is beginning not to feel so mean.

He smiles nervously. "Look, I'm sorry I said that about her. Your friend. You hear things. People talk a lot of shit."

"Actually," I confess, "she was someone I wish I knew better. Someone I should have known."

The boy nods respectfully. He understands. There are lots of people in his teenage life he wishes he knew better.

"Do you like working here?" I ask. I'm trying to save us from awkwardness, but the question just hangs there awkwardly.

"It's fine, I guess," the boy says. My question is irrelevant, not something he's ever considered. Whether he likes this job or not is not the point. I'm starting to bore him, like the rest of the adults in his life.

"I've gotta go back inside." He pitches his cigarette into the street. "Big day and all that crap."

"Take care," I say, an older person to a younger person. Our age difference stretches for miles between us. There's room for whole continents.

I climb into the Chevy and sit for a minute in the wall of heat, closing my eyes to picture Star clearly, her hair shining bright like a light in my mind. *You don't know me. You never did*, she whispers. Her light goes out and I'm left sitting in my mother's car, all alone the way Dennis predicted.

Down the street, Captain Score, the video arcade of my youth, has been transformed into Java.com, an Internet café. In that parking lot, Dennis leaned close—the cinnamon gum barely masking his cigarette-and-beer breath—and taught me how to drive a stick shift. Afterward, we played Frogger and Ms. Pacman ("What's this 'ms.' shit?" Dennis used to say. "*Ms.* Pac-*man*? It's

Pacman with a bow on his head.") until our quarters ran out. We'd find an excuse—cigarette? air?—and go outside to cinnamon-kiss in the dark, pushing each other deeper and deeper into the pitch-black woods that are no longer there, the same woods where Star was murdered. Scratched by tree branches, tripped up by rocks and stumps, we made love for the first time in wet leaves, trembling with the fear of murder, death, and nature. We trembled at the thought of something bigger than what we were doing, bigger than our own experience. One night, Dennis claimed that he saw something in the woods over my shoulder. "It's a sign," he said, but neglected to say of what. He didn't need to specify. He was grasping for something outside of us to make what we'd done love. Whatever was in the woods that night, I felt it too. It moved underneath the skin of life, the raw material of flesh and the huge cold shoulder of night colliding.

THE circles of sweat under my arms dry and stiffen in Temporama's air-conditioning, but the red marks on the backs of my thighs, where my shorts end, leaving my bare legs to press against the hot vinyl of the Chevy's bench seat, linger. I walk past Marla's surly, ravenous colleagues, gathered in today's mix-and-match wear around the refrigerator, past the desperate temp wannabes flipping through the pages of magazines in the waiting area, to her desk.

"I'm putting myself at your mercy," I say, standing directly in front of her desk. "I can't do Priscilla anymore. I want to be somebody else."

"Don't we all," she says, looking up from her paperwork. She seems tired today. At first it looks as though she is missing an eyebrow, but then I realize she hasn't applied her usual layers of mascara and eyeshadow. Her eyes recede into the costume party of her face like guests in street wear.

"Are you all right?" I ask. I imagine Marla confessing all her secrets to me over margaritas at the happy hour at the one Mexican restaurant in Standardsville, En Queso Emergency.

"Don't worry about me," she says dismissively. "Worrying is my job. Now, what in the hell are you wearing? And what's with the hair? Don't you know you're supposed to look at the color on the box first?"

"Don't you have any other temps you could torture?" I am grateful for her attention.

"None that love to be tortured as much as you," she says. She stands and starts to walk away.

"Where are you going?" I panic.

"Silly girl." She takes me by the hand, her partner in stealth, her representative on the outside. "Follow me," she says, leading me into the bathroom.

She pulls a plastic bag out from underneath the sink and begins to unpack her tools. An assorted box of colored contact lenses, a fake-beauty-mark kit, a wrinkle-free pink pastel pantsuit not unlike the blue pastel suit that Marla wears today, and red high heels.

"What is all this stuff?" I ask.

"My just-in-case kit," Marla says. She pushes me into a stall with the pantsuit, the heels, and a stick of deodorant, closing the door behind me. "Just in case I need to go undercover."

"Undercover for what?"

"I don't know. Love, war," she says vaguely. "A woman has to be prepared."

When I step out of the stall—a vision in pink—Marla goes

to work on my face. She sticks a beauty mark on my jaw, in the same place she has one naturally, and gives me a pair of blue-colored contacts to slip in over my brown eyes. She uses a curling iron to flip the front of my hair back in little wings, a revised Farrah Fawcett. When she is done, we stand next to each other facing our reflections. With the beauty mark, the fiercely bright blue eyes, the hairdo, and the carnivalesque face, I could be Marla's sister.

"You look terrific," she says solemnly. She gazes proudly upon me as she prepares to send me out into the world.

"Thanks," I say. I'm not sure how else to respond. I'm touched that Marla would want me to stand in for her.

"Wait, wait," she says. "One more thing." She rifles through the plastic bag and pulls out two putty-colored molds that look like shoulder pads. She hands them to me.

"What are these?"

"Breast Helpers," she says. "I'll go get the address and the questionnaire. You fiddle with those." She leaves me alone in the bathroom to consider my chest.

THE Edge, at the edge of a strip mall, is surrounded by an iron fence with electric wire running along the top to keep high school kids from shimmying over and having late-night parties in the private pool. A whole section of the adjacent strip mall burned down a year ago—Shoesaholics, a discount shoe store; Nothing Like the Sun, a tanning salon, where the owner was rumored to have drilled a hole in the wall of the tanning casket for his viewing pleasure; and Treasures from the Dust Bowl, a Southwestern jewelry store whose window was lined with chunky turquoise rings. I like to think it was arson—a purist, someone enraged by the idea of convenience, who hated the idea of everything at your fingertips. The arsonist was someone who believed deeply that the search for what you need is more valuable than finding it.

The Edge saw its chance—a burned-up vacant lot—and took it. In the beginning, the elaborate fence was the focus of angry letters to the local paper from strip mall store managers and customers who said it was a blight on the landscape. But the Edge stood firm, defiantly separate but equal.

"We're on the funky end of community-living establishments," Fletcher, the manager, says, greeting me at the gate. He dismisses the gatekeeper who asks me for two forms of ID. "She won't be needing those. I can tell right away she's our kind of tenant."

He offers me his hand through the car window. "Nice to meet you, Carla," he says when I introduce myself. He's younger and hipper, relatively speaking, than Marv or Kent. The collar of his zingy red polo shirt is turned up to meet his five o'clock shadow. He raises the wooden arm manually and steps out of the way as I drive into his domain—identical town houses with individual flourishes. Somebody's planted a vegetable garden here, somebody's children have built a communal fort out of a cardboard box over there. Fletcher waves me into a parking space in front of a particularly festive yard where a table with a built-in pin-striped umbrella is surrounded by chairs that match each stripe. A giant flag hangs over the doorway: PEACE, LOVE, AND UNDERSTANDING 2000.

Fletcher takes my arm—a gesture I'm now certain is in every gated community's sales manual: Establish physical contact, touching your client's arm in a friendly yet nonaggressive way as soon as possible. Having done that, he guides me to the door of the PEACE, LOVE, AND UNDERSTANDING 2000 town house. Before knocking on the door, he gives me a clipboard and asks me to provide my full name and the standard contact information.

"My clients do my selling for me," he says softly, just between us. "Carrie and Kevin have been here since the get-go." He rings the doorbell with gusto, then whispers, "They'll give you the real dirt on the place."

A woman about my age answers the door. She's wearing flattering short shorts, a faded orange T-shirt that is probably her husband's, and blue sandals with thin straps that climb up her delicate ankles like vines.

"Hey there," she says, running fingers through tendrils of wet hair.

Carrie is my age, but with three times the energy. She takes my nail-bitten hand in her smooth and manicured one, stroking it absentmindedly, and smiles before she turns to call to her husband. She eyes my Marla/Carla get-up curiously, the way one might study an unfamiliar meal in a foreign country before eating it.

"I just love natural hands," she says, fingering my torn cuticles.

"Kevin, hurry up and bring the drinks, honey," Carrie scolds. Kevin appears, wearing a Standardsville Rugby League T-shirt and sporting sculpted calf muscles. In his tan, square hands he carries a tray with tall frosty blue glasses and a bowl of trail mix. He bumps Carrie playfully with his hip as he moves through the doorway. It's a signal to the world, a tribute to years of exciting sex, the kind I've only read about. Fletcher is breathless beside me.

"You all are my best customers," he says. He wants in on this life of hip-bumps and wearing each other's clothes. "So make me proud and tell Isabelle all about us." Carrie touches Fletcher's shoulder as if to say, but of course. Apparently, she has the same rule about establishing physical contact immediately—to get inside a person's mind, you must first lay hands on him.

"Drinks first," Carrie says. We follow her as she heads for the picnic table. She lifts the tray swiftly and efficiently out of Kevin's hands, raising it above her head without so much as the rattle of a glass.

"Carrie used to be a waitress," Kevin says. His smile follows his wife's sashay, his eyes greedily conjuring images of Carrie surrounded by men slipping bills into the cinched waist of her French maid's cocktail-waitress outfit.

We pull our chairs under the shade of the sheltering umbrella while Carrie slides the piña coladas around the table with the brisk authority of a blackjack dealer. Kevin, Fletcher, and I are hypnotized as Carrie sips from her own drink. Froth lingers on her upper lip until she laughs and tongues it away.

"How long have you lived here?" I ask.

"A year," Kevin says, looking to Carrie.

"A year," Carrie says, nodding in confirmation. "We were married during the first week. Right here in the front yard."

Fletcher nods in time with Carrie and, as I slurp my piña colada, I notice the boundaries of Carrie and Kevin's life—the edges of their green, green yard and the beginning of the asphalt parking lot—containing us. Kevin touches my leg lightly with his square, tan fingers and points to a nearby town house with a hose running snakelike through a square patch of flower garden. "Some of our best friends, another couple, live right over there."

"One of my best friends is a neighbor," I say. The sweet drink starts to hit the backs of my knees.

"That's nice," Carrie says, giving me a smile for my effort, as if I actually had something in common with this couple who watched their grass seed grow to healthy maturity as they sat in their color-coordinated lawn furniture next door to a couple who would eventually become their best friends with whom they would sip drinks, admire each other's yards, and eye each other's sculpted calf muscles. "We just have so much in common with those guys. It's crazy!"

Maybe Carrie and Kevin are swingers. Fletcher is still nodding. "I told you they were great," he says, leaning toward me but loud enough for them to hear. They smile. Fletcher's turned-up collar is like a fence around his head, protecting him from real thoughts.

"You know, Carla, I'm in sales too," Kevin says. He gives Fletcher a pat on the shoulder. Maybe they swing with Fletcher.

I nod as Carrie pours me another drink. "Vitamins," Kevin says, showing off a bicep that looks like there's a small animal trapped inside his arm.

I reach over and touch it. "Kevin is naturally muscular," Carrie says. "Makes you want to touch it, doesn't it?" She puts her hand next to mine on Kevin's arm, letting me know that she does every day.

I imagine Carrie and Kevin in the morning before work. They must have fluffy matching robes that they wear around the house while one showers first and the other makes the coffee and the egg-white omelets, depending on whose day it is. They watch a morning show on their huge color TV that's never snowy. They occasionally fight, and some days Carrie can't stand to look one more time at the hard stone of Kevin's bicep, but they've got the routine of love down. Every casual caress and the way they refer to each other in the third person, like deities, is proof. Fletcher and I are their audience, and, in return, we get to be part of the act, this vehicle in which they've chosen to ride through life, as real as Marla's pastel suit, red heels, colored contacts, and Breast Helpers.

"What sort of people live here?" I ask dutifully, true to the questionnaire.

"Oh, *all* kinds." Fletcher is not falling for that old trick. "Very diverse." Even with a few piña coladas under his belt, he's sticking to the real-estate code of honor: Never answer this question in any detail. But I know the truth. Behind every door lurk people just like Carrie and Kevin. Town house after town house of hip-bumping, naturally muscular people with healthy tans.

"The people here are so friendly," Carrie says. "We haven't had *any* problems."

"The friendliest," Kevin agrees. "It's a very *select* group."

Underneath the love routine lies disdain for everything that lies outside the barbed wire-rimmed iron gate of the Edge. They don't want to know about the rest of the world. It's not just that they don't want to hear about obvious horrors like racism, poverty, and homelessness, they don't want to hear about any of the little messes either—unambitious, sporadically employed people, people who eat cereal for dinner or canned peaches out of the can for breakfast, people with potbellies and lovehandles, people with stacks of half-finished projects they will never finish, or people staggering through the wide-open, shabby loneliness of life. Marla's bravery wells up in me, filling me as I slip my feet in and out of her red heels.

"We must all learn to dance on a shifting carpet," I pronounce.

"Excuse me, Carla?" Fletcher asks, putting his hand on my shoulder.

I shake it off. "I *said*, we must all learn to dance on a shifting carpet." I'm not quite shouting. As much as I mocked Clifford's highway psychic babble before, right now—my body gone pleasantly numb from the heat and the piña coladas— these words seem downright prophetic.

"Is that from *Zen for Dummies*?" Kevin asks.

Carrie tilts her head as if she were curious and smiles.

A dull ache has started at the base of my neck. I need more than anything in the world to get home to Raymond, to his sweet potbelly and gentle touch. His name was love this morning as he held my head in his hands, my hair going red. Not marry-me love. Not let's-show-the-world love. Not a love that we have to tell anybody about. It's a love that shouldn't even be constrained by the word "love." It is beyond language, it's that pure. It is a feeling hovering modestly between us, lifting us both just a little bit above the earth.

"It's been real," I say, standing. "But I've got to go." I quiver a little on Marla's heels, regain my balance, and start to teeter quickly away from the table.

Fletcher and Carrie and Kevin protest.

"But you just got here," Kevin insists.

"You haven't even had the tour," Carrie says.

"There's a Jacuzzi in the bathtub," Fletcher says. After several piña coladas, it sounds like, "Thersha Jacuzzi in the bashtub."

"I just remembered something," I say, turning around and walking back. "I'm not very good in select groups." But Carrie and Kevin have turned their attention to Fletcher, who sways slightly as he stands. They both reach out to him, a hand on each shoulder. I put my hand down my shirt, pull the Breast Helpers out of my bra, and lay them on the table.

"Wow," Carrie says. "I never would have guessed. Those look really natural."

" 'Bye, 'bye, then." Fletcher waves good-bye and plunks down in Kevin's chair, empty because Kevin has jumped to his feet to steady Fletcher.

The gatekeeper lifts the manual arm as soon as he sees the Chevy in all its junky glory pull out of the parking lot filled with SUVs and perky-colored Saabs. When I look over my shoulder, Fletcher is holding the Breast Helpers up to his chest and prancing around the table. Carrie is laughing but not very convincingly. "Honey," she calls after Kevin as he heads back into the house carrying the tray of empty glasses and the bowl of trail mix that no one has touched, like evidence that needs to be destroyed.

It seems like years have passed when I turn the corner onto the cul-de-sac. My mother stands on the front steps with her purse over her shoulder. It isn't until I get closer that I see she's just stopped crying, just pulled herself together. This time, she isn't dressed for a date. She wears a business suit that she hasn't worn in twenty-five years. My heart tries to beat its way out of my chest. It's the suit she wore the day after my father left, the day she decided he never existed.

"Raymond's in the hospital," she says fiercely, implicating us both. She's through crying. She means business.

12

I DRIVE as fast as the stoplights allow. Images of Raymond race through my mind, his leg in traction—did he fall in the shower studying his movie-star Scientologists shower curtain? or his arm in a sling—maybe he got it stuck in the mailbox? I'm afraid to ask.

"Honey," my mother says. I wince, preparing for the worst—heart attack, stroke, aneurysm. "Have your eyes always been blue?"

"Contacts," I say matter-of-factly.

"And did you do something to your hair?"

"Dyed it," I say. "What is going on?"

"Did you always have that beauty mark?"

"What do you care?" I pull the beauty mark off my face.

"Oh, thank God," my mother says, putting her hand to her chest and exhaling with relief. "For a second I thought I was going crazy too."

"Too?" I run a red light.

"You do know you are beautiful just the way you are," my mother says.

"Why are we talking about this? What the hell happened to Raymond?" I look in the rearview mirror and my mascara is running. I look like an evil clown.

"Raymond asked his social worker to call me," my mother says. "He's in a psychiatric hospital."

"What are you talking about?" I'm confused and I'm headed to the wrong hospital. "Why didn't you tell me? Can't you see I'm driving in the wrong direction?" A flash of possessive jealousy pulses through me. Why would Raymond ask his social worker to call her? Raymond has a social worker? Why wouldn't he ask his social worker to call *me*?

"He finished four bottles of antacids and then called the psych hospital." My mother speaks in soft tones. I would prefer hysterics, something penetrable. "Take a left up here," she says. "That'll get us back on track."

The lawn of the hysterically pink hospital, tucked behind one of the malls, is neatly trimmed. The television ad for this hospital makes it look like Club Med. Beautiful patients sit in perfect circles and consult with handsome doctors who aren't doctors but play them on TV. At the end of the commercial a disclaimer flashes across the screen: For the confidentiality of our staff and patients, what you have just witnessed is a reenactment of actual groups held at our hospital. These people are not real. A placard on the front door reads: HELPING PEOPLE HELP THEMSELVES FOR TWENTY-FIVE YEARS.

"They must be exhausted," I say, but neither of us laugh. I

take a moment to check my reflection in the window, using my sleeves to wipe away the smeared mascara underneath my eyes.

We walk down a long hallway, also hysterically pink, to the door where the check-in nurse sits reading a book. On the cover, a woman explodes out of her corset, her breasts like too-full water balloons. The nurse's eyes move up our bodies to our faces with a look that says she has been interrupted several times already just as the hero is about to unzip his pants.

"Are you family?" she asks when we tell her Raymond's name.

"Yes," we both answer without hesitation.

The nurse smiles dismissively and points to a clipboard where we should sign in after a long list of other frantically scribbled names.

She ushers us into a room filled with clusters of huddled families. There are giant NO SMOKING signs posted on each wall next to finger paintings done by patients. The finger-paintings, a caption explains, were an exercise in expression. The finger paintings are mostly bright red and shocking blue. Someone has written ANGER and SADNESS at the bottom of one of the paintings. On another someone has scrawled "bored out of my mind." No one in the visitor's lounge is smoking, but everybody smells like smoke. The giant TV mounted on the wall is turned on without the sound. Raymond sits alone in a cluster of empty chairs, watching the silent TV as it appears to document the real lives of five teenagers, strangers to each other until now, thrown together in one apartment for one summer, the written explanation under the show's title reads.

"Cable," Raymond explains with a smile when he sees us. Then he touches his face with his hands, a southern-belle, sodelighted-you-could-drop-by gesture. He looks remarkably at home.

"I'm glad you came," he says, as if he had invited us to a party.

"How are you?" my mother asks.

"Fine," he says. His eyes wander up to the silent TV. The footage is shaky, taken by the teenagers themselves. The camera zooms in on a tickle fight in which the entire household piles onto one bed, diving under the covers, then cuts to an interview with one of the boys, his mouth moving frantically, pointing angrily at a jar of empty peanut butter.

"What happened?" I turn Raymond's face away from the TV toward us.

"We're just glad to see you, Raymond," my mother says when he doesn't answer. "We're glad you're okay, Raymond." She uses his first name with the flattened negotiating tone of someone who trying to make a deal. It's the first time since the accidental night around the hot pot that I've seen Raymond and my mother in the same room. Despite my mother's confident tone, her hand shakes and she reaches into her pocketbook, pretending to fish for something in order to hide her trembling.

"Talk to us," I plead. I grab one of Raymond's hands. "What is going on? What's wrong? Talk to *me*."

"I just needed a break," he says. He uses his free hand to stroke our joined ones, comforting me as if I were the one in the hospital. "I was just so tired."

"From what? Why didn't you tell me? You could have talked to me. I could have helped." I'm frantic.

"Isabelle," my mother says, first-naming me too. "Calm down."

"Don't tell me to calm down," I hiss. "And don't say my name." Other families stare at us from their quiet circles.

"Keep your voice down," my mother says. Her voice is even and subdued. It is no longer the voice of a negotiater; it is the voice of a terrorist. "You're making a scene."

All my keeping watch from across the street couldn't keep Raymond from this. All this time, I thought we were in on this together. Our loneliness was like our own weed-filled garden—something we shared and tended together, carefully cultivating the weeds curling up and up.

A tall bald man breaks from one of the huddles, walks past us, and pats Raymond's shoulder. "Hey guy," he says.

"Who's that?" I ask.

"Just a friend," Raymond says casually, as if he'd always had friends, effortless relationships filled with slaps and pats. He pulls a crushed pack of cigarettes from the back of his jeans and fishes for one that isn't broken. When he finally digs one out, he puts it in his mouth unlit.

"I didn't know you smoked," I say.

"We all smoke here," Raymond says, world-weary as though he'd been in the hospital for years instead of one night. In an adjacent room, visible through a square window in the wall, two tough, svelte teenage girls play pool, showing off thin arms in sleeveless, heavy-metal T-shirts. Cigarettes dangle from their lips and they blow smoke out of the side of their mouths.

"I don't really inhale," Raymond says.

"You look good smoking," I offer, because he does. Leaning into the couch, taking a fake drag from his cigarette, he looks more comfortable than I've ever seen him in his own house.

"We should go," my mother says just as a man in jeans and

a tucked-in white oxford shirt approaches us. He holds a stack of manila folders and a pen in one hand. Around his neck swings a chain with a hospital identification card on it. On the card is a picture of him wearing the same white shirt.

"Good afternoon, Raymond," he says. Like my mother, he believes in the power of first names. He says it precisely and emphatically like a reminder: This is who you are, remember?

"Hey," Raymond says.

"Would you like to introduce me to your friends?"

"Isabelle and Adeline," Raymond says.

"I'm Raymond's social worker," the man says. As he reaches for my hand, I see in the contours of his adult cheek the pudgy boy I baby-sat for one summer when I was in high school and he was in junior high, back when age was carefully ordered by grade. My sweaty teenage thighs stuck even then to the vinyl seat of the Chevy when I dropped him off at swim practice at the public pool. I'd wait in the parking lot filled with little children, their small chubby arms stuffed into water wings, escorted by their older brothers and sisters, towels wrapped around their waists, until he reached the door. Every day I watched him dance across the burning pavement in bare feet. He refused to wear the flip-flops his mother gave him.

"Frank?" I hold his hand even after our handshake is finished.

"Frank Robbins," he corrects me, pulling his hand away. He is stunned out of his social worker smooth talk.

"Isabelle," I say. I point at myself to clarify. "I baby-sat you years ago."

"Oh wow." Frank takes a step back to get some perspective.

"Wow." He puts his hand on his brow. "I thought you'd left town. I thought you were long gone."

"She was," Raymond says.

"She's here for a visit," my mother says. Their covering for me makes me wince.

"Let's talk in the hall," Frank says.

One night in the hospital is long enough for Raymond to understand that this does not mean him unless he's referred to by name.

"I'll go have a smoke," he says, wandering out into the hall, toward the room with the thin-armed, pool-playing, smoking girls.

My mother and I follow Frank. "Raymond says he has no family," Frank says. "He says that you two are the closest thing he's got."

I should have known Raymond was trying to tell me something when he dyed my hair. He said I didn't know everything. I didn't know this, but I should have known something. I should have known to stay with him, by his side, watching.

"We'll do whatever we can," my mother says. She has grown more and more businesslike since we arrived at the hospital, as though she wants to live up to the promise of her businesslike clothes.

"So what happens now?" I ask. I want Frank to tell us he's kidding, that this is all a big hoax. Raymond will return with his prop cigarettes. He and Frank will join hands and take a bow, and then we can all go home.

"We wait and see," Frank says.

"Thank you very much," my mother says.

"That's it? Wait and see? Frank, I once walked in on you

jerking off in the bathroom before you had pubic hair. Wait and fucking see?"

"Isabelle, get a hold of yourself." My mother turns to Frank, who remains unflappable in his lanky earnestness. "We'll be back later. Will you please tell Raymond we said good-bye?"

"I know this is upsetting," Frank begins.

"Oh, shut up," I say.

"I'll be here if you need to talk," Frank says.

"Thank you very much." My mother takes me firmly by the arm and escorts me down the hall, past the nurse still reading her book. From somewhere down the pink hall, the sound of someone weeping rises up, a ghost of despair.

My mother takes the car keys from me and drives home with her jaw set.

"How can you just . . ." I begin.

"Just be quiet," she says, looking straight ahead as we ride past mall parking lots, past the strip malls, past Modern Pizza with its shiny new red roof like a beacon in a sea of anonymous gray. I want so much to know what she is thinking so that I can think it too. I want to climb into her mind and rest there. Instead, silence buzzes between us.

At home, we go silently to our separate bedrooms. I lie on my bed, surrounded by the sturdily indifferent furniture that's been there all day, in the same place, oblivious. It's been arranged this way since before my father disappeared, since my mother circled this room telling me about Henry and San Francisco, since high school when Dennis and I watched the fireworks from our blanket. I understand now why Raymond looks for meaning in the wood of the banister that supports him as he makes his way up the stairs every night. I want to believe that these objects that surround me, that have surrounded me for years and years, might tell me something about my life too. But my bedroom furniture just sits there, obstinate and mute, a reluctant witness refusing to give anything up.

I jump out of bed and kick the bedpost until my foot throbs. The quick pulse of pain distracts me from my mother's quiet sobbing across the hall. Out the window, Raymond's empty house is like a person staring, forcing me to look away.

WHEN the phone rings, I'm still wearing the pink jacket but have managed to wriggle out of the slacks in my sleep. They're in a crumpled ball under the covers. My foot throbs slowly now, a dull thud of pain to remind me of yesterday.

"Marla?" I'm so relieved—someone willing to go a little berserk. I am desperate for one of her roller-coaster rants. I peel the jacket off and shove it under the covers with the slacks. I stand in the middle of the hallway in a T-shirt and underwear, my face wrecked with slept-in makeup.

"How could you do this? How could you let it happen?" As usual, she skips the hellos, but this time she's angry. "I groomed you, Isabelle. I picked you because I trusted you. *You.* You were the one."

"Hi Marla," I say. My savior. The one person right now who makes sense. I try to remember all the way back to yesterday afternoon, to whatever it was that I did that could have been so bad. Even if it was catastrophic, why would it matter? They think I'm Carla. "What's the problem?"

"You left my business card. Right there on the chair." Marla pauses to let this information sink in. "Mr. Fletcher didn't-give-his-last-name called me, very suspicious. Asked me if you had been working for Temporama long. Of course I denied it. Said you'd been with us ages ago, before you got your new job. 'New job' was the best I could do. Since you'd abandoned Priscilla, I wasn't sure whether you'd abandoned Prints Charming too. Then he asked me why you had written the number to Temporama and said it was your mother's. How was I supposed to explain that?"

"It's *your* pantsuit, it must have been *your* business card." My quota for Marla's ranting and raving has been filled. Now, I want to get back to the hospital to see Raymond.

"Well, what kind of mystery shopper are you that you don't even check your own pockets? Don't try to push the blame off on me, young lady. This is serious stuff. You nearly blew the whole operation. Fortunately for you, I think on my feet. I told him that your mother and I are old friends, that I'm like a second mother to you. I said that you and your mother were having a tough time living in such close proximity and that your writing my number next to her name must have been a Freudian slip. Can Freudian slips happen on paper, or can they only happen out loud?" Marla finally takes a breath while she considers this. "Anyway, we're lucky because I think I convinced him." She's saying "we" again. We're back to being part of a team, making the world of gated communities a safer place.

"Marla," I say wearily. For a second, I consider telling her about Raymond, about how scared I am right now, but she's made it clear that, in it's own peculiar way, this is a professional relationship. "I didn't mean to leave the card behind. It was an accident and it'll never happen again."

"I know you didn't mean to, sweetie," she says, my relenting second mother. "But remember: Sharp as nails. Eyes in the back of your head. Tough as tacks. Cross your T's and dot your I's."

"I'll talk to you later," I whisper.

"Wily as that coyote, but as smart as the roadrunner," she's saying as I hang up the phone, continuing to enumerate the many crafty qualities required of a mystery shopper.

THE other patients, including Trash and Belle, the tough pool-playing girls with whom Raymond trades cigarettes when he's in the mood for menthol, have dubbed the couch in the pool room "Raymond's couch." Raymond tells me this with a certain amount of pride when I visit him alone this afternoon. My mother insisted work had been so busy lately that she couldn't take time off to come during afternoon visiting hours. She has a date with Mr. Jones this evening so that rules out evening visiting hours.

"Too many visitors at one time isn't a good idea," she said on her way out the door this morning, as if she'd had a vast amount of experience in these matters.

"Two visitors," I said. "You and me. That's only two."

"I'll go another time," she said, closing the door behind her, effectively ending the discussion.

"Your own couch, wow," I say to Raymond, patting his leg as he sits across from me in our two-person huddle. There are two other huddles today—a patient and his wife or girlfriend locked in an embrace and a teenage boy with his family. One of the adults in the family has a toddler who occasionally breaks free from this group and teeters over to cling to our knees, then teeters away.

"Just another couch, in the same old town," Raymond mock-country sings. "This time I'm wearing a hospital gown."

"You're not wearing a hospital gown," I say adamantly, stupidly, instead of laughing.

"It's just a song I made up," he says. Now he's the one patting my leg. "It'll be okay."

Frank stops me in the hall on my way out. "We are still trying to determine the best course of action," he says, fiddling with the identification card hanging around his neck.

"I'm not sure what that means." Everything is mixed up. My masturbating ex-ward is trying to explain something to me, but I don't understand each word separately, much less all of these words strung together in a sentence.

"Just hang in there," he says.

I drive to the nearby mall where teenagers are still making smoking history. Inside, the breeze from the air-conditioning is so cold it gives me goose bumps and, humiliatingly, makes my nipples hard. I fold my arms across my chest and take a seat in the gazebo in the center of the mall, where I have a good view of a former high school classmate who now manages the corn-dog stand. I sat behind him in math—he used to borrow my pencils and never return them, which was fine because he chewed them all the way around. He must have borrowed fifty pencils that year. I'm surprised he isn't dead from lead poisoning. Instead, here he is wearing a red apron depicting a smiling Snoopyesque dog being lowered into a vat of bubbling deep-fried batter. A bubble over the dog's head reads: HOT DIGGITY DOGLICIOUS!

The pencil chewer maneuvers gracefully among his workers, making suggestions. He is neither bossy nor annoying. He is, from all outward appearances, as cheerful as the dog on his apron. The teenage girls working for him seem content in their matching red aprons as they dip naked hot dogs on sticks into boiling batter. They smile at their customers and make small talk. The pencil chewer commends them on their good work—a particularly well-dipped dog earns one of the girls a pat on the back—nothing sexual or scary, just a simple, kind, thank-you-for-doing-your-job-so-well kind of pat.

For a moment, sitting in the mall gazebo, next to the trickle of the multilevel waterfall, I remember the phone company in San Francisco with pleasure. There were days when I'd finish copying the last of that day's site maps and experience a rush of adrenaline at a task completed. It was a job with a beginning, a middle, and an end. It was straightforward. I felt useful. During breaks, Louise and Simon and I would meet around the coffee station to discuss the way coffee was ruining our lives—kept us up all night, gave us the shakes, made us sweat, fueled a Monday headache like nothing else—while we shared another freshly brewed pot.

On my way to my car, I join the smoking teenagers and ask for a cigarette. None of them speaks to me—I am clearly out of place, a wolf in teen's clothing—but they honor me with the inclusive silence of teenagers. They are sullen yet respectful in their black T-shirts and lace-up boots as I lean beside them against the concrete wall. When I'm finished, one of the girls, recognizing a state of confusion when she sees one, says, "Good luck with everything."

On my way home, I stop at the Laundromat where Dennis used to work. I haven't spoken to Dennis since our roll in the dirt, and I should call him, but I'd rather pretend it's just one of those utterly normal days, nothing in particular going on, nothing to ponder. The dirty clothes have piled up to that tipping point and there's nothing to do but head to the Laundromat and waste a few hours watching the washer and the dryer spin and shake. Since I don't have dirty clothes of my own, I mime laundry, opening and closing empty washers and dryers. I try to guess the ages and professions of the other Laundromat people. I study the way they organize themselves—do they use fabric softener? do they bother to separate the colors and the whites? do they handle their underwear boldly in public? I tell myself I'm providing a public service. This is the career they left out of the career counselor's catalog—certified voyeur, life witness.

"May I help you, ma'am?" A suspicious attendant catches me opening somebody else's dryer—I saw my chance and took it, a woman turned the dryer on and left the premises. I've stuck my arm up to my elbow in her hot clothes.

"No, I'm fine," I say. I respond as though the attendant were actually asking me if I needed her help instead of kicking me out. I pull my arm out as casually as possible, then head for the door.

With Raymond no longer crouched in the bushes outside my mother's house to observe our lives, I could disappear—fade into the cottony thick summer air or spontaneously combust like the children I once saw on a segment of a news journal show. The children simply exploded into dust. One mother swept her child up in a dustpan, unaware. She shook him into a garbage bag and put him out on the curb. By the time she realized what she had done, he was in the back of a garbage truck, stuck to everybody else's moist coffee grounds, old socks, and food scraps. I go home and crawl under the covers, hoping for combustion.

No such luck. A car's horn blares in my mother's driveway. Someone's leaning on it. I hear someone, probably Mrs. Morton, the neighbor who wanted to send Creampuff into exile, scream, "Shut up! It's called a doorbell. Use it."

"Isabelle!"

I peek warily outside and there's Dennis, standing underneath my window the way he did when he was fifteen.

"Who do you think you are?" Mrs. Morton shouts. "Brando?"

I open the window slightly and then crouch under the ledge.

"I saw you," Dennis says. "I can see the top of your head, Isabelle. I know you're there. You can creep around all you want. I just came over here to tell you that I'm through with you. You spend a night driving around naked with a guy and you can't even stand up and look him in the eye? You're a big liar, Isabelle, and a sucky one at that. You think you're so great, always holding out for something better. Well, this is it. This is your stupid life. It's happening right now and you're missing it."

I hear a car door slam and Dennis drives away, leaving me and my desperate, cowardly heart and equally cowardly mouth on the floor. I climb back into bed and try once again to achieve spontaneous combustion.

"LIFE has to go on," my mother takes to saying whenever I ask her to come with me to the hospital to visit Raymond. She waves her hands in the air like a conductor to illustrate how futile any attempt to stop life from going on will be. "And on and on," she says. She is ready for the next movement, pleased at the way her new life full of love and Mr. Jones has pushed her out onstage again. She and Mr. Jones spend every night together. Her life has lost the jaggedness of single living, that solitude that allows a person to feel the proximity of death, that ultimate solitude, a little more keenly. She no longer plans her meals alone in the car on the way to work. Sometimes she lets Mr. Jones handle dinner all by himself.

In the mornings before she goes to work, she comes into my room, leaving Mr. Jones in her bed surrounded by the debris of day-to-day couplehood—his socks on the bedroom floor, shaving cream in the bathroom, an extra toothbrush, an occasional pubic hair embedded in the soap.

She is afraid her happiness will injure me so she doesn't tell me much. The other night when she and Mr. Jones went to another movie to escape the heat—a movie about a plague that was the result of an environmental disaster and the hero got giant boils on his face—Mr. Jones turned to my mother and said, "I think I could get used to this, Adeline. You, that is. Not the giant boils." She offered this detail reluctantly. She felt the obligation to share, but I can tell by the way she leaves things out, keeping the best things for herself, that she has fallen in love.

"The summer will be over soon," she says more often than not, sitting on the edge of my bed like a nurse. Saying this is part of the routine of her new life too. She says it wistfully, but she is comfortably resigned. This summer is disappearing into memory. Life goes on and on, with or without us.

I've told her that my boss at the graphic design firm is looking into a permanent job for me at one of their branches in another town. I've told her I'm saving my money, that I have big plans. Huge, life-altering plans. She doesn't ask for details.

I spend my days visiting Raymond. I get to know Kristina, the nurse at the front desk who reads the bodice rippers and whistles through her teeth when she talks. She is sometimes even friendly to me. Some days Raymond tells me he is dying, though Frank whispers in my ear that Raymond is healthier than a horse. He wants your attention, Frank says, and I picture Frank's closet, a rainbow of preppy shirts that help him to feel normal.

"You aren't dying," I say, spoon-feeding Raymond the words like medicine, and sometimes, like a miracle cure, it works. But some days there is no consoling him and we sit there with our eyes closed, surrounded by the low tones of the other patients and their visitors. Sometimes, Trash or Belle or the tall bald man will be a part of one of those huddles and, on the way in or out, says hello to Raymond but never to me, though by now I am familiar. Though Raymond tells me about Trash and Belle teaching him how to play pool, about their chain-smoking so that they don't have to ask the staff for the lighter they're not allowed to have themselves, these are not things we can share. He exists in another world that belongs only to him. He sometimes explains the music videos he watches from his couch, on the TV that is on twenty-four hours a day in the pool room. The other day he told me about one he saw during a flashback weekend—a woman painted with wild-animal stripes, savage feathers pasted to her body, running through a jungle in pursuit of, or being pursued by (it was hard to tell, he explained), five blond men wearing headbands and cut-off T-shirts.

"The woman leaned against trees, trying to blend in, but the men always found her," Raymond says.

"Hmm," I say, hating myself for envying Raymond's life without me. I have lost him, my ally, to this alternate universe.

"I think the idea was, make sure you're camouflage is foolproof," Raymond says. His hands and eyes are puffy with medication.

Frank has told me that Raymond's condition seems to be worsening. There is no exact diagnosis yet. "We can be sure that he suffers from acute depression," he told me the other day. "That much we know." I wanted to spank him.

I feel lucky that I am the one who Raymond expects, the one for whom he puts out his cigarette (a big sacrifice as he inhales now and his cigarette supply is dwindling—I've started to bring him cartons so that he can pay back the patients he's borrowed from) to go wait in the visitors' lounge. He has rings underneath his eyes and his skin is sallow from being always inside and in the smoke-filled lounge area. One day when I arrived for afternoon visiting hours, he had his legs folded underneath him and his eyes closed, as if he were taking a yoga class. When I sat down in the chair next to his, he opened his eyes and said, "You are my witness." I sat down and tucked my feet up underneath me too, thinking that as long as we were safely contained in these bodies, we would only stray so far. There, in the visiting area, surrounded by huddled strangers whose faces had become as familiar to me as my own mother's, Raymond and I achieved an underwater stillness, like walking out into the ocean over your head and discovering that you can breathe easily, a soft, blue calm.

WHEN I get home from visiting hours tonight, I find my mother and Mr. Jones grilling in the backyard. The smell of burnt meat is in the air. I surprise them on the back patio, in the midst of layering their shish kebobs with sliced vegetables and steak. They are sitting side by side, arranging. Their silence is the sort of comfortable, close silence that follows a deep talk about missing husbands and former wives.

"Honey," my mother says as I slide into a patio chair around the table heaped with food. "Sweet pooch." She touches my arm and in her face I see hope for my own face years from now, slack with time, proof of dues paid. We have faces suited to the lines that have emerged across her forehead and the crow's-feet around her eyes. Her wrinkles have sculpted her once-smooth face into something that makes me want to read it with my hands.

"Hi, honey. Hi, sweet pooch," Mr. Jones says, kidding around. The coals under the grill are blue with heat and the smell of lighter fluid rises up with the burnt-meat smoke and blows down the street—a toxic ghost.

"How was Raymond?" my mother asks.

"He's fine," I say. I won't tell her that she should be a good neighbor, a good friend to her longtime admirer, and go to the hospital and see for herself because Mr. Jones is here. Mr. Jones is always here. So this tiny scrap is all I'll throw her.

"Good, good," she says. The scrap suffices.

My mother challenges Mr. Jones to a duel with her skewer, which wobbles under the weight of dinner. *"En garde,"* she says. "Don't mess with me and my daughter." They've had conversations about me, about the secrets of my life.

Mr. Jones puts his hands in the air as if my mother were sticking him up. As he begs for mercy, I see the change in my mother. It's not just finding Mr. Jones, it's a shift in the terrain of her face as if, after all these years, something has settled. As Mr. Jones takes up his loaded skewer and he and my mother duel their way to the grill, I see how my mother and I were never in the same boat so much as I wanted to be in hers, lying on the bottom to feel the rhythm of the water, listening to it slosh and pitch while she did all the rowing.

After dinner, I excuse myself to go across the street to pick up Raymond's mail. He claims he's expecting something important, though he won't say what. He has been asking me to do this all week. The second day he was in the hospital, he gave me the keys to his house. He knew even then that his stay would be indefinite.

"You take care of these, Isabelle," he said. "They're the only set I've got."

"Do you want me to make copies?" I asked.

"No, I trust you," he said, preferring to see this as a matter of who he trusted rather than a trip to the hardware store.

My mother and Mr. Jones hold hands across the table while they eat their dinner. There must be some other way to describe how old a person is—something other than childhood, adolescence, early adulthood, middle age, old age. Some descriptive term that encompasses mood as well—I am joyous-years-old or I am tired-years-old. My body will grow and grow, expanding until I split the seams of the house if I don't leave.

I turn around when I reach Raymond's front door. My

mother's house is lit like a stage to accentuate the players. Since I've been home for the summer, the living room curtains have remained open. Now, standing on Raymond's front steps, looking back, I recognize the invitation to observe. Watch this. Keep an eye on us. Imagine the parts you can't see.

Without Raymond in it, his house is even more spare and anonymous than usual, like a motel room but with less furniture. There is not one stray book or picture, no scrap of paper with his handwriting, not one pile of useless stuff. The floors are naked, swept clean. The mail consists of a neighborhood coupon book. I throw it away. It's less depressing to bring him nothing than to bring him an envelope screaming his name in capital letters from someone who doesn't mean it.

In the kitchen, I open empty cabinets. In the space under the sink, there is an econo-size bottle of dishwashing liquid, a small pile of dishes, and a lone pot. In the drawer next to the sink, I find a loose set of silverware—one fork, one spoon, one knife. Through the kitchen window, I see our house, the car in the driveway, the bright living room glaringly empty, between scenes.

I go upstairs to use the bathroom. The empty box of hair dye is still in the trash can. I take my time, examining the celebrity Scientologists shower curtain. A resurrected disco star and his wife stare accusingly at me. The idea of these movie stars, with their pouting mouths and exaggerated eyelashes, watching Raymond shower makes me sleepy and sad, so I venture into Raymond's bedroom and lie down on his pink-and-yellow crocheted bedspread. It smells like rain, musty and damp. Lying on my back, I follow the path of a single black spider as it crawls upside down across the vast, white expanse of the ceiling. I am eye level with my own room across the street, where the gauzy curtains wave with the light breeze coming through the cracked window.

Raymond's bedside table is bare, and I press my fingertips to the dusty top, leaving five faint marks. In the living room, my mother and Mr. Jones take their places on one of the couches. My mother goes over and fiddles with the stereo.

My hand wanders to the drawer of Raymond's bedside table, and I fiddle with the handle until the drawer falls open just a little. Inside is a stack of papers, an oasis in this desert Raymond calls home. I slide the drawer open a little more, until I can see that the stack of papers is a stack of envelopes, a stack of letters. I don't hesitate, telling myself that I am doing this in Raymond's best interest, that if Raymond wanted me to bring his mail inside, he probably wanted me to look around his house, that, in fact, he probably wanted me to find these letters. I tell myself that what I'm doing is simply an extension of what Raymond and I have been doing all summer, trying to sneak inside someone else's life.

At first, the familiarity of the tall scratchy handwriting on the envelopes fills me with knee-jerk love. Her handwriting, on letters she sent to college or San Francisco, always seemed vulnerable traveling across state lines, passing through the hands of strangers, a risk she took for me. But then the rush is gone and I go wooden in preparation as I reach in to pull out the soft, worn envelopes.

The first letter is dated the month after Raymond moved in, soon after I'd moved to San Francisco. I remember the smell of that month, the deliciously optimistic smell of the remnants—orange peels and coffee grounds—of the breakfast I had every morning by myself. I had thrown everything in my old life over, and, even then, just lonely enough to be excited by that feeling's sharp edges and looking for permanent work, the city still echoed with my mother's tragic adventure and seemed filled with possibilities. This is what I told my mother when we spoke on the phone. Things could happen for me here, I'd said. You just have to make it happen, she told me. Just make it happen.

Dear Raymond, I hope you enjoyed the dinner—I wasn't sure, you didn't finish everything. It was sweet of you to say you liked it. You are the most marvelous dancer. Sincerely, Adeline

Raymond's plate filled with small offerings to her—a bite of chicken, a spoonful of peas, a small pile of mashed potatoes. She cleared his plate, leaning over him so that he could smell her flesh through the haze of drugstore perfume. She took his hand, stood him up, and put his arms around her waist until he thought he would faint from being so close to her. She felt that innocence, the way he was untouched by years of marriage, his chest soft and malleable compared to the hard wall of my father's and the men who came after.

Raymond, Tragedy always lingers on the horizon but we can have the perfect romance, you and I. You on your side of the street. Me on mine. We'll watch over each other from afar, then meet in the middle. Look out your window just before you come over tonight. I'll be upstairs, trying outfits on and off for you. Let your opinion drift across the street to me and I will know what to wear. Fondly, Adeline

Raymond, his face pressed against glass. Did he change his clothes too? Slip out of his worn, familiar jeans?

All of the letters—fifteen of them over the course of the last year—traveled through the regular mail. They made their way from my mother's mailbox to the mailman's sack to the post office where they passed through stranger's hands along with other letters, bills, credit card approvals, birth announcements, death announcements, wedding invitations, coupons, voter registration, catalogs for household appliances, then back to the cul-de-sac of their birth and Raymond's mailbox.

Dearest Raymond, Your crooked face is handsome close-up. We dreamed this together, something bigger than just two people. It drifted out of our houses, filling the street with desire. Let's not be old-fashioned. We cannot expect to be the only ones in each other's lives. That is a recipe for disaster. Let's rise above. I will never close the curtains on you. Yours, Adeline

Raymond, his face still pressed against the glass, watching my mother's other dates escort her up the walk. Watching shadowy fumbling through windows, curtains open. Watch this too. Watch over me. Be my witness, the one who will never go away, trapped, compelled by desire to sit in his front-row seat across the street.

Lovely Raymond, What is the last thing you think of before you go to bed at night? This is me, thinking of you. Love, Adeline

At the bottom of the page is a rendering of Henry's stick-figure drawing of my mother in bed, thinking of him, only here there is an added caption:

Adeline thinking of Raymond. The last thing she thinks about before she falls asleep.

I can hear my mother's voice as I read, echoing in Raymond's empty house, ricocheting off the walls all the way back through time to my childhood bedroom. My mother's recycled love makes me queasy, but what makes me sick with fear is my own ignorance. Like high school geography—so *that's* where the Caspian Sea is—I'm in awe of all I don't know.

Dear, sweet Raymond, It is so kind of you to understand my tears the other night. I guess a loss like the one I've suffered isn't something to which I will ever grow accustomed. He died so young. Such a young, ridiculous death. Sometimes I wonder what would have happened if we'd never taken the bus that day. Sometimes I wonder why I've been allowed to continue living. I am old and ridiculous. But you are such a sweet, sweet comfort. You remind me of him. The sweetest. My love to you, Adeline

She told him all her secrets, even Henry. Raymond carried these letters inside, not wanting her to see his trembling hands as he read what used to be the secret my mother and I shared alone. He opened them in his foyer, shy even as he hid behind the door. She was like a god, seeing all, while on the West Coast I tried to forge a life that would achieve the wide openness she had described those years ago. I wasn't looking for tragic love necessarily, just a moment of skinlessness. But San Francisco was her town. I was trying it on like a dress she'd cast off, beautiful but never mine completely. Raymond too, beautiful but always hers.

Raymond, Last night. I'll say no more. With those two words, I hear the moon glowing through the window, sensing competition, determined not to be outdone. XXOO, Adeline

The last letter, written at the end of May, arrived a week after I lay bare-breasted across the warm copy machine. I was on my way home. This envelope is softer than the others, the mark of worried hands searching for clues. I unfold it slowly, so as not to tear the worn crease.

Raymond, my daughter is coming home for the summer and I'd prefer that she didn't know about us. This will be the last time I write. This marks the end of the affair. I think it best. I am not ready for this. Though years have past, I still have not recovered from my husband's death. Love, Adeline

My eyes rush over the letter again and again, studying each word individually for error. Her letters surround me on Raymond's bed. They are unfinished maps to the vast terrain of her private life, the one she's been living in all along without me. But no matter how many times I read the sentence, "husband" and "death" remain side by side on the page, indelible.

*   *   *

MY mother and Mr. Jones slow dance in the living room. The lights are dimmed. The stage is set.

"Look," Mr. Jones says, when I enter the room. "It's sweet pooch."

"Is Mr. Jones a marvelous dancer too?" I ask. Mr. Jones breaks free, retrieves his wineglass from the table and sways to the music, showing off. He closes his eyes for a moment as he sways. Maybe I'll disappear.

"Do you want a glass of wine?" my mother asks. She has no idea as I follow her into the kitchen.

"What is going on with you?" she asks. When I stand solidly in front of her like I'm ready for her to throw a punch. I try to stare through her, into her, as she uncorks the wine bottle.

"Don't bother. I don't want any," I say. "How could you do that to Raymond?"

"Honey, this is not the time nor the place," she says. She puts her hand on my shoulder and her firm grip tells me she knows what I'm talking about. She knows, but it's ancient history to her. In her eyes, tipsy with love for someone else, I see how much she needs me gone.

"How could you do this to me?" I shake her hard hand off my shoulder.

"What did Raymond tell you?" she whispers. "I knew this would happen."

"He didn't tell me anything," I say. "Don't try to blame this on him. I saw the letters."

She lets her hands fall at her side like broken tools. "I didn't know he kept them," she says finally. What I don't know about her is everything she doesn't offer me. She could be a twice-seen stranger, a woman I rode the bus with more than once.

"Did Dad die?"

"Oh, honey, no," she says. The blush starts at her neck, the way mine always does, and fans out across her face. "As far as I know, your father is still alive." She reaches out to touch my face, drained of blood and cold as ice.

"Don't." More than relief, I feel like a fool.

"I'm going to tell Mr. Jones to go home so we can talk." She heads for the living room, but Mr. Jones is already coming around the corner.

"No, I think he should hear this. Or is it too late? Have you already fed him on the dead version of my father too?'

Mr. Jones puts a protective arm around my mother.

"Yup," I say. "Too late. Did she make a Henry drawing for *you*?"

Mr. Jones doesn't look at me as he escorts my crying mother up the stairs.

Crossing the street, I trip and fall. The black tar pebbles leave tiny pockets in my palms. I press them in deeper, wanting something to leave a physical mark. I want to feel pain that I can see. In Raymond's bedroom, I bundle all the letters together with the twine Raymond uses for his recycling. On the top envelope, I use a thick, laundry marker to scrawl, *Return to sender (if this is your real name)* and a giant arrow pointing to my mother's name and address. When I'm done, my hands shaking and still filled with pebbles, I sneak across the street to my mother's mailbox and jam the letters inside.

Back in Raymond's house, I wish that he were here with me.

"We've all got to find our own freedom," he said the other day. At the time, it had the hackneyed and preachy ring of a self-help philosophy Frank might have fed him. But tonight, curled up in Raymond's bed watching the lights go out across the street, these words are the balm of compassion.

13

I WAKE up with my face in Raymond's pillow, inhaling the faint smell of Bay Rum. Through the window, I watch Mr. Jones and my mother climb into his Dodge Dart, the way they always do at exactly this time every morning to take her to work. Her mailbox hangs open, empty.

I put on Raymond's robe and I'm immersed in his smell. Beneath the initial layer of Bay Rum, Raymond smells like earth—rich, dark soil. I go down to Raymond's mailbox expecting retaliation for the returned letters but instead find a single phone message. *Marla called.*

I cross the street back to my mother's, Raymond's robe pulled tight around me. Upstairs, I dig through my closet for a mystery-shop outfit and find a paper bag destined years ago for the Salvation Army shoved behind piles of old shoes, a wraparound skirt from junior high crumpled inside. If I suck in my breath and pull tight, it just makes its way around my waist.

The skirt reminds me of spending Saturday nights in early adolescence with certain friends and being invited to attend church services the next morning. Neither my mother nor my father were very religious—God hovered perilously in the back of their minds, a hangover from various, nebulous forms of childhood Christianity abandoned in adulthood. Every once in a while, my mother would whip out a Bible and flip through it to read me a passage, her voice sonorous and priestlike. The begetting and begetting, murder and betrayal, stories of generation after generation of confused human beings was something we could both relate to.

"See," my mother would say when she finished reading a passage. "They're just like us." Satisfied, she would close the Bible with a dramatic thud and put it back in the linen closet, where she keeps all things historical.

When my friends invited me into their holy territory, I would put on unlikely clothes in combinations I would never wear otherwise but that seemed somehow reverent. The wraparound skirt with a friend's borrowed blouse, ruffly at the throat and cuffs. One friend lent me nylons—the first I'd heard of them at age eleven or twelve—and I wondered whether my fake tan legs were emblematic of the wondrous changes that took place through her religion. I'd clunk into church in sandals that I'd forced my mother to buy specifically for these Sundays—dark brown leather with a thick heel that served as weights.

I clunked all over town in those sandals—into the Unitarian church with the woman minister who smelled like lentil soup, into the Episcopalian church with the especially hard pews and the ominous organ music, into the Catholic church, where I sat awkwardly as everyone else filed up to receive the blood and body of Jesus, and into the Reform Temple with my Jewish friend who, every December, patiently explained Chanukah to entire classes at the request of some well-meaning suburban gentile teacher. These shoes anchored me, a balloon rising up out of them.

When I left whatever house of worship I'd attended that day, I felt as though I'd gotten away with something. The real miracle on mornings spent listening to adults speak about miracles was that no one pulled loose the ties of my wraparound skirt and said, "What are you doing here?" After the service, walking back to the car—somebody's rust-stained blue Volvo, or a brown-and-white station wagon with towels laid over the backseat to protect our good clothes from dog hair, or a big red van with a sliding door that never closed properly, forcing my friend and me to huddle, thrilled, as if our lives were in great danger—I felt what I've now come to recognize as the mystery-shop surge of power and pleasure. I'd gotten away with it again—no one had seen through my disguise.

I finish the outfit off with a blouse tangled around the wraparound skirt in the same paper bag. Its sleeves reach midforearm. I put on a pair of my temp nylons and slip my feet into a pair of Dr. Scholl's, hidden deep in the clothes purgatory of my closet, where my mother throws everything that neither of us will ever wear again but that she can't bear to part with.

I take scissors from the kitchen drawer—the ones that my mother uses to cut the fat off meat—and go to work. In a matter of minutes, I've gone from demure, shoulder-length Cherry Persian to rock-and-roll haphazard, red, and tufty. I trimmed my hair in college a few times, but a trim is not my intention. It's not a half-bad job, not unlike the disheveled heads of models on covers of fashion magazines I've skimmed while waiting for Marla in the lobby at Temporama. I'm pleased with my handiwork. This could be the haircut I have for the rest of my life.

When I check myself out in my mother's full-length mirror, my little-girl-visiting-God outfit no longer seems like such a good idea. The buttons on the blouse threaten to burst, and the skirt barely reaches my knees. I look like a low-budget, porn-star cross between Lolita and the Incredible Hulk. I slip into a tank top and shorts. On my way out to the Chevy, I stroke my hair—a gesture inherited from my mother—in an effort to be my own sweetest comfort.

"I ALMOST gave up on you," Marla says. When I approach her desk at Temporama, her eyes are on the stacks of paper on her desk, but she uses the preternatural powers she's acquired from sessions with the Highway Psychic to intuit my presence. She looks me up and down. "From the looks of you, maybe I should have."

"I've got a change of clothes in the car," I lie.

"The clothes are the least of your problems, Isabelle. What have you done to your hair now?"

"I'll wear a wig."

"For the rest of your life?" Marla opens a file drawer, puts her hand in one of the overflowing folders, and pulls out a piece of paper. "The questionnaire for Paradise Found," she says triumphantly.

PARADISE Found, as it turns out, is a mile down the road from Twilight. In fact, Marla told me, they've agreed to refer their clientele to Twilight when they reach that sunset age.

Sweating men with shovels and a minibackhoe dig up a small square of dirt just outside the gates as I pull into the circular drive. I check to make sure my bra straps are safely hidden under my tank top as I stride wigless under the matching gargoyles above the arched doorway.

"May I help you?" A short, squat man in a suit that's a size too big for him stands under an enormous chandelier in the foyer. There are no refreshments anywhere.

"I want to look at an apartment, Skeeter." I read the name off his name tag.

"Would you like to look at our brochure first," Skeeter suggests, rubbing his tiny hands together. Like Mr. Jones swaying to the music with his eyes closed, Skeeter hopes that this will make me disappear.

"No, that's all right. I'll just look at the apartment," I say.

"You are aware that we have a dress code here." Skeeter uses two fingers to smooth the thin hairs of his sketchy mustache. A picture window directly behind him looks out onto an enclosed yard surrounded by a sidewalk loop. Two women, wearing sundresses and big floppy hats, push toddlers in strollers around and around the loop. In the center of the loop is a mound of dirt next to a slide. A sign reads: NO PLAYING UNTIL 2002.

"No, I was not aware. But perhaps you could cut me some slack and just show me an apartment."

I will bring Skeeter to his knees. I'll start a revolution. I'll enlist the receptionist and the women with the floppy hats. We'll picket: Paradise Found out of our wardrobes!

"I'm afraid that I'm going to have to ask you to leave," Skeeter says. He looks toward the office where the receptionist types furiously away. She looks quickly back at her keyboard to disguise a smile.

"That's fine." I consider my options. There aren't many. "Because you know what? I can't afford to live here. I don't have a real job; I'm not married. I don't have any real aspirations to speak of; my ex-boyfriend won't speak to me; my best friend is in the nut house; and my mother, I've just discovered, is a bigger liar than I am. Besides which, those gargoyles you have hanging over your front door are hideous."

"Okay," Skeeter says. "All right now." Sweat trickles from his temple even though, inside Paradise Found, it's cold as a freezer. The clickety-click of the receptionist's fingers flying over the keyboard builds to a crescendo.

"Don't worry," I say. "I'm leaving." I walk back out the door, under the hideous gargoyles, through the gate to the Chevy, which takes up most of Paradise Found's circular driveway, and there's Mr. Jones. He's heaving dirt with the sweating men.

"Isabelle?"

"What are you doing here?"

"I added a landscaping component to my construction business." He wears a dark blue Standardsville High School T-shirt, drenched black with sweat. Beads of perspiration gather in the wrinkles of his forehead before rolling down his face. "I didn't recognize you with your hair . . ." He pauses and points to his own head. "Like that."

"I must ask you to exit the premises," Skeeter says, trundling up behind me.

"It's okay," Mr. Jones says. "She's a friend of mine."

"How unfortunate for you," Skeeter says.

"Go fuck yourself," I say.

"Isabelle." Mr. Jones says my name softly, the way he did when he'd catch me smoking during lunch in high school, authoritative but like he's been there too. His sympathy is the last straw. I jump in the Chevy and gun it. Skeeter and Mr. Jones shield their faces from the flying gravel as I peel out of there.

"DID you lose weight?" Kristina asks, putting her bodice ripper down to search for what is different about me when I sign my name in at the hospital.

"Something like that," I say, glad that my hairdo is only this noticeable.

Raymond looks disoriented when he walks into the visiting area. He moves so slowly it looks as though he's passing through something solid, not air. When he sits down next to me, he says, "This is it." He gestures to the too-bright lights and the nubbly brown carpet.

He looks at me. "I like your hair. It looks like mine." He rubs a hand through his own salt-and-pepper hair. All our lives, our hair just grows. It grows and grows, oblivious. I knew before I got here that I wouldn't ask him about my mother. I don't want him to know I was snooping, but more than that I don't want her to intrude on my relationship with Raymond.

"Thanks."

"You're leaving," he says. It's not a question. "That's good."

"Yes," I say, holding myself perfectly still. Maybe he can tell me where I'm going too.

"I was allowed to go outside today," he says. "We pulled chairs from the dining room into the yard to soak up the sun. Trash wore huge, glamorous sunglasses. When I looked into them I saw a tiny reflection of myself with an abnormally large head."

"Your head's not abnormally large," I say.

"It was the kind of sunny day that splits you wide open," Raymond says.

"I'm sorry, Raymond." I move closer to him until he leans his head on my shoulder. We embrace awkwardly, still sitting in our chairs. I wonder, as my shoulder goes damp where Raymond rests his mouth, whether he is thinking that this is the closest he will ever get to my mother.

At first, the low moan from Raymond sounds as though he's clearing his throat. I hold him tightly, in the ancient way of comforters, with all my strength, as if physical strength could save him, as if I could unzip my skin and let him inside. The two of us in one costume, we would be all right.

I HEAD over to Temporama to tell Marla that my stint as a mystery shopper is officially over. Raymond's right. I'm leaving. I can't stay in never-never land forever.

A police siren wails and I check my rearview mirror. I'm going fifty-five in a thirty-five-mile-per-hour zone. But there's no police car behind me. Up ahead in the Temporama parking lot, I see the source of the siren. A police car, its lights on, is surrounded by a bevy of temp counselors, including Marla, milling in their pastels. I squint and it looks like an Impressionist painting.

Then I see the familiar back of a man's head, uncombed hair sticking up like a rooster's. Dennis is spread-eagled against the police car, being frisked by the police officer who discovered me the night I tried to break into Modern Pizza. Marla looks on, her hands folded indignantly across her ample chest.

"You need help, Isabelle," she says, her hand on the door handle, opening it before the Chevy coughs to a stop.

My face contorts into a demented smile. It's the only expression available to me at the moment.

"Don't you laugh." Marla's face beats red with the heat, overshadowing the already dramatic blush strokes. "I am concerned for your mental health."

I start to say something, anything, but the truth is, I'm concerned too. The sound that comes out of my mouth is more a grunt than a word.

"Don't start with me," she says. The police officer still has Dennis sprawled facedown against the police car while he takes the shrill reports of Marla's coworkers.

"Just look at him," the pixie blonde says, indicating Dennis with the wag of a bony finger.

Marla takes my chin in her hand. She snaps her fingers in front of my face. "Snap out of it, kid." She flails her arm behind her at the Temporama sign in all its loopy, neon glory. "Your unwashed boyfriend just waltzed right in, not making any sense. I personally thought he was a crazy person. He wanted to know where you were. Not knowing him from Adam, I said I had no idea. He became hostile, said he knew you worked here. He held up one of your time sheets with *my* name on it, then sat down on the floor, refusing to leave until I told him where you were. You know my lips are sealed when it comes to the mystery shops so he sat there until we called the cops." Marla pauses for a breath. "Just tell me you'll get help, Isabelle. I knew when you came in with that crazy haircut that things weren't right."

Dennis, released from his position against the car, looks at me with the disdain he usually reserves for people who willingly wear coordinated outfits.

"Do you want anything, officer?" the take-charge poofy blonde calls over. She is huddled around a take-out menu with the other temp counselors. Dennis is no longer frightening. He's a welcome interruption to an otherwise tedious day. "Rehydrating protein shake?" the pixie blonde asks sweetly.

"It's me," I say to Dennis, holding up my hands as if he were the one doing the arresting. "Isabelle."

"No kidding," Dennis says. He sits down on the curb and puts his head in his hands.

"You seem familiar," the officer says to me, but before he has a chance to recognize me, Marla winks at nobody in particular and pulls him off to the side to let him know that she doesn't want to press charges. Her day has been made more interesting by this event too. I take a seat on the curb beside Dennis.

"I was going to call you," I say, regretting the inadequacy of this sentence as it leaves my mouth.

"Shut up," Dennis says. He looks at me as though I'm an inanimate object—a cardboard box that used to have something inside of it. We are alone on the curb. Everyone—except Marla and the policeman whispering near his car—has gone inside, air-conditioning preferable to drama.

"Nice haircut," Dennis says.

"Leave my hair out of this," I say.

"No, I mean it. I really like it." He runs his fingers through it. "It suits you."

I try to hold his hand, but he pulls it away. "Not so fast," he says.

Marla walks over. "There will be no charges," she says sternly to Dennis, who rolls his eyes at her. "Put some cucumber slices on your eyes and lie very still on a comfortable couch," she advises me. "You need a break from this business. You're burned out."

I nod. She smiles, pinching my cheek gently. "All of the best shoppers, the ones who really put their heart into it, have to take time off." She turns and disappears through the doors of Temporama.

"You guys are going to melt," the officer calls from his window as he pulls out of the parking lot. He presses the automatic window button to seal himself once again in cold air.

"If only we could." Dennis says.

"Can I give you a ride home?" I ask.

"You *better* give me a ride home," Dennis says. "I nearly died of heatstroke walking over here. Stan needed my car to go get beer. The Mustang finally broke down."

We get in the Chevy and drive aimlessly. "Standardsville looks so different when you're not naked," I say, testing the waters.

Dennis ignores me.

"Look, Dennis," I start. I'm not sure how to finish.

"You think you're different," he says, still looking out the window. "But underneath it all, you're just a stupid human being like the rest of us."

"I'm sorry I didn't call, Dennis," I say.

"You know that's not what I'm talking about." He turns to look at me. "For once, don't make this about me being the loser."

"I'm not sorry *for* you. I'm just sorry." I hope these simple words will carry much more on their small backs as they travel to Dennis's heart.

"I need to tell you something, whether you want to hear it or not," he says.

"Can this wait?"

"No, this can't wait. You've made me wait long enough."

"Please, I'm not sure I can handle anything else today."

"I'm leaving town," Dennis says.

I realize I'd expected him to profess his love for me. Maybe even ask me to marry him, giving me the opportunity to say no. But since he didn't, I wonder if Dennis was an important exit on my life's path and I wasn't paying close enough attention. I've missed the turnoff, and now I'm stuck on this ridiculous path all alone.

"Stan is really serious about his band. He wants to go to Detroit. He thinks it's going to rise again as the next big music scene now that Seattle's over and Austin's peaking. He said I could come along." Dennis looks intently at the denim of his jeans as he rubs it with his palms.

"You're going to be a roadie?" I ask. Bitchiness is the only thing I have left. Dennis has never left town. What does he think he's doing? Life is taking place all around me, stowing away in the back of dirty vans and leaving for Detroit.

"You are un-fucking-believable, Isabelle."

The space between us grows. "I'm just jealous," I say. I mean it, but I also want it to bring him back to me. "I miss you already."

"I miss you too," he says. He made this decision years ago, or on his way over to Temporama without me.

"We leave tomorrow." Dennis wipes his hands on his jeans, through with all this.

"Can't you stay a little longer?"

"Don't, Isabelle," he says. "I'm serious."

Stan is on the front porch, playing his guitar. "Dude," he calls out when we pull up. "Where've you been?"

"Shut the fuck up," Dennis calls out the window. Then he rolls up the window and turns to me. "You were the one good thing this summer," he says.

"You were better," I say.

We embrace, saying good-bye quickly, not wanting to dwell in the way of close friends who don't know when they'll see each other next. Dennis climbs out of the car, into the arms of Stan, who fake-weeps on his shoulder, leaving me terrified of everything that lies between now and whenever Dennis and I meet again.

14

I SPEND my days in Raymond's house, watching my mother and Mr. Jones come and go. Yesterday I watched as my mother dropped something on her way in to the house. Mr. Jones bent to pick it up, lingering on bent knees and looking up at her. The living room curtains are as always pulled open, so I catch glimpses of them having a cocktail before dinner or relaxing after work on the couches. One night Samantha came over and there was a lot of gesturing and laughter. At one point, she stood to demonstrate a dance step.

My visits with Raymond are usually spent quietly holding hands until Frank comes and tells us that visiting hours are over.

"If before I was born I was dead, then we've all been dead already," Raymond said the other day, and then fell silent again.

"What do you mean?" I asked. The bright colors of a daytime drama flickered softly on the screen above us. I recognized one of the characters from another soap opera that had killed her off years ago.

"I mean that I'm tired and I want to go home," Raymond said.

"You'll go home soon," I say. Frank has told me that Raymond should be here for a while, until his medication is stabilized, until he is less depressed.

"How will you know? How do you measure those things?" I asked.

"There are signs." Frank's eyes scanned the hall behind me for other potential crises. "It means a lot to Raymond that you visit," he said, meaning it, and meaning that he had other things to do.

"Signs," I said, just saying the word instead of asking the question Frank didn't have time to answer. Even if he did have time, I was fairly certain the answer would be as mysterious and cryptic as the sign I was waiting for myself, the one that would tell me to leave town, how to do it, where to go.

Some days, on my way home from the hospital, I stop off at a Walgreens to cruise the aisles in search of what is next. Just yesterday, I searched for good advice from drugstore packaging in the Walgreens across from the Hotel Fugor, where the teenage knight and his horse still occupied the same patch of lawn just outside the hotel. The horse plunged its nose into a bucket, splashing water while the teenage knight cradled his helmet under one arm as he drank a soda. Only a few cars honked as they passed. At the end of the summer, the knight and his horse were no longer miraculous. They'd become a familiar part of the landscape. I imagined the boy was thinking of the inevitable change of season. He looked forward to the heat lifting. He thought of his friends who would return from camp, the new music he would buy, the girl he would love. He didn't, he couldn't, think past the time when his body would no longer be lean and smooth, to an age when time would not be so endless and hot and boring.

I loitered in the aisle with the hair dye. The same wide-eyed woman appears on every box but with different-colored hair, from lightest to darkest. Yesterday, when I examined this human rainbow, the woman seemed startled by her own image, the ease with which she moves from Tawny Auburn to Cherry Persian to Midnight Black.

Other days, after the hospital, I go to the Super Cineplex, where one of the pimply ushers has replaced Dennis as manager. The movies are more like liquid than anything solid, and the images on the screen seep under my skin. I watch big studio pictures in which movie stars lose love and happiness and, throughout the course of two hours, struggle to get it back. Life lessons, my mother would call them if we were speaking. Yesterday, she left a postcard from Louise and Simon in Raymond's mailbox. On the front of the postcard was a picture of a Mexican beach at sunrise. The message, in Louise's handwriting: *We're thinking of returning to Tucson and settling down for a while. Soon we'll be three!* I recognize the sketch of a pregnant woman's belly as one of Simon's office doodles. The caption under the Mexican sunrise read: *The weather is here. Wish you were great.*

Today, after a blockbuster in which a movie star loses love and happiness, finds it again, loses it again, and then finds it threefold, I sneak through the gap in the wire fence next to the Super Cineplex, over to the duck pond behind the gated community under construction when I first ran into Dennis. HEAVEN ON EARTH, a sign reads, is near completion. It's built to look like a castle, with twin towers of faux stone.

I lie in the short tufts of newly planted grass and throw the lonely duck what's left of my popcorn. The duck swims out of the water and waddles onto dry land to peck at the soil around me. He is pecking at my sneakers when a furry orange dog hurdles through the gap in the fence, pulling an old woman behind him. The dog rushes the duck, the woman falls down next to me, and the duck quacks its way back into the water.

"Are you all right?" the woman asks, though she's the one who's fallen.

"Fine," I say. "And you?" I help her to her feet. The furry dog, looking like he's wearing a glamorous orange mink, barks at the duck from the pond's shore. His black tongue lolls from the side of his mouth.

"The Chinese say their tongues are black because when God cut the stars out of the night sky, the dogs lapped up the fallen night," the woman says to me, in answer to a question I might have asked. With knobby fingers, she arranges her wispy blue hair so that it hovers around her head like a cloud. She retrieves her night-lapping dog and heads back for the slip in the fence. Before the dog drags her away, she turns to look at me.

"A girl your age shouldn't lie around duck ponds feeling sorry for herself, you know," she says.

"I'm not." I protest too much.

But her dog is already dragging her across the hot tar of the Super Cineplex parking lot and I'm left alone with the duck and my defensiveness.

I drive to the cul-de-sac. My mother is not yet home from work, so I go inside her house. The front hall smells different, now a combination of the drugstore perfume and the salty beach scent of Mr. Jones. In the linen closet, I find the photo album of my baby pictures, the one my mother left out to inspire me when I first came home, still wrapped in sheets. As I begin to unwrap it, I feel something hard beneath it, also wrapped in towels. Inside is a scrapbook I've never seen before.

The first page: A baby pink wristband with perforated holes from the hospital. A picture of a wizened baby looking more like old age than youth, covered with brown hair that will later fall out. At the bottom of the page, a small square cut out of yellow construction paper and in that pointy scrawl: *Out of the womb and into the frying pan.*

One page has a piece of gum with three small teeth marks and a yellow ribbon I wore for a day when I was seven. There's a lipstick-kissed version of my lips on a scrap of lined faded green paper. And a picture of me at age eight in my favorite purple polyester bell-bottoms sewed again and again at the crotch. There's a gap in my teeth that the dentist said I would need braces to correct but my teeth grew together naturally. In the picture, I hold my arms wide apart: I love my mother this much.

In these pictures, my father is the ghostly blur in the background—half a body, head turned to look elsewhere. He always chose to be behind the camera—for the Twister picture or the picture in the scrapbook of me and my mother pretending to box. Or the picture of me, three years old in a swing, my mother pushing. She's added a caption: *Spank me up to heaven!* His hand is in that picture by mistake, a blur of orchestration and encouragement.

On the last page of the scrapbook is a picture of my father, though my mother claimed never to have kept a single picture of my father after he left. But here he is, joyously extending his arms to the camera, beckoning her to him. At the bottom of the picture is my mother's tall, scratchy handwriting: *September 1966*. It was taken the month before I was born. My mother is eight months pregnant and my father is saying to us both: Come to me.

A car pulls up outside, and when I look out the window I see my mother alone in the street, looking at Raymond's house, considering her next move. I sneak out the back in a panic but run into her head-on as I round the corner.

"I need to talk to you," she says.

"Here?"

"Not here. Get in the car."

We get into Mr. Jones's Dart, and she immediately backs over one of Mrs. Morton's peonies bushes. The lush, lazy pink petals float in the air behind us.

"Don't say a word," she says.

"Mrs. Morton's going to find out anyway," I say.

"Until we get there, I meant."

"Get where?"

She ignores me, swerving out into traffic at the end of the cul-de-sac. We drive past the corner gas station where a group of high school kids in bathing suits douse each other with buckets of soapy water left over from a car wash. One of the boys yells after us, "You ladies could be next."

"I've been thinking a lot about gravity these days," my

239

mother says, bullying her way into highway traffic. "The force of gravitation for any two sufficiently massive bodies is directly proportional to the product of their masses and inversely proportional to the square of the distance between them."

How miraculous it is that the words we use reach each other at all, sent out like envoys to cross endless terrain. So much to translate and so little time.

"I thought you said not to say a word."

A gray blimp floats in the clouds above the tangled mass of highways. Crowds of people fill the grassy sections between lanes to wave and shout encouragement.

"I meant you. What I'm thinking of is slightly different. It has to do with you specifically," my mother says. She passes when she can, always dangerously close to the car in front of her. What others call tailgating she has always referred to as "gentle encouragement." "It has more to do with the phenomenon of staying on the ground when there's nothing to keep you there," she continues.

The blimp begins to sail through the sky and the crowd goes wild. "Come back!" a little boy holding a skateboard screams, outraged.

The landscape as we leave town is open and monotonous, the view from every gated community. We are surrounded by that eerie, unboundaried space. Finally, we arrive on a stretch of highway that runs along the Mississippi. The one other time we tried this, we got very lost. We have been down this road before; this road eventually becomes the road where I was born.

"I'm determined to find it this time," my mother says. I was born in the car as she and my father rushed away from a day trip to Nauvoo, then a sleepy agricultural town known for its wine and cheeses, now restored as a theme park re-creating the Mormon settlement on the Mississippi.

I push my body deep into the passenger seat. Green bunches of trees whip by and there is a sudden quickening of beauty as we get closer. The road back to the epicenter of motherhood is appropriately enchanted. With my eyes shut, we're flying, the car a few inches off the road.

The day I was born, my parents wanted to go somewhere they'd never been. Friends had recommended a day trip to Nauvoo since my mother was a fan of Joseph Smith. She still considers him a fellow storyteller, someone who used his seer stone to contact angels. So my parents packed the car with a picnic and drove this road, safe in the knowledge that my mother wasn't due for several weeks. My mother often says that, at that point, she had decided she wanted to be pregnant forever. She had dreams in which she realized that I would never leave her body, that she would forever be two people. In her dreams, she thought she'd discovered the secret to never being lonely again. She'd wake up and spend all day trying to recapture the feeling.

They ate their picnic on the banks of the river, where my father explained to my mother the difference between the Reorganized Church of Latter-Day Saints and the Church of the Latter-Day Saints, the two incarnations of one religion, as she looked out over the water toward the green of Iowa.

"Get out," she instructs me now. She parks outside the LDS Visitors Center, and we wander behind a horse-drawn carriage toward Joseph Smith's house. A young tour guide pokes her sincere, round face out the front door. "Welcome to Joseph Smith's lovely home," she says. We are the only ones on the tour, except for a very tall, thick-waisted teenager with a Brigham Young T-shirt on.

A wasp clings to the folds of our round-faced tour guide's skirt as if it were being saved. "Joseph Smith and his wife," the guide says in the kitchen, "ate their guests at every meal." She sighs, takes a deep breath of the oaky, old air, and starts over. "Joseph Smith and his wife," she says emphatically, "ate *with* their guests at every meal."

The giant teenager leans over to tell us what he's been waiting to tell us all along. "Joseph had a lot of wives, you know. You don't hear about *them* on the tour."

We follow the giant teenager to Brigham Young's home. "You know you can convert your ancestors," the giant says to us as we approach the front steps.

"We're looking forward to it," my mother says. She has not looked at me once since we arrived.

An older, saccharine-voiced woman, guided by the prophet himself, she explains, takes us into Young's root cellar, where she holds us hostage for five minutes with the door shut. There, in the dark, she describes plates that Brigham Young's wife left in the root cellar, rediscovered one hundred years later.

"Brigham Young said that nonbelievers can be like those plates—rediscovered," the giant whispers to us.

Without saying a word, my mother links her arm through mine. Maybe the giant's right. Maybe we could be like those plates. Maybe there's a way to die for a little while, buried in a cellar, and resurface years later to live out the part of your life you saved for later. In this dark cave that smells like cold mud, here where Brigham Young's roots and plates once were, I am my mother's daughter. In the pitch-black darkness, I finally see what she's given to me, essential as the dark and the mud. She's showed me the place in between stories and life where people really live.

The giant leans his big head toward us. "Our God dwells near the planet Koloba with his wife and his children whom he sends to Earth in order to test their faith."

"I'll take that under consideration," my mother says to the giant. "Could you please let us out of here?" she asks the tour guide.

When we crawl out of the cellar into the bright green patches of mown lawns and carefully gridded streets, my mother and I wander away from the tour guide and the giant, though the tour isn't finished yet.

"Ladies?" The guide's saccharine voice follows us down the street. "Would you like to finish what you've started?"

"No, thank you," my mother calls back.

As we walk past Ye Olde Cobbler's Shoppe, my mother turns to me.

"Henry doesn't exist."

I sit down on a bench.

"I mean, he never existed, even before he died," she says, sitting down next to me. People dressed in olden-day wear worn in olden-day theme parks throughout the United States—knickers and bonnets, knee-high boots and long hoop skirts—walk happily by, greeting tourists.

"Hello, ye fair lasses," an olden-day man says. He stops to doff his tricornered hat at us.

"Please go away," I say.

"Just doing my job," he says, walking on.

"I couldn't deal with your father leaving. It was too much," my mother says. The tap, tap, tap of shoes being cobbled emanates from the Shoppe.

"Have you even been to San Francisco? What about that picture with the pigeons?" I'm not sure where to start, where my questions begin.

"That picture was taken in a park in Standardsville, by your father."

"And the recurring dream about Henry diving into the water from the San Francisco pier and the seals and the water? You standing there, paralyzed?"

She pauses to smooth her face with her hands, adjusting her expression, regaining her composure before she's even lost it. "Your father hovered around the two of us the way men sometimes do around a girlfriend and her best friend. He stood at the edges of rooms, even when you were a baby. But I let him fade away. I let him disappear into the corners of the house like dust. I wanted him to come back, but neither of us could figure out how to make that happen. Henry *was* really in my dreams. That's where *he* was born," my mother says. "And I always wanted to go to San Francisco."

"So why didn't you come visit me?" I never invited her, not once. I wanted the experience for myself. I thought she'd had all that she deserved. The question is easier than acknowledging her missed opportunities.

Several tourists stop to watch us, until they realize that we're not reenacting anything.

"You actually did it, Isabelle. Don't you see? You really went to San Francisco and I never had the courage."

"I'm sorry," I say, because I never invited her to visit and because her heart ever had to break.

"Don't be sorry. I admired your bravery as much as I envied it," she says.

"How could you do that to Raymond?" I'm angry all over again. I want her to take the blame for Raymond sitting catatonically in the visiting lounge. I want her to somehow account for every ounce of his pain. I want her to make him better.

"You believed in my stories. You went off to San Francisco and tried to make something happen for yourself. Here I was, fearful of growing old alone and just fearful in general. And yes, Raymond was a distraction from that. He was someone I turned to. Yes, I lied to him. But look who's accusing me, Ms. Patron of the Hotel Fugor. And yes, I've moved on. If that means I've abandoned him, hurt him, then I've done that too. I'm just trying to make a life for myself like anybody else."

"And what about Mr. Jones?"

"What about Mr. Jones? He wants to hold my hand when we go to the movies. He thinks I'm pretty. He enjoys my company. I enjoy his, and he could leave at any minute, which terrifies me. I've told him everything. I've tried to come clean, as clean as a person should."

I look dubious.

"I've told him *everything*," she says. "And he's still here, so we'll see. And by the way, the scene you made at Paradise

Found almost cost him the job." She doesn't ask me what I was doing there. She doesn't want to know, the way I don't want to know about the conversation she and Mr. Jones had about it, the way I don't want to know anymore about her and Raymond. The mean trick of love stares me in the face: The distance between us keeps us close. She takes my arm and I stiffen, but I let her do it. I want to punch her, but I also don't want her to let go, which means we're doing pretty well. We're back where we started, back where we belong.

"Can we go home now?" she asks. She's finished with this conversation. She is tired, the way she must have been tired after her nights of Henry stories, when she left my room and crawled into bed. My father gone, I can begin to see why she would need me as an audience for the lies that would protect her from his absence. I understand the need to lie out loud, to let it ring out beyond yourself until it is louder than the truth.

"I want to go home too," I say.

A family of tourists that has gathered to watch us applauds. "Get a life," my mother says to them over her shoulder as we walk back to the car.

Once we are on the road again, we pass a sign marking the sight of the Great Swamp Fight. Next to it is a restaurant called, simply, Restaurant. My mother pulls into the parking lot.

"What are you doing?" I ask.

"Follow me," she says.

So I do, into the lobby where two slot machines stand side by side.

"Your father and I stopped here because I thought my contractions were hunger pangs," she says.

"What have we got to lose?" I say.

Standing hip to hip, we put quarter after quarter in the slot machines. Lemon, orange, banana. Two bananas and a lemon. Restaurant's owner sticks his head around the corner.

"You ladies hungry?" he asks hopefully. Does he imagine our lives elsewhere? Does he suspect that, thirty-three years ago, my mother and father came to Restaurant, as they waited for me to be born, their whole lives ahead of them only imagined in the colors and shapes of dreams. Quiet days spent at home with the junk of life—piles of old news-papers, candy wrappers, juice-stained books, unmatched socks, half-used bottles of shampoo, last night's dinner crumbs still under the dining room table—and all of us there.

"I wanted to show you something real, something true," my mother says, staring at her losing combination. She means the beginning—where I started from.

My mother must have been astonished as she began to give birth in the car, my father still driving, kneading her shoulder with one hand to help himself and her stay calm. Out of the corner of her eye, the trees whipped by but in her pain they weren't trees. They were what pain looked like—pure and without a recognizable shape. It hurt her to look but look-ing was part of helping me to be born, so she did. At that moment, by accident, her life was the way she had always tried to make it, the way she had told it—real-life, high-speed adventure. They pulled over and I was born on the side of the road.

"I know," I say. I take her arm and lead her back to the car, away from our losing fruit and Restaurant's owner still waiting for legitimate customers. I take the keys and drive to show her that I am competent, that I've learned things since the baby pictures tucked away in the linen closet. The lush beauty disappears behind us, like the fading landscape out the window of a rocket leaving earth.

15

〜

Before leaving Standardsville, I plan to spend my last
night at Raymond's. I called my old boss, the history professor
in my college town for whom I did research on Benedictine
monks. He told me his latest research assistant left to go to
graduate school on the West Coast. He's writing a book on Las
Vegas and the desert re-creations of the world's greatest feats of
architecture—the Taj Majal, the Eiffel Tower, the Pyramids.
He's exploring the effect these re-creations have on the way
Americans view the original sites. I'll live cheaply in the apartment attached to his family's home, baby-sitting his two young
children in exchange for half the rent. It's a small, hip city—
familiar and manageable. It's a temporary plan. I called my ex-
boyfriend who has, over the course of the last year, married.
He says he's very happy and his new wife is pregnant. He said
he's so happy that he'd even like to see me again. I always
knew we'd make better friends than lovers, he said. For the
sake of our future friendship, I chose not to take offense. I

called Marla and she told me that Temporama has a branch there. She'll even give me a referral.

"You're a piece of work," she said. "The best kind. Gotta run. Love you."

I could hear the receptionist over the intercom, letting Marla know that her next appointment had arrived.

After I finish making the phone calls that will decide my future, at least for a little while, I wander across the street. My mother called me at Raymond's to invite me over for coffee before I go to evening visiting hours at the hospital to say goodbye. She isn't in the living room, so I look out back, figuring she might be taking advantage of the slightly cooler weather today. On the radio this morning a DJ announced glumly that the heat wave had broken. "But only for today, ladies and gentlemen," he added triumphantly. "So watch out!"

My mother doesn't hear me coming and I watch her for a minute without her knowing. She sits in a patio chair with a glass of wine in the magic, dusty red light of dusk. Her eyes are filled with the setting sun, her cheekbones distinct in the shadowy light.

"I thought you said coffee," I say. "I don't want to walk into the hospital smelling of alcohol. Kristina will kick my ass."

It is only when she turns to look at me that I see she is crying.

"Mr. Jones?" I ask. I can't form a full sentence in the face of these tears.

She shakes her head and cries into her hand silently so that I know it's worse than heartbreak.

"Frank called," she says.

"Raymond?" I rush forward to stop her from telling me any more.

She lifts herself out of her chair and I see how much sadness weighs. She comes toward me as though she has to physically bring me this news.

"He'd hidden a razor blade." She touches her own wrists to illustrate.

"I didn't know," I say. What exactly didn't I know? That Raymond was capable of this? That things were this bad? That he had such violence in him? Death wasn't a onetime thing, he'd said. It was something you returned to. What I didn't know is that Raymond would leave me like this.

What wells up in me is raw. I am sure I will drown with whatever is filling me. I know suddenly what it is like to be an animal, driven by instinct, driven by wild hunger. The sound that comes out of me sends my mother stumbling back, but she moves forward again to hold me as I jerk in her arms like something newly dead.

THOUGH I punch and pull the pillows on Raymond's bed, they don't offer anything except clouds of silvery dust. I want them to tell me what Raymond thought. He once said that the phone sitting in his kitchen reminded him every day that the lawn needed mowing, though the boy he hired rarely came, and when he did he dragged the lawn mower behind him in lazy zigzags. His welcome mat—spiky green astroturf—told him to head back down the lawn to check the mail. His TV not turned on told him that everything must someday come to an end. One night, watching TV beside me on my mother's couch, he announced that the long neck of the standing lamp in his living room informed him that my mother was a very astute woman.

The sound of Mrs. Morton's bare-assed cherub spitting floats through the window from next door. It's working again after neighborhood kids choked it with a pencil, lodged so deeply in its throat that she was forced to call a plumber. Now the cherub dribbles contentedly. Through its gargling, the voices of Mrs. Morton and a friend drift into Raymond's kitchen thick with the silence of someone never coming back. Ice clinks in afternoon cocktails like the jewels of the living.

All I wanted this summer was to disappear. A gentle fade—into a costume, under a wig. With Raymond gone, the cruelty of that wish reveals itself to me—my true, ungentle intention. I wanted to go with him. A part of me wanted to leave this world.

I bang drawers open looking for anything that will explain Raymond's departure. Most of them are empty, except for a small packet of soy sauce and a pile of straws whose wrapping is coffee-stained. I hurl these things on the floor. When I first see the list, Raymond's tiny, neat handwriting startles me. Like finding my mother's letters, it's as though his voice is trapped in a drawer. The list is divided into categories: Family, Friends, and Other Helpful Numbers. Under "Family" are "Mom and Dad" with an address in southern Illinois. The address is crossed out with a giant X, meaning, I assume, that they died.

Under "Friends," I find: "Adeline," and in a different color ink, probably added at the beginning of the summer, "Isabelle." Our phone number is listed though Raymond never called once. He probably fantasized about calling my mother, looking through his window to our house with her voice held captive in his ear. Under "Other Helpful Numbers" is the number to the community mental health center, the one where

Samantha works as an adminstrator, the one Raymond called to receive a referral to the psych hospital after he finished off the antacids, back when he fooled us all into thinking he was only capable of joke suicide.

After listening through the many options of the phone menu: self-esteem, assertiveness training, eating disorders, healthy relationships, body image, healing workshops, I press 0 to get a real person on the other end of the line.

"Can you describe the pain in more specific terms?" the voice asks. It is a high female voice that sounds as if it's coming through a wind tunnel, like she is someone who has used nose spray wildly. Her nostrils are hairless and smooth.

I begin to try. I explain that it feels something like when the gynecologist checks my ovaries, one hand inside and one pressing from the outside as if, but for the skin, the doctor would have an ovary in her hand. I tell the voice that it's like that but not quite. I tell her that the pain seems to be floating in my abdominal area and I worry that it may land and become something serious. I tell her that I have delicious fantasies in which this pain does in fact turn out to be something tragic and this fatal diagnosis slices the fatty part off my days until they are sculpted and meaningful. I begin to tell her that the pain began during the past year when I realized how close I was getting to my mother's age in the picture of her, nonchalant and filled with things to say in the park I thought was in San Francisco but which turned out to be in Standardsville. It began when Raymond killed himself. It began after my father left. Maybe it was there before I was born, in the womb, but the windy voice is giving me another number. It is the number of a counselor who, she thinks, will be better able to help me. As she gives me the number, I tell her that this pain is my own personal damage, but as I pretend to write the number down, saying it back to her at the speed that I would be writing it if I were actually writing it, I look around Raymond's barren kitchen and know that this pain doesn't set me apart at all.

My mother and Mr. Jones drive me to the train station.

"I'm sorry about the other day," I say to Mr. Jones.

"Don't worry about it," he says. "I did all kinds of crazy stuff when I was your age." He pauses, puts on an exaggerated thinking face. "Well, by your age, I was much more mature. But don't worry about it. There's still hope for you."

My mother slaps him affectionately on the shoulder. She and I have made a deal. We will treat my leaving as if it were only for a weekend instead of the last time we'll see each other indefinitely. We will simply ignore the fact that after this trip, I'm going straight to my new life. We'll deal with it later, in the privacy of our own homes.

"See you in a couple of days," my mother says, handing my suitcase up to where I stand on the steps of the train.

"See you soon," I say back, blowing her a kiss. "I'll be back in a flash."

Out the window of the train, everything rushes toward me and then disappears, the quick tug of curiosity hooking me into the fleeting landscape. Who lives there? And there? If you grew up in a house overlooking the train tracks—movement whizzing constantly by your kitchen window—would life rushing by surprise you years later when you found yourself at the same kitchen window still watching?

There are rows of parked schoolbuses in an empty lot packed together like an elusive rare species caught. It's surprising to see easily so many of the things you searched for in the distance as a child—down the street, is that it?—wondering if it would ever come, as if schoolbuses themselves were random, temperamental creatures. Now, abandoned cars in somebody's driveway, power lines like mammoth totems. Mounds of dirt and a tractor, then again and again. Graveyards filled with earth and bones.

When I was in kindergarten, my father's way of greeting me was to stumble back in fake astonishment—is this my daughter?—before he came forward to embrace me. It was a joke that made us all laugh because it was silly and then because it was predictable, a signal that we recognized.

A small girl's face flies by as a train passes us going in the other direction. She studies her own reflection in the window, distracted and annoyed by images from the outside world rushing through her reflected face. I want to stop the rushing too. I'd like to hold a minute in my hand, capture it like a fly, study it before it buzzed away again.

In the station parking lots, there are people standing outside their running cars waiting for loved ones, children, parents. They prepare for that moment when they will move suddenly from being alone to being with someone else. They collect their thoughts—gather them up like favorite objects rescued in a fire—to best represent themselves.

The urn with Raymond's ashes is tucked between my feet. I am taking him south to the farm where he once lived with his parents. He told my mother the name of the town once, and I'll put my mystery-shop sleuthing skills to good use once I get there to find the exact address. I'll get a hotel room in a small town undisturbed by tangled highway systems. After all those nights on the couch, Raymond is taking me somewhere.

The man sitting beside me smells of oranges and carries a briefcase. When we first got on the train, he leaned in conspiratorially and asked, "Where are you going?"

"South," I said.

"You need some flowers for your vase," he said, unconvinced by my abruptness.

"I have ashes," I said.

"Ashes are good," he said, looking toward the empty aisle.

Now we ride in the silence pungent with his citrus smell, looking out the window—little boy with a hose filling a baby pool, scrubby bushes and dirt, then forest, forest, forest.

I cough and the man beside me, waiting as we all do for an entrance into someone else's life, says eagerly, "Bless you."

"Who is in the vase?" he asks, genuine concern wrinkling his brow.

"A friend," I say. And when I stop laughing, he tells me about a field he saw once on this same train trip that was so green and beautiful that just looking at it helped him through his divorce.

"It was one of those moments, you know?" he says.

We are moving into dangerous territory with the mention of his divorce, and I check the destination on the ticket stub sticking out of the top of his seat to find out whether he is getting off soon or whether I will need to tactfully change seats, but I nod in agreement because I know exactly what he is talking about.

The landscape opens suddenly as we leave woodland for

cornfields, and I remember watching one night as Raymond crossed the street back to his house. An unexpected wind cut through the thick heat of summer, spiriting a stray picnic napkin past his feet. He looked up, lifting his face into the momentarily cool air, seeming to understand that survival too will end. He closed his eyes, turning his face completely to receive the blissful, random opportunity for relief. I turn my face too and for a precious, buzzing minute, looking at this green field, I am filled with the elusive beauty of the world.

wm WILLIAM MORROW

New in hardcover from Maud Casey!

DRASTIC
Stories
ISBN 0-688-17696-8 (hardcover)

In this stunning collection of powerful and piercing short stories,
Maud Casey explores how to survive modern crises of loss and love.
Her characters, emotional and geographic nomads, are haunted by
loneliness. Though they flirt with madness and self-destruction,
Casey's characters—whether compulsively, gently, or haphazardly—
reach toward life.